ROYAL FAMILY

Praise for Jenny Frame

The Duchess and the Dreamer

"We thoroughly enjoyed the whole romance-the-disbelieving-duchess with gallantry, unwavering care, and grand gestures. Since this is very firmly in the butch-femme zone, it appealed to that part of our traditionally-conditioned-typecasting mindset that all the wooing and work is done by Evan without throwing even a small fit at any point. We liked the fact that Clementine has layers and depth. She has her own personal and personality hurdles that make her behaviour understandable and create the right opportunities for Evan to play the romantic knight convincingly...We definitely recommend this one to anyone looking for a feel-good mushy romance."—*Best Lesfic Reviews*

"There are a whole range of things I like about Jenny Frame's aristocratic heroines: they have plausible histories to account for them holding titles in their own right; they're in touch with reality and not necessarily super-rich, certainly not through inheritance; and they find themselves paired with perfectly contrasting co-heroines...Clementine and Evan are excellently depicted, and I love the butch:femme dynamic they have going on, as well as their individual abilities to stick to their principles but also to compromise with each other when necessary."
—*The Good, The Bad and The Unread*

Still Not Over You

"*Still Not Over You* is a wonderful second-chance romance anthology that makes you believe in love again. And you would certainly be missing out if you have not read *My Forever Girl*, because it truly is everything."—*SymRoute*

Someone to Love

"One of the author's best works to date—both Trent and Wendy were so well developed they came alive. I could really picture them and they jumped off the pages. They had fantastic chemistry, and their sexual dynamic was deliciously well written. The supporting characters and the storyline about Alice's trauma was also sensitively written and well handled."—*Melina Bickard, Librarian, Waterloo Library (UK)*

Wooing the Farmer

"This book, like all of Jenny Frame's, is just one major swoon."—*Les Rêveur*

"The chemistry between the two MCs had us hooked right away. We also absolutely loved the seemingly ditzy femme with an ambition of steel but really a vulnerable girl. The sex scenes are great. Definitely recommended."—*Reviewer@large*

"This is the book we Axedale fanatics have been waiting for…Jenny Frame writes the most amazing characters and this whole series is a masterpiece. But where she excels is in writing butch lesbians. Every time I read a Jenny Frame book I think it's the best ever, but time and again she surprises me. She has surpassed herself with *Wooing the Farmer*."—*Kitty Kat's Book Review Blog*

Royal Court

"The author creates two very relatable characters…Quincy's quietude and mental torture are offset by Holly's openness and lust for life. Holly's determination and tenacity in trying to reach Quincy are total wish-fulfilment of a person like that. The chemistry and attraction is excellently built."—*Best Lesbian Erotica*

"[A] butch/femme romance that packs a punch."—*Les Rêveur*

Royal Court "was a fun, light-hearted book with a very endearing romance."—*Leanne Chew, Librarian, Parnell Library (Auckland, NZ)*

"There were unbelievably hot sex scenes as I have come to expect and look forward to in Jenny Frame's books. Passions slowly rise until you feel the characters may burst!…Royal Court is wonderful and I highly recommend it."—*Kitty Kat's Book Review Blog*

Charming the Vicar

"Chances are, you've never read or become captivated by a romance like *Charming the Vicar*. While books featuring people of the cloth aren't unusual, Bridget is no ordinary vicar—a lesbian with a history of kink…Surrounded by mostly supportive villagers, Bridget and Finn balance love and faith in a story that affirms both can exist for anyone, regardless of sexual identity."—*RT Book Reviews*

"The sex scenes were some of the sexiest, most intimate and quite frankly, sensual I have read in a while. Jenny Frame had me hooked and I reread a few scenes because I felt like I needed to experience the intense intimacy between Finn and Bridget again. The devotion they showed to one another during these sex scenes but also in the intimate moments was gripping and for lack of a better word, carnal."—*Les Rêveur*

"The sexual chemistry between [Finn and Bridge] is unbelievably hot. It is sexy, lustful and with more than a hint of kink. The scenes between them are highly erotic—and not just the sex scenes. The tension is ramped up so well that I felt the characters would explode if they did not get relief!...An excellent book set in the most wonderful village—a place I hope to return to very soon!"—*Kitty Kat's Book Reviews*

"This is Frame's best character work to date. They are layered and flawed and yet relatable...Frame really pushed herself with *Charming the Vicar* and it totally paid off...I also appreciate that even though she regularly writes butch/femme characters, no two pairings are the same."—*The Lesbian Review*

Unexpected

Jenny Frame "has this beautiful way of writing a phenomenally hot scene while incorporating the love and tenderness between the couple."—*Les Rêveur*

"If you enjoy contemporary romances, *Unexpected* is a great choice. The character work is excellent, the plotting and pacing are well done, and it's just a sweet, warm read...Definitely pick this book up when you're looking for your next comfort read, because it's sure to put a smile on your face by the time you get to that happy ending."—*Curve*

"*Unexpected* by Jenny Frame is a charming butch/femme romance that is perfect for anyone who wants to feel the magic of overcoming adversity and finding true love. I love the way Jenny Frame writes. I have yet to discover an author who writes like her. Her voice is strong and unique and gives a freshness to the lesbian fiction sector."
—*The Lesbian Review*

Royal Rebel

"Frame's stories are easy to follow and really engaging. She stands head and shoulders above a number of the romance authors and it's easy to see why she is quickly making a name for herself in lesfic romance."—*The Lesbian Review*

Courting the Countess

"I love Frame's romances. They are well paced, filled with beautiful character moments and a wonderful set of side characters who ultimately end up winning your heart...I love Jenny Frame's butch/femme dynamic; she gets it so right for a romance."—*The Lesbian Review*

"I loved, loved, loved this book. I didn't expect to get so involved in the story but I couldn't help but fall in love with Annie and Harry...The love scenes were beautifully written and very sexy. I found the whole book romantic and ultimately joyful and I had a lump in my throat on more than one occasion. A wonderful book that certainly stirred my emotions."—*Kitty Kat's Book Reviews*

"*Courting The Countess* has an historical feel in a present day world, a thought provoking tale filled with raw emotions throughout. [Frame] has a magical way of pulling you in, making you feel every emotion her characters experience."—*Lunar Rainbow Reviewz*

"I didn't want to put the book down and I didn't. Harry and Annie are two amazingly written characters that bring life to the pages as they find love and adventures in Harry's home. This is a great read, and you will enjoy it immensely if you give it a try!"—*Fantastic Book Reviews*

A Royal Romance

"*A Royal Romance* was a guilty pleasure read for me. It was just fun to see the relationship develop between George and Bea, to see George's life as queen and Bea's as a commoner. It was also refreshing to see that both of their families were encouraging, even when Bea doubted that things could work between them because of their class differences...*A Royal Romance* left me wanting a sequel, and romances don't usually do that to me."—*Leeanna.ME Mostly a Book Blog*

By the Author

A Royal Romance

Courting the Countess

Dapper

Royal Rebel

Unexpected

Charming the Vicar

Royal Court

Wooing the Farmer

Someone to Love

The Duchess and the Dreamer

Royal Family

Wild for You

Hunger for You

Longing for You

Wolfgang County Series

Heart of the Pack

Soul of the Pack

Blood of the Pack

Visit us at www.boldstrokesbooks.com

ROYAL FAMILY

by

Jenny Frame

2021

CREDITS

Editor: Ruth Sternglantz
Production Design: Stacia Seaman
Cover Design by Sheri (hindsightgraphics@gmail.com)

Acknowledgments

Thank you to all the BSB staff for their tireless hard work. Thank you to Ruth for always helping my books be the best they can be.

Thanks to my family for their support and encouragement.

Finally, thanks to Lou and Barney for helping me cope with my stressful approaching deadlines!

To Lou

"We three are family…"

Chapter One

Veronica Clayton moved gingerly from behind deep undergrowth to the cover of a large tree. Her heart and breath were steady despite the exertion of tracking the target she was stalking. Clay's training as a police protection officer kept her emotions in check and her head clear.

She was the best shot in the protection command. In fact she'd always been the best marksman in every team she'd been in, from army cadets as a girl, to police training and her first assignment to the firearms squad.

Clay heard the low murmur of voices, and then caught her target in her vision. She kept her weapon close to her side and edged around the tree trunk to get a better shot. She'd only need one—one opening, and her target would be down. She raised her weapon, and in a second... *boom*.

There were screams followed by shrieks of laughter.

Holly wiped snow from her jacket, and Princess Edwina, or Teddy as she was known, bounded up and down on the thick snowy ground.

"Get her, Holls," Teddy shouted.

Holly shot her a glare. "I'm going to kill you, Clay."

Clay gathered more ammunition from the snowy ground and ran out into the gardens of Sandringham Estate. The royal family were gathering to celebrate Christmas at Sandringham, the Queen's Norfolk Christmas retreat, in observance of an old tradition. Tradition was very important to the family, especially at Christmas, and this was a time they treasured.

Clay laughed at Holly's threat. "You can try, but I'm too fast for you."

Teddy started to lift snow and throw it in Clay's direction, but being only three years old, her missile didn't get very far.

Holly shouted to Jack, one of the new members of the protection squad, to help them. After Beatrice, the Queen Consort, had her second child, Jack was placed under Clay's command, to be an extra pair of eyes on the royal children. Clay got on with Jack really well and trusted him to help with the protection of Teddy and her three-month-old baby sister, Princess Anna. Jack ran across the snowy garden at top speed and gathered up a big pile of snow. The Queen's dogs—Rex, Shadow, and Baxter—chased around and barked loudly.

Teddy and Holly chased after Clay as fast as Teddy could run on her little legs, but when Jack's snowballs hit Clay square in the back, she fell to her knees dramatically, as if she had been shot.

"I got her, Princess Teddy," Jack said in triumph.

Clay played up her death scene as the princess and Holly hurried towards her. "I'm dying—you got me. Don't shoot."

"We've no sympathy, Clay. We're going to get you, aren't we, Teddy?" Holly said.

Teddy picked up handfuls of snow and threw them all over Clay as she sat on her knees in the snow.

"I got her, I got her, Holls." Teddy jumped up and down.

"You sure did," Holly told her.

Clay loved spending time with the Queen's children. She loved them like her own little sisters and would die to protect them. Being a protection officer meant she didn't get the Christmas holidays off work, but since her mother had died a few months ago, she didn't care.

Her mother's sudden death left Clay with no immediate family, and the quiet loneliness of her own flat was too much to bear. So she threw herself into her job. Protecting these two important children was her life now, and the hustle, bustle, and excitement of a royal family Christmas dulled the grief that she felt deeply inside.

There was a lot of focus on the royal family at Christmas, and the protection team had to be on their toes. Despite Christmas being a private family time for most British families, the royal family had to be on display at this time of year, leading the nation in their celebrations.

The snow rained down on Clay from above, and the dogs barked with excitement, until she said, "I'm dead." She went still and feigned her death.

The snow stopped, and Teddy said, "You okay, Clay?"

"Don't trust her, Teddy," Holly said.

Just then Clay made a grab for Teddy, and she squealed. Clay held Teddy above her head. "I'm going to get you, Princess."

This was her family now, and without her mum, this was the best way to spend Christmas Eve.

❖

Queen Georgina heard shrieks of laughter from outside. She got up from her desk and walked to the window. She smiled when she watched Teddy, Holly, and Jack have an all-out snowball fight in the garden.

This was the life she had longed for—spending Christmas with her family and children at Sandringham House. She had so many happy family Christmases at this, the Sovereign's private estate. She only wished she had more time to spend outside playing with her children, but the affairs of state didn't stop just because it was Christmas Eve.

Although she had Christmas Day off from the boxes that came to her daily from her government, Christmas Eve was no exception. Now George knew how her father felt when he was always apologizing for having to slip away over the holidays.

But she was glad to see her daughter Teddy was still having plenty of fun with Clay and Holly. Holly had been filling in, when she could, for the nanny, who'd been let go just last month, after it was discovered she was selling stories to the press.

George sighed. After her own childhood nanny, Mrs. Baker, had retired when they returned from their American trip, it had been hard enough for Beatrice to choose this nanny. But now her wife trusted outsiders even less, and they had to start the whole recruitment process all over again.

When it came down to it, she knew, Bea just hated having to rely on a nanny. She wanted to be the one looking after the children. But it just wasn't practical with all the engagements they had to attend, both during the day and in the evening. Relying on staff to help was a normal part of life for George's family, and it was just taking Bea a little bit of time to relax about it and not feel so guilty.

One thing that was secure was Clay's position as Teddy and baby Anna's protection officer.

Teddy absolutely loved Clay, and Clay was young enough that she would be a stable influence on Teddy's and her little sister's lives for a long time to come. Above all both she and Bea trusted Clay. She had blossomed under Captain Quincy's influence, and now that Jack had joined them, the wall around her wife and family was secure.

She laughed as Shadow, her black Labrador, and Baxter, her boxer, chased Clay and Jack, while Rex, the honey-coloured Lab, stayed right next to Teddy. Rex, once her late father's dog, fell in love with Bea when George met her, and when Teddy came along he became the princess's unofficial chief of security.

George heard a knock at her study door, and she retreated to her desk. "Come in."

Sebastian, her private secretary, entered carrying two red government boxes. He bowed at the neck and said, "Your Majesty."

"Come in, Bastian. Let's get this paperwork done and get Christmas started."

"Yes, ma'am. Just two boxes today," Bastian said.

He put them on the desk, and George used her brass key to open them. She picked up the first folder and scanned the first page.

"Why don't you pour us both a sherry, Bastian, It's four o'clock on Christmas Eve, after all."

"Thank you, ma'am. I will." He walked over to the drinks table and poured two small glasses of sherry. "Here you are, ma'am."

George took her glass and raised it. "Cheers and Merry Christmas."

"Merry Christmas."

George looked back down to her papers. "It's mostly about the election today, I see."

"Yes, ma'am. I understand from government officials you may have to cut short your Christmas break and go back to Buckingham Palace earlier than usual to meet the prime minister, whoever he or she might be."

"Hmm…then my speech to the House of Lords will follow soon after. It must be done, I suppose."

Once a government was returned, the Queen, on behalf of her government, had to set out to the people their intentions for their allotted time in office. It was unusual to have an election at the end of January, but the current prime minister, the formidable Bodicea Dixon, had lost her majority in the House of Commons. She couldn't get an emergency budget through the Commons and lost a vote of confidence. An election was the only option.

Since Bo Dixon had come to power, her authoritarian leadership and questionable support of the troubled regime of the dictator of

Vospya had made her party's popularity plummet. Labour had lost MP after MP, and the party was in open civil war, the left of the party trying to claw back from the more right-of-centre Bo Dixon.

George sat back in her seat. "Do you think I'll be welcoming my second prime minister as Queen, or will Bo Dixon hang on?"

"It's a tight one, ma'am, but I'd put my money on the Conservatives ousting Ms. Dixon," Bastian said.

The opposition had appointed a new leader six months ago to replace his dull, boring predecessor. Raj Shah was young for a potential prime minister, and George secretly hoped he might win, not because of his politics—she believed strongly in her duty to be impartial—and not because she had come to dislike Bo Dixon.

But his premiership would be nice to see because it would mark another couple of firsts, for her reign as Queen and for the country. Raj would be the country's first prime minister of Indian descent, and the first married gay man. Number Ten would be home to Raj, his husband, and their two children. Another barrier would be broken down.

"Well, we shall see what the country wants very soon," George said.

"Yes, ma'am. The other main issue in your boxes today is the security arrangement for the visit of Queen Rozala and Crown Consort Lennox."

George smiled and picked up the next folder. "Excellent, I can't wait to see my cousins."

Rozala had blossomed in her role as Queen. George knew it was in no small measure owing to the help and support of her partner, Lennox.

"There aren't too many issues, are there? I assume MI6 and the royal protection squad are liaising with Denbourg secret service?"

"Yes, ma'am, but there are strong opposition voices within the Denbourg government and officials to her coming at this time, including Crown Consort Lennox, I believe."

The trip to Britain in February was important to Queen Beatrice and Queen Rozala. Beatrice had come up with a new campaign for the new year. This year her charitable focus would be on supporting families.

George was really proud of Beatrice and all the hard work she had put into it. She had even managed to get the UN to designate the year as the Year of the Family, and many European countries were engaging in their own campaigns. Denbourg was one.

Queen Rozala was getting her UK charity, Dreams and Wishes, to work with Beatrice's Timmy's and other charities. It would all kick off when Rozala visited.

George put the folder back in her red box. "Is Lennox worried because Queen Rozala is so late in her pregnancy?"

"Yes, ma'am. She will be in her seventh month and hit her eighth month when they visit, but Queen Rozala is determined," Bastian said.

George knew how stubborn Rozala could be. "I would be concerned if it was my wife, but we'll make sure we look after her. I understand her pregnancy has been very healthy so far."

Bastian nodded. "Yes, but her officials have long memories, and the Queen's mother died giving birth to Rozala."

"I understand that. Maybe you could put together a contingency plan to give the Denbourg officials, detailing how we would react if there were any problems? It may allay their fears."

"Excellent idea, ma'am. I will do."

"And the documentary? Is everything still set to start in the new year?"

To celebrate the Year of the Family, Bea had been asked to have cameras follow her campaign, for a documentary for the BBC. The documentary would depict their family in the Year of the Family.

Letting cameras into their private lives wasn't ideal, but it was essential every now and then to let the public see what the royal family did day to day, and to document something close to Bea's heart. Her father had done a few, which had been a great success.

Bea only agreed if she could choose the filmmaker. Aziza Bouzid was an old friend of Bea's who produced exceptional documentaries and had won awards for her work. Bea had told her they met through her former role at Timmy's.

"I better get on with these then." George picked up her father's fountain pen and began to sign some of the papers. After a few moments, she realized Bastian hadn't left, and she looked up. He was looking a little nervous.

"Was there something more, Bastian?"

"Ma'am, you asked me to try to find a suitable nanny for the princesses."

"Yes, since my wife has found something wrong with the last hundred applicants, especially after the disastrous last appointment." Clay had discovered their nanny was taking private photographs and videos of the children, then selling them to the highest bidder. George and Bea couldn't understand how press photographers were getting that close and how they were getting hold of some deeply personal information on the family.

Clay had her suspicions and fed some bogus information to the nanny to see if it appeared in the press. It did, and when George found out, she wanted to rip the nanny limb from limb, figuratively speaking.

Bastian grasped a folder. Government files for the Queen's eye tended still to be on paper, so they couldn't be hacked online.

"There is a nanny, just qualified from the prestigious Landsford School, who might suit, and she has an acute understanding of this world and I believe will be very trustworthy."

George was intrigued. "Who?"

"I have her secret service file." Bastian held it out to George.

"You asked for her to be vetted before consulting me?"

"No, Your Majesty. She already had a file. The late king asked for it to be kept top secret unless you ever asked directly about her." George frowned in puzzlement and curiosity and took the folder. She opened it up and Bastian said, "Her name is Katya Kovach."

CHAPTER TWO

Katya Kovach scooped up her shoulder-length hair and wiped the sweat from her brow. There weren't many people in the large gym at Landsford nannying school. Most of the students and graduates had gone home for Christmas, but she didn't have to leave until tonight.

Katya loved exercise. Feeling fit made her feel in control and gave her a sense of security. After a hard run on the treadmill, she was stretching and warming down.

All of a sudden she heard a voice whisper in her ear, "Hey, my lady."

In a split second Katya whirled round and took her assailant's feet out from under him. He fell to the floor, and Katya pinned him with her fist inches from his face.

"Hey, it's me!"

The familiar voice penetrated Katya's consciousness, and the fog started to clear from her eyes. Her fist was inches from her best friend and fellow Landsford graduate, Artie Davidson. She jumped up quickly and tried to calm her breathing from the adrenaline rush coursing through her body.

"What have I told you about sneaking up on me, Artie?"

"I'm sorry, Kat. I forgot."

Katya shook her head and then offered her hand to Artie. "No, I'm sorry."

Artie took her hand and stood up.

"I didn't hurt you, did I?" Katya asked.

Artie smiled and brushed down his clothes. "Only my pride. Don't worry about it."

Katya looked around the gym and noticed that everyone was looking at them, something that she hated.

"Let's go over there." Katya lifted her water bottle and towel and walked over to the side of the gym where there were a few benches along the walls.

"I just wanted to say goodbye for now," Artie said, "I'm off home. Mum and Dad are expecting me in an hour."

Katya wiped her face with her towel. "Say hi to your parents, and make sure you phone me."

Artie smiled. "I will certainly, my lady."

Katya rolled her eyes. "I wish you wouldn't call me that."

Ever since they became friends, Artie had called Katya *my lady*, due to her cut-glass English accent. He said she sounded more like the people they would eventually be working for than their nannies.

Landsford was situated in London and was the country's most prestigious nannying school. It catered to the aristocracy, politicians, and the very wealthy. With their brown uniforms and hats, Landsford produced nannies that echoed a bygone Victorian era.

But as Katya had just demonstrated, they had moved with the times and recognized that the children they looked after might need protection.

All Landsford nannies were trained in self-defence and skidpad driving, by former secret service agents, to give them the best chance of protecting the children under their charge.

Both Katya and Artie had graduated at the top of their class in the summer but had agreed to stay on and mentor the new first year students until their first placements were due to start in the new year.

Unfortunately, Katya's post had fallen through.

"When do you leave for Miss Dorcas's house?" Artie asked.

"I'm to be there for nine. I've got plenty of time."

"Listen," Artie said, "I know holidays, especially Christmas, are hard for you, so call me at any time, or if you want, come and stay with my family for a while. I don't start working until February."

Katya smiled and squeezed Artie's hand. He was so kind and the best and only friend she had. She didn't make friends easily. She didn't trust anyone and very few got past her defensive barriers.

Artie had been so persistent in trying to gain her friendship since they first enrolled together that she'd eventually given in and let him in. But even he didn't know much about her past. He knew she was an orphan and had essentially been brought up by Miss Dorcas, her former boarding school headmistress.

"Thank you, Artie. I appreciate it, but I'll be fine. Miss Dorcas and I will have a lovely time. Then I have a few interviews lined up in January."

"As long as you know the offer's there, Kat."

Katya smiled and gave him a kiss on the cheek. "Of course I do. Now go home before old St. Nicholas arrives with your presents."

Artie kissed her on the cheek. "Okay, have a nice Christmas."

Once he was gone, Katya went upstairs to her room, took a shower, and finished packing her bag. She looked over to her bedside table and gazed at the picture there. It was a photo of her family. Mother, father, aunts, uncles, grandparents, and cousins. Strictly speaking, she wasn't supposed to have it out on display for prying eyes to see, but all of that was a long time ago, and she didn't think the other students would be very interested.

She walked over and picked it up. Katya reverently traced her fingers over her mother and father. This photo was of the last time they had gathered together as a family—the last time before their world, and hers, was turned upside down.

Don't.

It was time to go. Katya gathered her bags and went downstairs. She would catch the bus and be at Miss Dorcas's house in no time.

Thirty minutes later she was exiting the lift of her former headmistress's retirement building. She approached the door and dropped her rucksack. Just as she was about to ring the bell, the door opened and the tall, elderly figure of Miss Dorcas appeared, or Dora as she was known to Kat.

"My little Kitty Kat, come in. I've been watching out of the window for you."

Kat opened her arms to hug the woman who had brought her up, who'd stepped into the shoes of a mother when Kat had none.

But instead of reciprocating, Dora took her hand and reverently kissed the back of it.

Kat sighed. "I keep telling you—I'm just a nanny. You don't need to do that, Dora."

Dora cupped Kat's cheek and said, "You will always be much more, Kitty Kat. Anyway, come in, come in. We have our Christmas Eve to get started." Dora led her by the hand through to the living room. "What do you think?"

Kat gasped. Dora's living room always looked like Christmas had exploded out of a can, but every year she managed to make it bigger and better.

"You've added more?" Kat said.

Dora looked quite pleased with herself. "Yes, don't I always? It's my favourite time of year."

Kat pulled Dora into a hug. "Thank you. It's wonderful."

Dora had been doing this since Kat's first year in Britain as a refugee. She was ten, in a foreign country, and in boarding school, with no one to go home to at the holidays. But that first year after losing her family, Dora took her into her cottage on the grounds of the boarding school, and they began to make new Christmas traditions.

Back then, Kat knew, their holidays together were always focussed on giving Kat something she didn't have any more, after the loss of her family. But in recent years their time became about Dora, and giving her the love and attention she so deserved in her later years.

"Come in and have a drink while dinner is cooking," Dora said.

Kat took a seat on the sofa while Dora poured them two snowballs, their traditional Christmas Eve drink. The TV news played in the background, its sound down low, but the pictures of fighting, gunfire, and people crying while speaking to TV reporters made the country's identity clear.

It was the country of her birth, Vospya.

Dora handed her a drink. "I'm sorry. I forgot I left the news on."

"It's okay. It breaks my heart to see Vospya in such turmoil, but the people are fighting back, and that gives me hope."

During the years since she had left there as a refugee, Vospya had turned from being a liberal, prosperous republic to being a harsh, authoritarian dictatorship, with an awful human rights record. But the uprising against the dictatorship of President Loka, led by the Liberty Freedom Fighters, had been building slowly, and now their numbers were getting greater with every passing day.

She watched as the news showed the rebels, carrying the former flag of Vospya, storming one of her country's greatest museums and waving the flag from its steps, claiming the building as their own. Kat prayed that one day the true Vospyan flag would be flying over the government buildings again.

Dora raised her glass and said, "To Vospya and the Liberty Freedom Fighters."

Kat smiled and clinked her glass against Dora's. "To Vospya and liberty."

They each took a sip, and Dora said, "Now, there's something I want to talk to you about. A possible job for you."

Kat was desperate to get to work. Being independent and in control meant the world to her. When she arrived in Britain with not a penny to her name, she vowed never to be in that position again. She had worked in cafes and shops since she was sixteen years old, then bars and clubs when she turned eighteen. She was determined to pay her own way through college and nannying school, since a kind benefactor had paid for her school fees and living expenses.

Kat studied English, history, and foreign languages on her own time. She spoke German, French, Italian, and a little Spanish, all of which she knew would help her on her way through life. She hated not working and would be so pleased if she could get a job quickly.

"Nannying? Have you heard of a family that needs help?"

Dora chuckled. "Yes, I've heard of a very special family that needs a nanny, and your childhood experience in Vospya will be of a great help."

"Tell me—I'm intrigued," Kat said.

Queen Beatrice stroked the fine soft hair of her baby daughter. The three-month-old was sleeping peacefully. She kissed the tips of her fingers and placed them on her daughter's brow.

"Sleep well, Anna."

Princess Adrianna Sarah Sophia quickly became Anna when she came home from the hospital. Beatrice and George wanted to name her after all the strong women in her life, the ones she could count on.

Bea heard the door of the nursery open, and George whispered, "Are you ready, Bea? Mrs. Bruce is here."

"Yes, she's fast asleep."

Bea felt George's presence behind her. George wrapped her arms around her middle and said, "Of course she is. She's an angel."

Unlike her boisterous big sister, Anna had been a calm, contented little girl.

George sighed. "I can't believe how lucky I am. Three beautiful girls to look after. Thank you, Mrs. Buckingham."

Beatrice turned around and kissed George on the lips. "You're welcome, Bully. Did you speak to Theo?"

"Yes, apparently she had an unavoidable holiday in the Caribbean."

Bea sighed. Theo's girlfriend had been invited to spend Christmas with the family. Not an invitation the Queen gave lightly, but Lady

Celeste and Theo had been together for six months, and it was getting to the stage where the family needed to try to include her in family occasions.

Bea had met Celeste at events where she came as Theo's guest and wasn't impressed by her attitude towards the staff or other guests who she thought were beneath her.

"She never seems to miss being on Theo's arm at film premieres or parties, but anything else, she's too busy."

"I think Theo's a bit embarrassed, to be honest," George said.

"I don't like her, but I'm sorry for Theo's sake."

"Neither does my mama, or Granny. I just wish he could meet a nice girl, like I did. Someone who cares, who would share his desire to do good in the world."

Bea put her hand on George's chest. "He's not going to find her in his circle of overprivileged friends."

"I know that. He was always happy with girlfriends who weren't serious, but in the last year I've seen him longing for what we have. I think he's lonely."

"He'll find it. He just needs to look in different places. We better get downstairs before Teddy explodes with excitement," Bea said.

George nodded. "She'll probably be even worse with her Uncle Theo making her more excited."

After dinner the family all retreated to the drawing room for their traditional Christmas Eve celebration, while Bea checked on Anna, and George and Theo got Teddy into her jammies. Bea had found the Buckinghams' traditions a bit odd at first, but she grew to enjoy them and add her own along the way. Unlike other British families, the Buckinghams opened some presents on Christmas Eve, a tradition inherited from their German ancestry. Bea had adapted this to one family present each, wanting to keep the magic of Santa Claus alive in her children.

She adjusted the stocking on the end of Anna's cot. "I hope Santa Claus is good to you, sweet pea."

They walked out of the nursery bedroom to find one of the older housemaids, Mrs. Bruce, waiting for them. She curtsied to Bea.

"Are you sure you don't mind keeping an eye on Anna, Mrs. Bruce? It's a shame you're missing the staff party."

The kitchen, housemaids, pages, chefs, and security staff were all having a get-together downstairs in the kitchen, while the family enjoyed their own celebration upstairs.

"Not at all, Your Majesty. Let the young ones have their fun. It'll be too noisy for me anyway. I'll sit with my book and be quite happy."

"I'll have one of the pages bring you up a sherry, Mrs. Bruce. We're very grateful," George said.

But first, they had invited some of the staff and security team into the drawing room. They were having a surprise for Quincy and Clay before they went off to join the staff party downstairs.

George held open the nursery door for Bea, and they walked out to the corridor. George took Bea's hand and could feel the tension in her wife, and she was sure she knew why. Now was as good a time as any to bring up the nanny subject.

"We can't keep doing this to the staff, and your mother and father, having them look after the girls," George said, "It's not fair. And the staff didn't sign on to be babysitters."

"I know that," Bea said a little too forcefully. "I'm sorry."

George squeezed her hand. "I may have a nanny for you to see."

Bea sighed.

"I know how you feel, my darling, but even if we weren't part of this life, we'd still need childcare. We'd both be working people."

A page walking up the corridor towards them stood to the side and bowed his head to them.

"Thank you, Tom," George said to him.

Once they were past, Bea said, "I can't shake the feeling that I'm dumping my children on some stranger. A stranger I know nothing about, in the heart of our family bubble. You know what that *woman* did."

George stopped and hugged Bea. Both of them felt such guilt for not realizing their last nanny's character. "I know. I feel awful every day about it, but this woman I have in mind—I trust her, and I haven't even met her."

Bea pushed away and looked at George quizzically. "Why?"

George smiled. "Because she was brought up in our kind of world. I'll tell you about her later. Let's go—Teddy will be getting impatient."

❖

Clay was always nervous around the extended royal family, and the drawing room was full of them, along with the protection squad. The room was chaos with people chattering, dogs chasing the children, and children running and squealing around the room.

She took in everything around her. There were people who would give anything to have this job.

Every scrap of the royal family's personal life was sought out hungrily by the press and the public, but few knew the truth.

All of the Queen's immediate family was there to celebrate Christmas. George's mother, Queen Sophia, was talking to Bea's mum, Sarah. Then there was Reg, Bea's dad, who was talking to George's uncle, the Duke of Bransford. The duke's wife, George's aunt Grace, was laughing with the Dowager Queen, Adrianna.

George's cousins Lord Maximillian and Lady Victoria were helping Prince Theo to entertain the children—Teddy and Elizabeth and Fabian, the children of Viscount Anglesey. Since Viscount Anglesey had been dishonoured and banished from the family, after a plot to oust the Queen and usurp her throne, Queen Georgina had purposely brought his children into the bosom of the family, to make sure they were not punished for the sins of their father.

Clay had heard that the children were living with their grandparents, Princess Grace and the Duke of Bransford, virtually full time. The gossip was that Marta, their mother, was happy to leave them there while she attended parties and holidayed around the world.

Theo and Teddy shot past Clay, and she laughed when Theo grabbed Teddy and turned her upside down, holding her by the legs. Teddy giggled incessantly.

She turned to Jack beside her and saw that he was really tense. "You okay, Jack?" Jack was new and still getting used to being around the family.

"I'm a bit nervous. Do you know why we've been called in here?"

Clay looked along to Captain Quincy, who was chatting to Major Cameron, who'd been Captain Cameron until a few months ago. "It's a surprise for Captain Quincy. Just wait and see." All the protection squad were standing near Clay—Boothby, Jones, and the others—murmuring and gossiping about what was happening.

The only person not present was Inspector Lang, who had retired after a short illness before Christmas. Captain Quincy had been acting commander of the royal protection squad in the meantime. No police officer in their group had a problem with Quincy's rapid promotion, or her command. After she took the bullets meant for Queen Beatrice during the American tour, she became a hero to the nation and to every one of her fellow officers.

Clay saw Jack gulp hard as Lali Ramesh, Queen Bea's personal assistant and Major Cameron's wife, walked towards them with her friend Holly. They were two beautiful women, and Clay had always had a little crush on Holly, but now she was a good friend. But then Clay seemed to have crushes on everyone.

"Jack, Clay," Holly said, "save us from Cammy and Quin's boring army talk."

Lali laughed, and Clay started to speak, "Well—"

The drawing room doors opened, and Major Cameron announced, "The Queen."

At that command everyone who was sitting stood respectfully. It was always strange to see Queen Georgina's family bow to her, even in private, but it was tradition, and besides Queen Georgina commanded respect.

The Queen walked in with Bea. Teddy ran to George as soon as she spotted her. George lifted Teddy in the air and spun her around.

"Presents, Mum," Teddy said.

"Soon, Teddy bear. We have our surprise first, remember?"

Teddy clapped her hands. "Yes, the secret."

George put Teddy down and said, "Please sit, everyone."

Once the family was settled George turned to one of the pages and nodded. She brought over a silver platter with two flat boxes on it.

George picked up the first and said, "I've asked you all here tonight to make a very special announcement. After an exemplary career in the Royal Marines, Captain Quincy joined the royal protection squad and hasn't been with the police force for long, but she has shown herself to be an exceptional officer, just as she was in the Royal Marines. Her act of bravery, saving Queen Beatrice, can never be repaid, and since stepping into Inspector Lang's shoes, she has further shown her professionalism and dedication to the job."

George opened the box and revealed two epaulettes for the rank of inspector.

Clay looked over at Quincy. She looked shocked, and a beaming Holly held tightly onto her arm. It was so nice to see the unflappable Captain Quincy so happily surprised.

George continued, "Bea, Teddy, if you would do the honours."

"Gladly." Bea took the epaulettes and handed them to Teddy. They walked over to Quincy and Bea lifted Teddy. "Do your stuff, Teddy." Teddy handed over the epaulettes to Quincy, and Bea said, "Congratulations, *Inspector* Quincy."

Quincy bowed. "Thank you, Your Majesty."

Holly immediately threw her arms around Quincy's neck. Clay looked on enviously. *It must be amazing to have someone to love you like that.*

"But that's not all," the Queen said. She produced another box and handed it to Teddy. "Remember, we practised?"

Teddy nodded and to Clay's surprise ran over to her. Clay had no clue about what was going on.

She knelt down to Teddy's level and looked at the presentation box. It was a pair of sergeant's epaulettes. Clay was beyond shocked. She looked up at Bea and then at Queen Georgina, who walked over to stand next to her.

"Attention, Clayton," the Queen said. She stood up to attention and the Queen continued, "Scotland Yard allowed me to do the honours and inform you of your promotion."

"Congratulations, Sergeant Clayton." The Queen winked at her and smacked her on the shoulder. "You deserve it."

All of her friends and colleagues started clapping and cheering loudly. Then each in turn came to congratulate both her and Quincy.

Wow. The Christmas party was going to be an extraordinary celebration now.

❖

Oh God, my head is sore.

Clay felt like there were two pieces of barbed wire being pushed and pulled inside her head, and yet she had to be very alert.

It was Christmas morning and one of the most public events the royals held all year, the Christmas Day church service. It was a tradition that the family walked to the church on the grounds of Sandringham House, apart from the Dowager Queen, the Queen Mother, and Bea's mum, who were driven.

George and Bea led the procession of the family past crowds of well-wishers, who'd queued from early morning just to watch the family pass. They were due out of the service any time now, and then Clay and her colleagues would be on high alert as they walked back past the crowd.

Tradition dictated that the family stopped and talked to the people waiting and took gifts of flowers and a whole host of other items, especially gifts for the royal children. That meant Clay had to be especially alert and keep an eye on her charges.

The raging hangover she had wasn't helping. What a night they'd had in the Sandringham kitchen. Queen Georgina had provided the champagne and other wines and spirits from her drinks cellar. Clay was not used to champagne. It was like a fizzy drink and went down far too easily, hence the dreadful hangover.

Quincy came out of the church door and indicated to the assembled protection officers, including the extended royal family's protection officers, that they were about to move.

They all walked down the steps of the church and moved out of the way to allow the family out. Queen Georgina emerged from the church with Queen Adrianna on her arm, then Queen Beatrice with Queen Sophia and Teddy. Anna was too young yet for this event.

Once the Queen Mother, the Dowager Queen, and Bea's mum were safely escorted to the waiting car, the family began to walk down the path back to the house.

The path was flanked on either side by throngs of people, who mostly wanted the attention of Princess Teddy. They had cards, stuffed animals, toys, and some gifts of sweets, which would be accepted but of course never given to her.

Clay put her hangover to the back of her mind and made sure that no one got too close to Teddy. Bea and Teddy stopped at an old lady in a wheelchair who was holding a helium balloon for Teddy. Bea was helping Teddy engage with the older woman, but she needn't have bothered—Teddy was great with the public, a proper little show-off, and was making the lady laugh.

The Christmas arrival and departure were always shown live on TV, and Clay thought about how her mum, if she had been alive, would have been sitting with her auntie, watching this right now and being so proud of her.

Making her mum proud had meant everything to her. She had made a lot of sacrifices so Clay could get to where she was, and all Clay wanted was to make her mum proud. Now there was no one watching her with pride. She was quite alone in the world.

After slowly making their way through the crowds, the royal party finally arrived back at the house, and she was off duty till later.

The staff were all going to have Christmas dinner together, after the royal family had been served, and make a nice night together, even though they were away from their own families.

Clay checked her phone—she had six missed calls from her aunt. Clay didn't get on with her aunt. A rarity these days, she was fervently against the fact that Clay was gay, because of her religious beliefs. Her aunt had been pushing her to sort through her mum's house, pack up the things she wanted to keep, and get the house up for sale.

But she hadn't been able to face it. Clay was terrified of packing up her mum's house, because if she did, the last part of her mum would truly be gone.

She looked around the room at everyone so happy and celebrating, and a feeling of tightness began in her chest and panic spread throughout her body. *I can't do this.* She hurried upstairs to her room and slammed the door shut.

CHAPTER THREE

The royal car drove through the gates of Sandringham House, carrying Katya to her interview. The recent snow had given the large Jacobean style house a romantic, picture-postcard look.

She would be there in minutes, so she took out her make-up mirror to check her appearance. Her brown Landsford uniform was designed to be traditional and plain, and Katya liked it that way. Standing out was the last thing she wanted to do.

Katya had learned that anonymity was safety, and in every way she could, she faded into the background. The brown uniform was the unchanging Victorian style of brown work dress with short sleeves, brown hat, thick brown tights, and brown brogues. Her coat was a thick, heavy brown wool.

A Landsford nanny wasn't supposed to be noticed or to upstage the children or their important parents, and that suited Katya. She went even further, pinning her shoulder-length blond hair up into a bun, and wearing minimal make-up.

As she approached the house, she felt some nerves. When she graduated from college, she never thought she'd be offered an interview for a position like this, or if she should accept if offered. Perhaps it was all too close, too high profile, but Miss Dorcas said the royal couple were desperate for someone they could trust.

The car stopped outside the front door where a beautiful woman was waiting for her. A male page opened the car door, and she stepped out.

"Ms. Kovach?"

"Yes."

The woman smiled and extended her hand. "I'm Lali Ramesh, Queen Beatrice's private secretary."

"Pleased to meet you, Ms. Ramesh, and call me Katya, please," Katya said.

"And you must call me Lali. Let me take you in."

Katya followed Lali through the entrance to the home. It wasn't as large and palatial as Windsor or Buckingham Palace, she knew, but grand enough for a country estate. Most in her position would have been bowled over by the size, the grandeur, but not Katya.

She was taken through to a large ornate drawing room, with grand paintings and a decorated ceiling surrounded by white decorative plaster.

"Take a seat, and I'll get Queen Beatrice for you."

Lali left, and it wasn't long before Queen Beatrice was walking into the room. She stood immediately and curtsied as the Queen Consort approached.

"Katya? So pleased to meet you," Queen Beatrice said.

"You too, Your Majesty. Thank you for seeing me."

"Take a seat."

Queen Beatrice was even more beautiful in the flesh, and as warm as people said. A few moments later a page entered the room with tea. He set it on a trestle table and the Queen Consort poured out two cups.

"Milk? Sugar?"

"Just milk, please," Katya said.

Queen Beatrice handed over the cup and said, "You must know that we've had a problem employing a nanny."

"Yes, I did read about your last nanny, but I never trust everything I read in the media."

The Queen Consort smiled. "Good answer. But some elements were true. Our nanny did sell stories and took some very personal photographs of the children in their nursery. Fortunately our lawyers intervened before they were published."

Katya was shocked. "That is disgraceful. For a nanny to do that? It's shameful."

"Yes." Queen Beatrice looked down with what looked like guilt. "You can imagine how wary I am of trusting someone with my children."

"I understand, Your Majesty. Trust is so important," Katya said.

The Queen Consort took a sip of tea. "Queen Georgina trusts you, and she hasn't even met you."

Katya got the impression Queen Beatrice knew more about her than she was saying.

"I know you were brought up in places like this. I know who you are. Princess Olga Bolotov of Vospya and Marchioness of Romka."

Katya's heart started to race. "That's who I was, but that was another life."

"George's father didn't tell her about you. He kept your identity on a need-to-know basis. She was only told about you before Christmas."

"The secrecy was felt necessary for my safety. Only two Bolotovs survived after the revolution in Vospya, myself and my uncle, who was out of the country at the time. My uncle doesn't know I made it out. It's a secret even from him," Katya replied.

The Queen Consort sat forward in her seat and said, "Why does someone like you want to be a nanny?"

Katya's mind played the old movie in her head, like it always did. The screams, the shots, the confusion, and the fear. She looked Queen Beatrice in the eye and said, "Someone like me saved my life, and I want to be that person for other children. As for the rest—this may have been my world, but it is no longer my life any more. I want to have nothing more than an ordinary life."

Queen Beatrice stood. "Well, I'd better take you to meet the children."

Clay was surrounded by boxes in the living room of her mother's home. She took the last picture off the wall and stared into the frame. It was Clay and her mum at her police passing out parade. Her mum looked so proud, *was* so proud of her. Even more so when Clay began working for the royal family.

Trinity Clayton and Ronnie, as her mother called her, had come a long way since their days living in Brixton in the South of London. Nobody would have thought that the girl who was brought up with very little, and failing at school, would end up with a career in the police force, guarding the Queens' children. It was all because of Trinity.

"Is this the last of the boxes, Clay?" a voice said behind her.

She turned around and saw Holly standing there with a box in her arms.

"Yeah, this is everything. Thanks for helping me," Clay said.

"Of course we'd help you. You're family. Isn't she, Quin?" Holly said to Inspector Quincy, who was coming back in from the van they had hired.

"Indeed. We're here for you. The Queen and Queen Bea are safely in for the day, so we can help you as much as you like."

"Thanks."

Quincy patted her on the back and said, "Just these few more boxes and we'll be finished."

"Is that picture going into storage with the rest?" Holly asked.

"No." Clay clasped it close to her chest. "No, this one's coming with me."

"Okay."

Before long, Clay and her two friends had finished loading the van. It was time to leave, and Clay was dreading it.

Holly took Quincy's hand and said, "We'll let you have privacy. Come out whenever you're ready."

They left, and Clay was finally alone with her memories—and her guilt. Clay grasped the picture closer to her chest and turned in the empty space. It felt like the sadness and gloom was in the air itself, suffocating her, while the guilt twisted in her stomach.

She hadn't been there for her mum. She'd been so tied up with her job, and now there would be no other chances to make memories.

"I should have been here more, Mum."

Her mother understood the nature of Clay's job. It was a vocation, all-consuming, not a nine-to-five affair, but still that didn't ease the guilt. She was alone now, and she was quite sure that the sun would never come out again.

Clay walked to the front door and said, "Goodbye, Mum."

She got into the van, and Quincy started to drive off. Clay looked into the rear-view mirror and watched the cottage becoming smaller as they moved away. She felt like she was leaving her mum behind, and tears filled her eyes.

She wiped her eyes, hoping that Holly and Quincy hadn't noticed, then felt Holly's hand grip hers. The effort of trying to keep her tears under control was making her chest feel like it had a tight elastic band around it. She couldn't breathe.

When would this pain ever ease?

❖

A black limousine pulled up in front of the Vospyan Embassy in London. Alexander Chak, the new ambassador, gazed upon the grand, old sandstone building and felt strong satisfaction that he, a once lowly infantry freedom fighter, had made it to Britain. Such journeys were not made without ruthless action and decisions, and Alexander was relentless in his pursuit of power.

Among government staff, the two best ambassadorial positions were the United States and Great Britain. Alexander had wanted the British post more than anything. Despite its modern and, in his opinion, weak liberalism, he admired the UK's imperial past, something he would like for Vospya.

Once the Liberty rebels were vanquished, he would be pushing politically for expansion of their borders into neighbouring territory. Another reason he wanted to be here was to enjoy the bright lights and entertainment of London's excess.

Alexander's driver opened his door and he stepped out onto the pavement. The first thing he saw was the British police, holding back protestors behind a barrier. They had rainbow flags, signs, and placards about human rights.

He was told that there was a level of protest every day at the embassy. He looked over at them and straightened his tie. How could a country allow this kind of protest on their streets? This showed the weakness of Britain.

Alexander stared at one of the most vocal protestors and straightened his tie. In Vospya they would be shot or tortured for information. It was hardly surprising the people behaved this way, when their Queen was a lesbian and, disgustingly, was allowed to have two children.

He thought of Queen Beatrice. What a beautiful woman. He had a thing for blondes. What a waste to be living a deviant life like that. Alexander was sure that he could change her mind, like most women he had come across.

His thoughts were interrupted by a voice beside him.

"Your Excellency."

He turned around and saw a small, well-dressed man standing beside him.

"I'm Victor, sir. Your private secretary. Welcome to London."

"Thank you, Victor. Are they here just for me or…?" Alexander pointed to the protestors.

Victor cleared his throat. "They are here most days, Your Excellency. Let me show you in."

Alexander followed Victor up the stone steps and entered into a rather grand entrance hall. It was filled with embassy staff who stood on the marble hall floor and all the way up the grand stairway. They all began clapping at his arrival.

He waved and smiled, and then a young woman caught his eye at the base of the stairs. She was standing next to an older woman. The young woman was petite and delicate and had long blond hair—everything he was attracted to. Like his wife, when she was a much younger woman.

Alexander leaned over to Victor and said, "Who is that woman?"

Victor narrowed his eyes. "The older woman, Excellency? That is your secretary, Margaret."

"No, the young woman next to her."

"Oh, that's Anita. She is an administrative assistant under Margaret."

Alexander didn't take his eyes off her and said, "She's my new secretary."

Victor went to protest. "But—"

He gave Victor a hard stare. "Make it happen, Victor."

"Of course, Excellency."

❖

The high energy children's song rang out loud in the Sandringham nursery. Katya held Princess Anna in her arms and danced around, while Teddy bounced on the tips of her toes.

"Hands up to the sky, Teddy," Katya said.

Teddy was all smiles as she followed the instructions in the song. "Up to the sky, up to the sky."

Anna giggled as she was bounced around by Katya. The two royal children were just adorable, and Katya was falling in love with them already. Teddy had been friendly and loving from the time they first met. She had a lovely, excitable, fun-loving personality, and by contrast Anna was a calm, laid-back little girl. Katya knew she was going to enjoy her new job.

The nursery door opened, and when Teddy spotted it was her mum, the Queen, she ran and jumped into her arms.

"Computer, mute music," Katya said.

"You having lots of fun, my little terror?" Queen Georgina asked.

"Yeah, we are dancing with Kat."

"Excellent."

George put Teddy down, and she ran over to her toys. Katya curtsied to George.

"It's a pleasure to meet you at last." George took Katya's free hand and kissed the back. It was a greeting common between royals, who were often related, and the Bolotovs were related to the Buckinghams through Queen Victoria. "Katya, are you settling in well?"

"Yes, Your Majesty. Your children are beautiful and very good-natured."

Princess Anna stretched out her arms to her mum, and Katya handed her over. George kissed her chubby cheek.

"This angel is," George smiled, "but Teddy the terror keeps us on our toes."

To illustrate this, Teddy was running around the room, hands outstretched, pretending to be an aeroplane.

"I'll keep her busy, then," Katya said.

George hugged Anna close and rubbed her back. "Katya? I have to ask this once, because I feel guilty. Are you sure you want to do this? Be our nanny? I mean, I know my father paid your school fees and helped you get a good education, but I didn't know you existed. If I had, I would of course have helped in any way I could. I mean, I still will. If this isn't what you truly want, then I'll help you do what you really want. Once a royal, always a royal in my book."

Queen Georgina truly was a good woman, as many people said she was. "Queen Georgina, I'm very grateful for your offering, and I know it may feel awkward for you to have a former aristocrat working for you, but you mustn't feel so. My royal life ended when I was ten, and I do not want to hang on to any part of it. I'm an ordinary woman, and I want to be treated as such, and I do want this job."

George nodded. "I just wanted to get everything out in the open, and make sure you were comfortable with it."

"I am, and it will be a pleasure looking after these two. One thing, though—please keep my identity private. I don't want anyone to treat me differently or anyone in Vospya to know I'm still alive."

"Of course. Your safety is paramount. I'm sorry you had to watch Queen Beatrice and me welcome President Loka to Britain. The very man who led the rebellion against your family. But I had no choice. I must meet whomever my prime minister wishes me to, but it gave me no pleasure."

It had been horrible to watch on the news. The red carpet had been rolled out for the man who orchestrated the murder of her family, but she wanted to reassure the Queen.

"Your Majesty, no one understands better than I the difficult position a constitutional monarch is put in from time to time by their government. That's what my uncle the King had to do."

"Thank you for your understanding. Now you'll be working closely with Veronica Clayton and Jack, the children's police protection officers. Sergeant Clayton is off on a short period of leave at the moment, but she'll be returning soon. The children are very fond of Clay."

Katya smiled. "I'll look forward to meeting her."

"Oh, you'll get on very well. Clay is upbeat, fun-loving, and caring. Perfect for the children."

CHAPTER FOUR

Clay sat on the edge of the bed and held her head in her hands. Her skull felt like it was being repeatedly hit with a hammer. She felt sick to her stomach.

Flashes of drinking shots, dancing, and snorting coke filled her head. The woman behind her stirred, and she was filled with self-loathing. Clay looked up and was faced with her own image in the woman's dressing-table mirror.

She didn't recognize herself. Her warm black skin was even darker under her eyes. She looked awful. Long gone was the chirpy, positive woman she truly was, and in her place was someone ill and sad. She was wasted. Finally dealing with her mother's house had been the straw that broke the camel's back.

The grief that she had managed to keep buried deep down had come pouring out, and she was struggling to cope. Luckily she had been given a short period of bereavement leave. She had hoped to heal and come back to her job with a renewed purpose, but instead she had been sinking deeper into her pain. She flinched when the woman she'd spent the night with touched her shoulder.

Nina was her name, she remembered.

"Do you want to stay for breakfast?"

Clay looked at the bedside table and saw a mirror with white powder on it and a pipe. This wasn't her. The last time in her life she had taken drugs was at a party at school. She had taken up with a bad group of friends, before her mum took them out of London. Trinity Clayton would be so ashamed of her.

"No thanks. I have to go. Thanks for everything."

Clay stood up and pulled on her jeans and T-shirt. She just wanted to get out of here.

"Can I get your number?" Nina asked.

She took one last glimpse in the mirror, ran her hand through her blond-tipped tight curls, and grabbed her jacket. "I don't think that would be a good idea. I…I'm not in a good place right now."

"See you around then," Nina snapped.

That was her cue to go. Clay walked out of the flat and downstairs to the street. It was half past seven in the morning, but the roads and pavements were busy. The morning light was making her head worse. She needed painkillers and coffee, but the last thing she wanted to do was go back to her empty flat.

That was the whole reason she felt so terrible this morning. She was on leave from work in an empty flat, with nothing but her feelings of sadness. That was why she had been out drinking most nights.

Anything to try to numb her feelings, but it all just made Clay feel worse. She knew what her mum would say if she could see her now. She'd be disgusted.

Clay rubbed her forehead. What could she do? Where could she go?

Then she remembered Quincy and Holly had the weekend off and were back in London. The Queen had given them a cottage on the Windsor Estate and an apartment at the palace since they were both integral parts of the royal household. They were taking the weekend to start packing up some of their things, as they were going to rent out their house.

Clay flagged down a taxi and jumped in. Twenty minutes later she was outside the Quincy house. She paid the driver, and he said, "Do I know your face? I'm sure I do. Are you an actor?"

"No," Clay said.

"A sportswoman? Boxer, are you that woman boxing champion? You've got the build for it."

This happened every so often. She was in the public eye alongside the royal family. "Nope, not me."

He squinted. "Who are you then?"

Clay tapped her nose and said, "Top secret."

She got out of the taxi and pressed the bell on Holly and Quincy's door. The door opened and a surprised Holly was looking back at her.

"Clay? You're up and about early. You look ill—are you okay?" Holly asked.

"I haven't really been to bed. I…" Clay's voice cracked.

Holly took her hand and pulled her inside.

"Quin?" Holly shouted upstairs.

She heard footsteps and Quin's voice. "I told you I'd move the box, and I will. You don't need to wail like a banshee."

Quincy stopped on the stairs when she saw Clay. "Oh."

Holly turned to Clay and said, "You see the abuse I have to put up with?" She looked back to Quincy. "Clay hasn't been to bed yet. She needs coffee and taking care of."

"Of course. Come through to the kitchen," Quincy said.

Clay sat at the table and rubbed her head. Holly gave her a cold bottle of water, and she glugged some down. "Do you have any painkillers, Holly?"

"Give me a sec." Holly went over to her handbag and rummaged through. "Here you go."

Clay took them straight away and hoped they'd work.

"I'll make coffee," Holly said.

"What's been happening with you, Clay?" Quincy said.

She felt embarrassed trying to tell Quincy what she had done. Quincy was so strong and steady. A hero.

Holly brought the coffee over, and Clay took a sip. It tasted good.

"Tell us, Clay. We won't judge you. We just want to help. We love you." Holly squeezed her hand.

That sentiment brought tears to her eyes. She didn't deserve such caring friends.

Clay sighed. "I've felt so alone since I've been on leave. I've just been sitting in my flat going over everything in my mind. I feel so alone without Mum. Since I put her house up for sale, it's hit me hard. I don't have anyone."

"You have us, and your mum's sister," Holly said.

"I was never that close to my auntie—she's really into her church and God and doesn't like me being gay. Besides, she has her own family. She doesn't need a grown-up to look after."

"As Holly said," Quincy said, "you have us."

"Thanks. I've felt so guilty that I wasn't there for her enough. I just wanted to block it out," Clay said.

"What have you been doing? Quincy asked.

"Drinking every night, one-night stands, just trying to block out the pain."

"That's not like you," Holly said. "I don't think I've ever seen you drink to excess before."

"I never did, really, but I don't feel like me. I don't know who I am any more."

"I know who you are," Quincy said. "You're Sergeant Clayton. Exemplary officer, brave, kind, honourable."

Holly squeezed her hand. "Quin's right. It'll take time to feel better. The pain of losing someone never goes away, but it gets easier. You're staying here with us till we go back to work." Holly turned to Quincy.

Quincy nodded. "Of course. I'll drive you to your flat to pack a bag."

"Then you can have a sleep and have dinner. You need looking after, Clay," Holly said.

Clay was quite overwhelmed. She wiped away some tears. "Thanks. I don't want to be alone." Those words echoed around her heart. She was frightened that she'd always be alone, and also frightened that she would meet someone.

What Holly and Quincy didn't know, what no one knew, was how guilty she felt every time she looked at Teddy and Anna. The guilt that rained down upon her since her mother died only amplified that.

She'd had the biggest crush on the children's last nanny. She always seemed to have crushes on women and fell in love easily. Nanny Angela had seen that interest in her and played up to it. Angela had flirted, laughed at her jokes, and generally made Clay feel there was something growing between them, but she had been played for a fool.

All the time Clay had been so distracted that she didn't notice the signs that Angela was abusing her position and didn't realize she was passing private moments to the press. No one blamed Clay. No one was anything but supportive of her in the team, and neither Queen ever said anything to her, but Clay felt responsible, and it was eating away at her.

She could talk to her friends, but in some ways Clay felt that she deserved the guilt, just like she did for her mother's death. She wasn't there for her mum. She was so caught up in her career that she wasn't with her at the last, and she would always regret that.

❖

It would take a while for Katya to find her feet in Buckingham Palace. She wasn't overawed by palaces like this, but it would take time to find her way around the seven hundred rooms.

The other staff had been really welcoming, so far. This morning she was meeting the chef and his kitchen staff. Chef Christophe was very open to her new way of doing things.

She sat in Christophe's office next door to the large royal kitchen, sipping a cup of tea and going over a new daily menu for the princesses. She and Queen Beatrice had planned the menu at Sandringham, keen to make sure that the children ate as healthily as possible.

Katya and Christophe looked at the holographic computer screen in front of them. Christophe ran his hand over his goatee as he considered the seven-day menu plan Katya had emailed him.

"That all looks excellent, Katya. This will be no problem." Christophe had excellent English but still a strong accent.

"Thank you," Katya said. "Would you mind if we had a meeting once a week to go over each new menu plan?"

"Of course not, it will be a pleasure," Christophe said.

"There was one other thing. Would it be possible to come down to the kitchen to have cooking and baking lessons with Princess Edwina? Queen Beatrice will be with us when her schedule allows, but most of the time it'll just be me. I think it's important to teach children about healthy food."

Christophe smiled and clapped his hands together flamboyantly. "Ah, anything for the little princesses."

There was one thing she noticed straight away on her new job—the genuine warmth between the staff and the royal family.

"The princesses mean a lot to the staff, don't they," Katya said.

"Oh, my dear Katya, we adore the little girls. Life in the palace has livened up once again, now that the Queen has a family. The Queen likes to think of us all as a team and is very kind and considerate to the staff. The little princesses are family to us, and we are very protective of them, especially after your predecessor's antics."

"Yes, I've heard about her. Don't worry. The children are safe with me, I promise," Katya said.

"You're from Vospya, I heard. Is that true? Because your accent is as English as tea and scones."

"I arrived as a refugee, aged ten. Hence the accent."

Christophe shook his head. "There are terrible things going on in Vospya. It must have upset you to watch from afar."

It did hurt. Every news report she saw of the fighting going on was like a stab in the heart. "It does. I can only hope the Liberty Freedom Fighters can find a way to give us our country back."

Christophe nodded. "I pray for that. When I look at the news reports of their treatment of gay people, it makes me thank God I live in Britain. My husband and I would be terribly persecuted over there."

"That's what hurts the most. The wonderful liberal country of Vospya has been overtaken with hate and intolerance," Katya said vehemently.

Christophe must have heard the emotion behind her words because he covered her hand with his and said, "We must have hope that good will prevail."

"Yes, you're right."

"Are you getting on well with the protection officers?" Christophe said. "Some of them can be—how do you say?—dull. But most of them are good fun, and all are very loyal to the family."

"Inspector Quincy is nice and very helpful, but quiet. Jack is a nice boy. I'll be working with him and his superior Sergeant Clayton, but I believe she is off at the moment."

"Oui, she is. You'll love Clay. Such a bright, happy-go-lucky young person. The little princesses adore her too."

❖

Beatrice sat on the floor in their family drawing room at Buckingham Palace, dressed simply in jeans and a jumper, helping Teddy with a jigsaw. Anna was on the floor between her legs playing with a toy, while Rex lay beside them, guarding them.

Shadow and Baxter were lying outside George's dressing room, waiting for her to come out. The television was playing in the background, the screen showing a house in a rather smart area of London. She and the rest of Britain were waiting for the new prime minister to leave his house.

Although they'd had to return to Buckingham Palace so George could appoint the new prime minister, Bea's official calendar hadn't started yet, as they were still meant to be on Christmas holidays. She was loving being able to spend more time with the children, although she still had her correspondence to deal with.

It was also giving her time to spend with Katya in the children's company, to put her mind at rest.

George walked out of her dressing room and the dogs jumped up in excitement. "No, down, you two. You can't get my suit all hairy. Has he left yet?"

"No, should be any minute," Bea said. She looked up at George and smiled. "You do scrub up well, Bully."

George straightened her tie and smiled. "I do try."

"Oh, here he comes," Bea said.

They both watched the screen as the door opened and out walked the presumptive prime minister, Raj Shah, with his husband, Mark, and their two children, a girl and a boy.

"Beautiful looking family," George said.

Bea nodded. Raj was the youngest prime minister in the country's history. He was extremely well-presented with a sharp suit and sharper haircut. His husband was the same, and together with their children, the Shah family made the perfect picture. She watched the screen and examined the feelings it was stirring. Tears threatened to spill from her eyes.

"It's so strange," Bea said. "The conservatives have been my political enemies all my life, and now I'm welling up at the thought of one becoming prime minister."

She turned to look at George, and her first tears dripped slowly onto her cheeks.

"Don't be hard on yourself. It's a historic appointment. The first openly gay prime minister, and married with two children? Besides, Mr. Shah has taken his party to the centre rather than the right."

Bea wiped her tears away. "I suppose you're right, and I suppose Bo Dixon was meant to represent the left, and she took the Labour party to the right in a lot of ways. Not to mention figuratively getting into bed with Vospya and President Loka. I don't think the public will ever forgive her for that."

"No, it was utter folly to do that, but now we have a fresh start for the country," George said.

Bea watched Raj and his husband get into the prime ministerial car, and they were waved off by their children.

"Should you go now?" Bea asked.

The new prime minister in waiting was heading to the palace to meet George and be sworn in.

"I'll wait until he gets up the mall," George said.

A drone camera followed the car along the road from above. There were some well-wishers by the side of the road, waving the car on. The car drove up the mall headed for the palace.

George buttoned up her suit jacket. "I suppose I better get going."

"Tell him…" Bea hesitated, then said, "Tell him we wish him well."

George smiled at her. "I certainly will."

❖

As she had done when Bo Dixon won the election, George stood alone in the audience room, waiting for her new prime minister. Shadow and Baxter had followed her, but Rex, as usual, stayed with Bea and the children.

This was now the second prime minister of her reign, and she was hopeful she could have a better relationship with this one than Bo Dixon. Bo had been made to resign from the party leadership, but rumours were that she wasn't going to leave politics.

George knew how cunning and ruthless Bo was. If there was a way back in, she'd find it. There was a knock at the audience room door. She got into position and the door opened. Major Fairfax led Raj Shah into the room.

They stopped and bowed at the door, and the major said, "Mr. Shah, Your Majesty."

George smiled, extended her hand. Raj walked forward and bowed once more before taking George's hand. He looked nervous so George knew she had to put him at his ease.

"What a night you've had, Mr. Shah. Congratulations on securing the election, and by a landslide too."

"Yes, Your Majesty. It was quite a night."

"Do sit down." George indicated towards the seat beside him.

He waited for her to sit, then sat.

"Your husband and your family must be very proud of you," George said.

Now that the formalities had ended for the moment, Raj visibly relaxed. "I hope so, ma'am. My family is everything to me, and if I can make them proud, I will be the happiest man in Britain."

"I agree—family is everything. Tell me about your two. I just saw them on the news, before you left."

"Chloe is six, and William is ten. They keep us busy," Raj said.

George chuckled. "I know the feeling. Our two keep us on our toes. Oh, my wife asked me to wish you well. We are both aware of what a historic moment this is for Britain."

"Thank you, and thank Queen Beatrice for her good wishes."

George sat back and crossed her legs. "Tell me, what are your plans?"

"I would like to have the Queen's speech as quickly as possible. There is so much to do."

The opening of parliament and the Queen's speech were ceremonies rife with pomp and circumstance, and an important part of George's role.

"What subjects will you cover, Mr. Shah?" George asked.

"Health, schools, business, and technology, and of course building some bridges with our allies and foreign governments. The last government broke some of those friendships," Raj said.

George couldn't flinch or show any kind of partiality. So she simply developed the conversation. "What areas of the world do you think we need to be involved in?"

"Firstly, we need to be more involved in a leadership role at the United Nations. Ms. Dixon's government pulled back from them and let other countries lead in the world's problems, mostly because it didn't suit her interests."

That was music to George's ears. She thought Britain should always be involved on the front line at the UN, carrying out relief to struggling countries and protecting the defenceless.

"What areas of the world in particular do you think are most important for the UN to be helping?"

"Vospya," Raj said seriously. "It's mineral rich, and yet the people are living in utter poverty. It is in open civil war. The Liberty Freedom Fighters are making gains, but they have been brutally slaughtered, as have the general population."

George sighed and nodded. "It is very sad. Vospya used to be at the top table of world democracies, and a good friend to this country. I only hope that the war is not prolonged."

"As I say," Raj said, "the Liberty Freedom Fighters are making more gains as time goes on and getting stronger, but they are still outgunned."

"I see they are using the former royal house of Bolotov on their banners."

"Yes, they represent their former liberal democracy. The rumours are that fighters are in contact with the last remaining member of the Bolotovs, Prince Louis of Vospya," Raj said.

Little did Raj know, but there was another member under this very roof. It reinforced why Katya's anonymity was vital. She knew Prince Louis had been subject to assassination attempts over the years. The government of Vospya saw him as the last link to their democratic past. The one that got away.

"Of course, I will know more once I get into Number Ten and see the security reports."

"Yes, indeed. Well, we'd better finish the formalities." George stood and Raj followed. "The duty falls upon me as your sovereign to invite you to become prime minister and to form a government in my name."

"I will," Raj said firmly.

George held out her hand and the new prime minister kissed it.

"Well, congratulations again, Prime Minster. I'm sure you're going to be very busy, so I won't keep you."

George touched a discreet sensor on the small table beside her, and Major Fairfax came in.

"Thank you, ma'am."

Once they left, Major Cameron entered the room and bowed. "Excuse me, Your Majesty. Inspector Quincy inquired if Sergeant Clayton might have five minutes of your time, at some point?"

George checked the time. "Yes, I'm just going to my office to do my boxes. Bring her to me in thirty minutes."

"Yes, ma'am."

Clay was nervous. Major Cameron led her down the corridor to the Queen's office.

"It's good to have you back, Clay. We've missed you," Cammy said.

"Thank you, ma'am."

"Is everything all right?" Cammy asked.

Clay was caught up in her own thoughts, as they were whizzing around her head. Cammy probably thought she wasn't herself, and she wasn't. Clay had always been bubbly, enthusiastic, positive, and now a gloom had settled over her. She had no idea how to lift the gloom from her soul, and all she could think of was to run away from everything that reminded her of her sadness.

Cammy stopped outside the Queen's office and knocked on the door. Queen Georgina told them to come in, and Cammy led the way.

"Sergeant Clayton, ma'am."

Clay's heart was starting to pound now. She was about to change everything in her life, everything that had meant anything to her.

George looked up from her paperwork and smiled. "Clay, come in. Welcome back."

"Thank you for seeing me, ma'am."

The door closed and Clay was left alone with the Queen. "How are you feeling now?"

Clay gulped hard. "Fine. Um…thanks for giving me the time off."

"Of course. It's been a difficult time, I know. What did you want to talk to me about?"

The urge she'd had to run far away was all that had occupied her mind for the last week. And now this was it, and there'd be no turning back.

"I spoke to Inspector Quincy about this, and I felt I had to ask your permission. I'd like to leave the royal protection command and take a post abroad, with one of our ambassadors."

Queen Georgina looked shocked. She sat back in her seat and said, "I wasn't expecting that, Clay."

Clay immediately felt guilty. "I'm sorry, ma'am. I love the princesses, and this was my dream job, but I need to get away. I realized over Christmas that there's nothing here for me now. No family. Everything here reminds me of what I've lost."

Her voice cracked and she was forcibly trying to hold back the tears. Her chest felt as though it was going to explode.

"Do you not have any other family, Clay?"

"My mother's sister, but we're not close. She's a Fundamentalist Christian and doesn't approve of who I am."

Queen Georgina got up and walked around the desk. She put her arm on her shoulder and said, "We are all your family here, Clay, a community that all pulls in the same direction. Queen Beatrice and I are so grateful to have you looking after the girls. We trust you, and in the position we are in, that means the world, but we care enough about you to let you go if that's what you truly want. Is it?"

"I think so, ma'am," Clay said.

"You don't sound too sure."

"I'm—I don't know what to think," Clay admitted.

Queen Georgina sat on the edge of the desk and said, "What did Inspector Quincy say when you told her?"

"That she didn't want me to go, and that I had a chance for a glittering career here, but she would help if I wanted and give me a glowing reference."

The Queen sighed. "I'll not lie to you, Clay. I would be disappointed to see you go. Teddy and Anna love you. I hoped you would be with them into adulthood, as long as you wanted to stay, and that gave Queen Beatrice and me comfort. The next year that's ahead of us will be challenging in lots of ways. We have the documentary starting at the end of the month. There will be more strangers around the girls, plus Queen Rozala will be visiting. There will be chaos, no doubt, and then there's the new nanny—"

Clay was surprised—she'd only spoken with Quincy about her transfer. They hadn't had the daily team meeting yet. "They've started already?"

"She, yes. Ms. Katya Kovach. I'm sure she'll work out much better than the last," the Queen said.

Clay sighed and hung her head. "I'm sorry—I should have noticed what was going on. It was my job to protect the princesses."

"No one blames you, Clay. We should all have noticed," Queen Georgina said.

But the Queen didn't know that Clay had been distracted by her crush on Nanny Angela. She should have known better.

"Nanny Katya comes from the prestigious Landsford School. I have every confidence in her. Now back to you, Clay. I suggest you take a month or two before making this decision. If you still want to go then, fine—you'll go with my blessing and a personal reference from me. What do you say?"

Giving it two months was the least Clay could do. The Queen had been good to her. "Yes, ma'am. I'll do that."

"Excellent. Why don't you go and see the children. Teddy has been missing you. Oh, and meet Katya. I think you'll like her."

"Yes, ma'am."

Clay bowed and left the Queen's office. She made her way up to the nursery, hoping she would find the princesses there. As she did, Clay resolved that if she was staying for the next few months, then she was going to make sure that she did all she could to protect the children, and that meant scrutinizing the new nanny and making sure she was honest and treated the princesses very well.

She'd allowed her own feelings to cloud her judgement once, and that would never happen again.

❖

"Come in."

Katya looked up from the arts and crafts project and saw someone she didn't know. Teddy squealed when she saw her and ran into her arms.

"Clay! I missed you."

The penny dropped. This must be the royal protection officer who had been off on leave. Wow. Nobody said she was gorgeous. Sergeant Clayton had warm black skin and short black hair, except for on top, where her ringlets were fashionably blond. She looked solid and strong under that suit, which was about as far away from the formality of the other protection officer's mode of dress.

All the staff had told her of Sergeant Clayton's bubbly, positive personality, but no one mentioned that she was so good-looking. So good-looking her stomach did a flip.

Normally Katya was never so affected by women's attractiveness, but the sergeant was apparently the exception. She quickly brushed the glitter from her uniform and went over to meet this Sergeant Clayton.

"I missed you, Princess," Katya heard Clayton say, and her heart melted.

It was so sweet for Teddy to have such a nice relationship with her guard. "Hi, I'm Katya, you must be Sergeant Clayton?"

She looked up at Katya and her smile disappeared. Katya felt like she was being silently assessed.

"It's Clay."

"Clay, okay." That was strange. There was a coldness in Clay's voice.

"Teddy, why don't you show Clay the pictures you've been making?"

"Yes," Teddy replied, dragging Clay over to the table.

Whoa, that was awkward. What had she done?

❖

Clay went to the security operations room in the palace hoping to find Inspector Quincy. She had serious misgivings about Katya. The new nanny spoke like the Queen and her family, like she was brought up in a posh family—or was that pretence? Whatever it was, there was more to Katya than met the eye.

Another thing that worried Clay was her reaction when she saw Katya. She was beautiful, in an understated sort of way. That was dangerous. And when Clay found someone attractive, her good sense seemed to fly out of the window.

Katya had agreed to meet her at a pub close to the palace to go over their new routine for the children, and it would be a good chance for Clay to assess her character.

Clay found Quincy finishing up a video call from Ravn, Queen Rozala's head of security.

"Excellent, Major. I'll be in touch in a few days' time," Quincy said. Once the call had ended, Quincy turned around and saw her. "Clay. The Queen tells me you're going to be staying with us a while longer."

"Yeah, I wanted to be sure."

"I'm so glad. So, what can I do for you?" Quincy asked.

"I'd like to see Katya Kovach's security file," Clay said.

Quincy crossed her arms. "Why?"

"I'm going to be working alongside her, and I feel like I should know. Especially after…"

Quincy sighed. "Clay, would you stop punishing yourself? If there's any blame to add, then we must all share in it. Nanny Angela had me fooled too."

"I feel like I should know her history," Clay said.

"If you like, but there isn't much in it." Quincy tapped her fingers across the virtual computer screen in front of her, and the file appeared.

Clay reviewed the file. "Born in Vospya. Came to Britain as a refugee, aged ten. Went to Roedean School." She looked up at Quincy. "That sounds weird—where's that?"

"It's a boarding school in Brighton."

"Boarding school?" Clay had limited knowledge of the people who went to boarding schools, but she didn't think the likely careers of those sorts of girls extended to being nannies. "Then an English degree at Cambridge, and after that Landsford nannying school. That's weird too."

"A slightly unusual path, perhaps, but ours is not to reason why." Quincy closed the file, leaving Katya's photo up on the computer screen.

That was the weirdest of all. Not only was Katya's security report scanty, and unusual, but Quincy seemed keen to end the enquiry. Clay was getting a bad feeling. Something was not right.

Clay gazed at Katya's eyes in the picture and noticed how unusual they were. One green, one half green, half blue. She was a beautiful woman, and her unusual eyes only added to her beauty.

She looked at her watch and left Quincy in her office. She had a couple of hours before she was to meet Katya at the pub. She had to think.

CHAPTER FIVE

George took in a big deep breath. It was so good to get out for a walk in the garden after being cooped up in her office for most of the day. She held Anna in a baby carrier against her chest, and Teddy ran ahead of them with the dogs.

They were still on holiday hours, so George had the luxury of no official appointments, apart from the prime minister, until the State Opening of Parliament next week. Normally she only got to give the children a bath in the evening and read a bedtime story, if she was lucky, so she wasn't wasting the extra time she had on anything other than the children.

Bea was happy for her to take the girls out for a walk before dinner and tire them out. To George, this was heaven—family life with time to enjoy it.

"Be careful, Teddy. Slow down," George shouted.

Teddy was running with a large stick, and the dogs bounded after her. "Yes, Mum."

"She's growing up so fast, ma'am."

George looked to her left and smiled at Quincy walking by her side. Normally Cammy would accompany her, but George wanted to talk to Quincy about a few things. She had told Clay to finish up early tonight and go home. With Quincy there, the children didn't need anyone else on protection for a simple walk.

"How's the new cottage at Windsor, Quin? Does Holly like it?"

"Yes, very much so. It's going to be so much easier for us both having the cottage at Windsor and the apartment here at the palace. Thank you very much for allowing us to stay there, ma'am."

"Our pleasure, and the Admiral? How are she and Holly getting on?" George said with a grin.

Quincy laughed. Her adoptive mother, whom she had always known as the Admiral, was a regimented military woman, and Holly's carefree, exuberant nature jarred with that. But after Quincy was shot on the royal American tour, and Holly dedicated herself to nursing Quincy back to health, she won the admiral's grudging respect.

"I don't think she understands Holly's view of the world, but she loves how much Holly makes me happy. The admiral's opened up to me a lot more since Holly came into my life."

"That's good to hear," George said as she placed a kiss on Anna's head.

Anna waved her little arms and legs and baby-talked lots of sounds as they walked along.

Quincy smiled. "Princess Anna is such a placid little girl."

"And thank goodness for it, with that little terror as a big sister." George pointed to Teddy, who was now rolling along the grass with the dogs jumping up and down.

"Teddy does have a lot of energy," Quincy said.

"Yes, I think we're going to need to find ways to channel that energy as she gets older." George sighed. "Family is both a delight and a worry, and not just the younger ones."

"Prince Theo?"

"Yes, he's taken his break-up with his girlfriend hard. Especially now that she's giving interviews to any magazine with enough money, not that she needs it with such a rich family."

"I did see some pictures of him coming out of clubs and pubs. His police protection officer is finding it hard to keep the photographers away from him. I wasn't sure if I should tell you or not. I didn't want to worry you," Quincy said.

"I knew, and we told him all along she was only interested in being the girlfriend of a prince, but he wouldn't listen. Christmas really brought it home to him, I think. I know my brother—he's had enough of parties. He's really knuckled down to royal life and giving back to the country. All he wanted was his girlfriend with him at Christmas. He was embarrassed that she stood him up," George said.

Teddy came running up to them and brought Quincy an interestingly shaped leaf. "Thank you, Teddy," Quincy said.

"Welcome," she replied and ran off.

"You're privileged, Inspector," George said. "If only her uncle was happier."

"It's a shame because he's really been working hard with his charities in the past year."

"Exactly. He's passionate about them, and he needs someone who will share that, and he isn't likely to find them drunk in a club. Mama is worried about him."

"What about Queen Adrianna?" Quincy asked.

"She wants to give him a clip across the back of the head, but I think being angry with him will just push him farther away," George said.

"I'm sure he'll find his way. He is excellent with the princesses."

George stroked Anna's head. "He couldn't be better. The perfect uncle, and they both just adore him."

They walked along in silence for a minute, watching Teddy chase around with the dogs, Rex always keeping close to his favourite human—well, after Bea, of course.

"How is Clay settling back in?" George asked.

Quincy pursed her lips. "Professionally speaking, perfectly, but in herself she seems lost. Her mother was her whole world, and after initially throwing herself into her work, Christmas really brought home to her how alone she is now, and her grief has come tumbling out. I think she just wants to run and hide. She's lonely. That time she stayed with us in London, she got herself much more settled, but then we moved to the cottage at Windsor, and she was alone again."

"Do you think she'll leave us, Quin? I would really like her to stay."

Quincy twirled the leaf Teddy had given her around in her fingers. "If we can show her she has friends that want to be her family, then perhaps not."

Then an idea hit George. "Quin, what if we gave her accommodation at Windsor and the palace? If we made her feel part of our community, part of the royal court, then maybe she wouldn't feel so alone."

"I think that would be an excellent idea, ma'am," Quincy said.

"What about the old undergardener house, down at Badger's Wood, Badger's Burrow? It's only one sitting room, and one bedroom and bathroom, but it would be nice and cosy."

"Yes, ma'am. I know which one you mean. Holly and I have taken a stroll down that way," Quincy said.

"It hasn't been occupied for quite a few years, so it'll need to be decorated and made shipshape."

"It'll be a good project for Clay. Give her something to focus on, and a base she can call home."

"That's settled, then," George said.

At that, Teddy and the dogs came hurtling towards them.

"Doggies want their dinner, Mum," Teddy announced.

George smiled. It was one of the things Teddy loved doing, taking care of the animals, whether it was the dogs, or horses, or the deer, or cattle at Windsor.

"Come on, then. We'll get these dogs fed, and then you two girls."

"Yay!" Teddy jumped up and down.

❖

Clay gazed through the window of the upmarket pub, and she was frozen for a second. It was the first time she'd seen Katya out of her uniform. The blond hair that had been pinned up in a conservative bun now hung loose and cascaded over her shoulders.

Katya was concentrating intently on something at the table, and the heart that had betrayed Clay when she first saw Katya did so again. Even more so when Katya leaned her head and her hair cascaded to one side, leaving her neck exposed. She was beautiful, and Clay could just imagine her lips kissing her soft neck.

She caught herself and squeezed her eyes shut tightly. What was wrong with her? Was she a walking hormone or something? Why did she have to drool over every woman she met?

Get a grip.

She pulled herself together and entered the pub. She went up to the bar and got a bottle of lager and wandered over to the table.

"Katya?"

She looked up and gave her a smile. "Veronica, hi."

Clay felt her hands sweating as she stood there, that smile making her shiver. "Can I get you a drink?"

"No, I'm fine." Katya raised her wine glass.

Clay sat down and finally saw it was a computer pad screen Katya had been working on.

"I'm glad we're getting this chance to talk, Veronica—"

"It's Clay," she said firmly.

"Okay, *Clay.* I'm glad we got this chance to talk. I wanted to talk to you about my weekly play timetable."

Clay noticed that as a few customers brushed past Katya, she flinched and then fanned her hair over that side of her face. It was as if she was trying to keep a low profile.

"Are you listening to me?" Katya asked.

"What did you say?"

Katya sighed. "I asked if you'd like to look at my play timetable, since it will involve your police presence at some of the outings."

Clay took the pad off her and read over what looked like a school timetable.

"This is for the next two weeks. Then the documentary will be starting, so there will be some changes, depending on whether the princesses are expected to go to events with Queen Beatrice."

One thing that jumped out to her, was weekly cooking and baking lessons in the palace kitchen. "What is this thing? The kids are not in the army—I mean, what if they don't want to cook that day?" Clay pointed to the screen.

"Children don't always want to do things at specific times—they need structure—but they do enjoy it once they get started. Cooking and baking are great fun for children."

Clay shook her head as she gazed at the screen. "There's no time left in the afternoon. I always take Teddy out to the palace gardens and play with the dogs. It's our thing."

"The children will be tired after a morning of structured play, but I can try to fit that in somewhere else."

"Structured play? When do they get to be kids?" Clay sounded annoyed and angry.

Kat should probably have used her experience and training to soothe the situation, but Clay was really aggravating her. She'd been nothing but nice to Clay, and yet Clay seemed to dislike her on sight.

"Children respond well to rules and routine and structured play. Rules mean safety," Katya said.

"You went to a school to learn this shit?"

Clayton's voice was raised, and some people were starting to look. Katya didn't like attracting attention.

"You don't seem to like me very much, Veronica. Everyone told me—Clay is so nice, so bubbly, so friendly, but not to me." Katya lowered the tone of her voice, as she would with any child in a tantrum, and that's what Sergeant Clayton was behaving like—a child in a tantrum. It was a shame because she was really good looking.

"It's *Clay*, and it's not about liking you. I don't know who you are, so I can't trust you. Protecting the royal family isn't just a job—I love those little girls, and someone like you hurt them."

Katya sighed and began to pack her computer pad away in her bag. "First of all, I'm not the last nanny who breached their privacy, and second of all, you're a police protection officer, look at my security report."

"I have, and there's nothing there. It might as well be blank," Clay said.

"That's because there's not much to know."

Clay leaned forward on the table. "I read that you were a refugee. How did you end up at your posh boarding school and get that posh accent then?"

Now Katya was really starting to get angry. "Who do you think you are? I feel like I'm going through a second interview here. The family hired me. Queen Georgina and Queen Beatrice gave me the job and oversight over the children. You're a police officer—it has nothing to do with you."

"I told you. I love those girls—they are my family," Clay insisted.

"You may love them, but you're not their family. You are staff—so stick to your job, Sergeant."

Clayton had such anger in her eyes at that comment. She was clearly restraining herself, and instead of saying anything, Clay got up and stormed out.

❖

Clay lay propped up in her bed looking at the virtual computer screen in front of her. It displayed Katya's security file. She couldn't stop turning everything over in her mind. There was something wrong, and she couldn't put her finger on it. The little things she had noticed at the cafe, the lack of information in the security file—it just didn't add up.

One of the strangest things was that the people who should care, who always cared about who people were, like Quincy and the Queen, weren't worried about the lack of background information. She knew the Queen went through all the background information to do with personal staff with a fine-tooth comb. She was very protective of her family.

Why was this appointment different?

She didn't know what to ask the computer to search for. There was nothing to go on. Then a thought hit her. Maybe by becoming friendly with Katya and asking questions, she could get the information she needed.

CHAPTER SIX

The next morning Katya was preparing for her day's work. She tied her hair up in a ponytail and sprayed on some perfume. Queen Beatrice had asked her to dress down today, since they were going to a public park this afternoon, and she didn't want them to stand out more than normal.

She wore jeans and a thin V-neck wool jumper, and in the afternoon she could simply put on a warm jacket to go out to the park. Katya looked at her watch. It was half past six in the morning, and she was going to have breakfast in the staff dining area before officially starting work.

Although it wasn't so much like work at the moment. Queen Beatrice liked to be a hands-on mum, where possible, and unlike most placements, where she'd be expected to give her charges care from morning till night, and through the night, both royal parents took on as much responsibility as they had time for.

Katya had heard that the traditional royal nursery used to be quite far from the private apartments of the monarch. Lali explained that when Beatrice became pregnant with Princess Edwina, she had the rooms next to their own private apartments repurposed as the nursery and children's bedrooms, so they had direct access day and night to their children.

Katya remembered her own nursery at her family's country estate. It wasn't next to her parents' rooms. When she was young, royal parents weren't quite as hands on, but her parents always made time all throughout the day to be with them.

Nanny Robinson, an Englishwoman who was always there for them, had been there for her and her older brother. She was there right till the end.

Katya's own room was also next door to the children's, and she was very pleased with it. She had a bedroom, a small sitting room, and a bathroom. The best bit was the view over the Buckingham Palace gardens down to the lake at the back. Last night she sat in the bay window with a glass of wine and read her book. It was beautiful in the early evening, as darkness slowly fell.

Despite having an easy start, she knew that her care would be needed much more when the royal couple got back to engagements next week.

Katya heard her phone beep and lifted the small device from the table. News notifications popped up. *Reprisals against the Liberty Freedom Fighters ramp up as they win more ground in Vospya.*

Katya closed her eyes. She knew what reprisals meant. Torture and death. They were so brave, fighting to get their country back, but she understood what that cost only too well. She blessed herself and sent up a short prayer to God for their protection. Katya's dream had been to one day go back and visit Vospya, but who knew if that would ever be possible. She took a deep breath and got her emotions under control.

"Breakfast."

She walked downstairs to the staff canteen in the lower floors of the palace. It was an office catering facility like no other. You entered the wood-panelled entranceway, adorned with a bronze of George's father's favourite horse and many gifts of artwork the royals had received from around the world. There were two dining rooms and an all-day cafe next to it, and they were both decorated in a mixture of the modern and the traditional. The furniture and relaxed atmosphere resembled any popular London coffee bar, except for the paintings from the royal collection, which adorned the walls.

Katya joined the line at the servery and got some porridge, fruit juice, and coffee. She turned around and looked for a table. This dining room was quite busy. She spotted Holly, Inspector Quincy, Major Cameron, and Lali enjoying breakfast together.

She hoped she wouldn't be seen. They were really nice people, but they were two couples, and she would feel awkward just herself.

I'll try the other room.

Just as she set off to walk she heard Holly shout, "Kat? Come and sit with us."

She had no choice now. Katya walked over to the table and smiled at everyone. "Morning."

"Sit down, Katya," Holly said.

"Thanks."

Everyone said hello and Cammy asked, "How are you settling in, Kat?"

"Great. It's an amazing place to work. I had no idea the palace had facilities like this," Kat said.

"It's nice, isn't it," Lali said. "Queen Georgina had it refurbished. Do you know, sixty years ago, it depended on your rank which room you'd sit in?"

"Really?" Katya wasn't surprised. This royal world ran on rules.

Lali nodded. "The footmen and kitchen staff in one room, and the private secretaries and officials in another."

"I think there's still some snobby officials who'd like it that way," Holly joked.

Katya sipped her fruit juice. "Is the cafe nice?"

"Aye," Cammy said, "it's great to have a place where we can meet for a cup of tea, whatever the time. We work some odd hours in this place."

"Finding your way around all right, Katya?" Quincy asked.

"I'm learning fast. It's a huge place," Katya said.

"You'll soon know it like the back of your hand." Quincy looked at her watch. "Cammy, we better get to it. We have the security briefing in an hour."

"Aye, you're right."

Katya looked over to the news channel playing over on the wall, while Cammy and Quincy kissed their partners goodbye. A part of her heart ached inside her. She doubted she could ever trust anyone enough to let them in and know who she was, far less fall in love.

That made her sad. It was a lonely life, but she was used to it. Isolation and loneliness meant safety.

"Clay is late this morning," Lali said.

"She probably got held up in the rush hour. I'm so glad Quin and I have an apartment here now and don't have to worry about the bloody commute any more," Holly added.

Katya knew a lot of the pages and kitchen staff had rooms here, as they needed to be available at all hours sometimes, but she wasn't sure about the security staff. "Do you both have rooms here?" she asked.

Lali nodded. "Cammy and I have since we were married, and Holly and Quin, much more recently.

"It's so much easier, and the apartments are nice. How is yours, Kat?"

"Really nice. Great view of the gardens."

"Not bad, is it? Wait till you go to Windsor Castle at the weekend. You'll love it," Holly said, and then she turned to her left. "Look out. Here comes trouble."

Katya looked over to the serving area and saw Clay holding her tray of food and walking over to them.

Oh no. This was going to be awkward. Last night's disagreement in the pub was only too fresh in her mind.

Clay arrived at the table and sat down. "Morning."

"Good morning," Katya replied along with the others.

"How was the rush hour?" Lali asked.

"A bloody nightmare, but I'm here now."

"Good," said Holly. "Lali and I have to go, but you take care of Kat for us."

When they left, there was an awkward silence. Katya tried to sip her coffee and keep focused on the TV news in front of her, but it was hard to ignore Clay. She had a presence that compelled her to look.

When she did, she found Clay's brown eyes looking back at her. They were deep, soulful, and she imagined very easy to fall into.

"So," Clay said, "how are you this morning?"

How am I? She's talking like we didn't have a whole argument last night. "Fine, thank you. Yourself?" Katya said politely.

"Okay, I guess."

Clay looked up at the TV and saw the news report was about Vospya. She had come to work today with the mission to find out whatever she could from Katya. There was something they all didn't know, and she was determined to find out. "You're from Vospya, aren't you?"

"Yes, when I was a little girl. You did read my security report, didn't you?" Katya said.

"Yeah, I'm just making conversation. I'm interested."

Katya sighed and turned her attention back to the TV screen. It showed the government forces bombing freedom fighters in the countryside not far from the capital. "I'm from the capital, Viermart. It was once a beautiful city," Katya said with sadness.

"Did someone in your family bring you here to Britain?"

"No, I came on my own. All alone."

"Then you went to boarding school and Cambridge? What college at Cambridge?" Clay asked.

Katya had to laugh inside. She had been distracted at first by the news reports but could now see what Clay was doing. She turned to her and said, "I hope you're very good at being a close protection officer, because you'd make a horrible detective, Sergeant Clayton."

Clay squinted. "What are you talking about?"

"Your questioning. I think a first year cadet could be more subtle," Katya said.

Clay took a sip of her energy drink and seemed nonchalant. "What are you talking about?"

"You don't trust me, and you're trying to find out everything about me by questioning because there's nothing on the internet."

Katya knew that for certain. Any significant person that the UK was keeping secret and out of public view had the protection of knowing that the cyber unit of MI6 deleted any new information that popped up on the web.

"Why would you be so certain? You're hiding something," Clay said.

"Aren't we all, Sergeant? Pain, emotion, memories? You don't leave a war-torn country without hiding a few things about oneself, but if you want to know the answer to your question—I went to Corpus Christi College, Cambridge. Okay?" Katya had had enough and stood up. She pointed to Clay's energy drink. "Too many of those aren't good for you, Sergeant."

Bea bounced Anna on her hip as she watched Teddy play on the playground equipment. St. James's Park next to the palace had a fantastic play area, and Teddy loved coming here, especially as there always were lots of children to play with.

Apart from nursery friends and relatives, Teddy didn't mix with as many children as Bea would have liked. Sleepovers were out because of security, and it was too much stress and pressure to put on a little friend's family.

Bea wanted Teddy to have as normal a childhood as possible, and they tried their best, but it was difficult. She looked around the perimeter of the playground, and the suited men and women stuck out like sore thumbs.

Quincy was a few feet behind her, and Clay and Jack had their eyes on Teddy on the play equipment. Around her were a lot of nervous mums, dads, and childcare people, watching their charges play alongside Teddy.

Life was always like this. People were either too nervous to be around them or being overfamiliar and trying to get near them because of who they were. She supposed that you didn't expect to see the Queen Consort and the heir to the throne of Britain at the play park.

She kissed Anna's head and held her little hand. Katya was right below where Teddy was playing, keeping close watch. Bea was really grateful to have Katya, after their last disaster of a nanny. She fit in really well, and her teaching through play approach impressed Bea. They must instruct the nannies very well at the Landsford School.

The one thing that she appreciated more than anything was Katya understood how this felt. Quincy, Clay, all the security people—they did their job and kept them safe, but they didn't know what it felt like to be constantly watched with morbid fascination.

Katya knew. She'd had a whole childhood that would have been similar to Teddy's and Anna's experience. If people only knew who was really hiding in plain sight.

Bea gasped when Teddy ran and jumped off the equipment rather than going down the fireman's pole.

"Teddy!" Bea shouted and all the other parents looked around at her. Katya got Teddy by the hand and walked her back to Bea. "Teddy, I've told you before it's too high to jump from there. You could hurt yourself," Bea said.

"Sorry, Mummy," Teddy said. "Go see pelicans?"

Bea smiled. The pelicans on the lake were the highlight of any trip to St. James's Park, as far as Teddy was concerned.

"If you're good, we'll go now," Bea said.

Katya took Anna from Bea's arms and said, "I've heard Teddy talking about the pelicans. Are they really in this park?"

"Yes, they are a lot of fun. Teddy and Anna like to feed the ducks and see the pelicans, don't you?"

"Yes!" Teddy jumped up and down on the spot.

Bea turned and nodded to Quincy, indicating that they were leaving the play area. Katya strapped Anna into the pram.

"Do you want me to push the pram, ma'am?" Katya asked.

"Yes, I'll hold on to this terror," Bea said, hugging Teddy to her hip.

As they walked off, Bea felt every eye of the adults around them on her and the children, some starting to take pictures as they left.

The security team formed a loose circle around them, Quincy on the right, Clay on the left, and Jack behind.

"I don't think I'll ever get used to that," Bea said.

Katya pushed the pram onto the footpath that led around the lake. "No, I don't suppose you ever do."

Katya remembered being four or five and waving to large crowds of people whenever she went out with her mother and father, and not understanding why the people wanted to see them.

Then came the feeling of loneliness at having such a closeted childhood. The best fun she had was when all her cousins got together at a family event. They ran wild over the gardens that surrounded Gorndam Palace. In fact, she had played with Princess Rozala, as she then was, when her parents came on a state visit to Vospya.

Katya thought that she heard Bea say something, but she'd been so lost in her memories that she'd missed it. "Sorry, ma'am?"

"I was saying, is that why you like to be anonymous now?" Bea asked.

"There's safety in anonymity, ma'am."

"And you're happy with that?"

"Yes. I miss being of service to Vospya and its people, but I don't think anyone would seek out this kind of public life."

"The best leaders never do," Bea replied.

They stopped at the ducks first, and Teddy got the bread they brought from home and threw it to them.

Katya crouched down beside the pram and held Anna's hand, while Bea helped Teddy. "Look at the duckies, Anna."

Bea walked back to them and Clay took her place and lifted Teddy up on her shoulders.

"She's so good with them," Bea said.

It was sweet to see the change in Clay. The only time she saw her smile was with the children. She suddenly remembered what she'd said last night at the pub when they were arguing. *You may love them, but you're not their family. You are staff, so stick to your job, Sergeant.*

That sinking feeling of guilt settled in her stomach. Clay had lost her mum—she had no family, so she'd heard—and Katya had said that to her?

They walked around to the pelicans with Teddy holding Clay's hand. They did look sweet together. Where was this soft, mushy feeling coming from? Clay had been nothing but rude to her.

She shook off the feeling and said to Bea, "Ma'am, how did pelicans end up in a London park?"

"George tells me they were a gift from a Russian ambassador in 1664, and they've been a traditional part of the park since then."

Katya looked out onto the water and saw them sunbathing on a rocky island in the water. "They are beautiful."

"Teddy," Bea said, "tell Kat the names of the pelicans."

They came to a halt at the bench looking out onto the viewing area. Quincy and Jack took up their positions.

"Mildred, Hugo, Star, Echo, and Mum," Teddy said excitedly.

Bea laughed and Clay looked back and smiled at them. A smile from Clay?

"Why Mum?" Katya asked.

"She's really called Georgina, but Teddy likes to call her Mum. When George became Queen, the park had a new baby pelican, and they named it after her."

"How sweet."

Kat's gaze again went to Clay and Teddy. Clay was crouching at the fence beside the water, and Teddy was hugged in close to her, while Clay pointed out different things about the birds.

Oh God. She was sweet.

Clay was happier than she had been in a long time. Queen George and Queen Beatrice had offered her an apartment at the palace, and a small cottage at Windsor. The cottage needed work, the Queen said, but she didn't care. She would be amongst her community of friends and not going home at night and leaving the only friends she had.

She hurried downstairs to the cafe. Clay hoped she would catch some of her friends in the dining area or the cafe after work.

She found Holly sitting with Katya. "Holls, the Queen's offered me an apartment here, and a cottage at Windsor."

Holly jumped up and hugged her. "That's great news. We'll all be together, then."

"Congratulations," Katya said.

Katya smiled sweetly, and Clay's chest tightened. How could someone with such a pretty smile be anything but what she appeared to be? But that's what she thought about Nanny Angela, and she was wrong then.

"I've got a great idea," Holly said. "Why don't you come out to dinner to celebrate? Quincy and I are going to meet Cammy and Lali for a pub meal tonight. We could make it into a celebration."

This was the bad part of having good friends. Having to make excuses not to go out with them and be the only one not in a couple.

"Um…" Clay stuttered.

"Don't say no, Clay. You always do. This is a celebration. I was trying to persuade Kat to come too."

Oh no. Even more awkward. Katya started to reply, but Clay said, "I'd like to go home and get my packing started, Holls. I want to move as soon as I can."

"All right." Holly sighed. "I'll let you off this time. I better go and get ready. Next time, you're coming too, Kat."

Once Holly left, it was just her and Katya, and she felt it would look bad to just leave, so she sat down beside her.

There was a silence, and Katya filled it. "It's awkward not being in a couple, isn't it?"

Clay ran her hand through her hair and let out a breath. "Yeah, they always try to get me to go, but two couples and me feels weird."

"Yes, before you came, Holly was trying to persuade me to come too. Everyone's really friendly—"

"Apart from me, you want to say?" Clay said. Clay's guard was down a little bit, and she thought, *Am I really right to be cautious about her?*

Katya sidestepped the question. "Everyone's really friendly but I'm not into socializing."

"Do you have a boyfriend or girlfriend?" Clay asked.

"No, as I said, I don't socialize," Katya said.

That was odd. "Kind of a weird thing to say."

"I prefer my own company. It's easier that way."

"What's easier?" Clay asked.

"Life." Katya went back to the computer pad.

That answer made Clay think, once again, that either Katya was really strange, or she was hiding something. Earlier when they had returned to the palace, Clay had looked up the college that Katya attended at Cambridge. She was shocked to find that Corpus Christi College was famous for its history in the world of spying. Many foreign and domestic spies were recruited from Corpus Christi.

Was Katya a spy? And whose side was she on?

She had to know. So she'd called an old friend of her brother's,

Rosco. A man whose business connections were on the shady side, but who had made it easier for her mother to get Clay away from the bad crowd she had met at high school.

Rosco owed her brother a favour, and he had a soft spot for her, so she knew he would help if he could. She called him and asked if he could find out anything about Katya and was eagerly awaiting a response.

Who are you, Katya?

Katya looked up from her computer pad and said, "Did you get the email I sent you?"

"No, I haven't checked," Clay said.

She took out her phone and saw she had a few emails. One was from Katya, labelled *Timetable*.

"Another timetable?" Clay said in frustration.

"Open it."

She did and quickly glanced along the boxes. Then she saw a new addition to the Princesses' day: 3 p.m. to 4 p.m., engagements permitting—Clayton Playtime.

Clay didn't really know what to say. Rules and structure seemed to mean everything to Katya. "You made time for me?"

Katya moved closer, and Clay could smell her intoxicating perfume and felt her body shiver.

"I saw how you were with the princesses today. You obviously have a close bond with them, and I was wrong to push you out."

"Thanks," was all Clay could think of to say.

"You're welcome." Katya got up and said, "I'll say goodnight then."

She squeezed past Clay and the edge of the table. Clay had the urge to grasp her hips and pull her onto her lap. Instead she said goodnight, and Katya walked away.

Who are you, Kat?

Kat was being nice to her, even after the distrustful way Clay had treated her. One thing she knew for sure was that she was so attracted to Kat, but as she had learned to her cost, attraction distracted her from her duty, and she could never allow that to happen again.

She kept watching Kat as she walked towards the door. Sam, one of the young pages, approached her and chatted for a few seconds. When Kat left, he came over to Clay's table and sat down.

"Hey, Clay."

"Hey, how's things going?" Clay asked.

"Busy as always. Do you know if Katya is available? If she dates men?"

"Haven't a clue, mate." That was the problem. She didn't know who Kat was, and she had to find out.

Sam sighed. "She's bloody gorgeous. I always seem to fall for the unattainable girls. First there was Queen Beatrice—"

Clay did a double take. "Queen Beatrice, you're serious?"

"Yeah, when she wasn't with the Queen, you understand. She came to the palace and Windsor for charity stuff, and I was in total love."

Clay laughed. "But then the Queen—"

Sam shook his head "Yeah, no competing with the Queen. Then there was Holly."

Clay was in the same boat. She'd had a huge crush on Holly at first, but she knew she had no chance when Quincy came along.

"Yeah, I get it," Clay said. She had crushes on most of the same unattainable women as Sam.

"But again, there's no competing against a tall, brooding war hero, who just happened to save the life of the Queen's wife." Sam looked in the direction of where Katya had last been. "Now it's happened again. I fall for a woman too easily, and I don't even know if she likes men."

Clay didn't know that either, but somewhere deep inside she felt it. She felt almost sure Kat liked women, but as Clay had found out before, feelings are not always the best things to go on. "Just be careful, Sam. We don't know who she really is."

George adored intelliflesh. In fact if she could do it anonymously, then she would buy a huge amount of shares in the company.

Intelliflesh made it possible for George to have full sensation in the strap-on they loved to use. Bea was on top of her, lifting and lowering herself onto the strap-on. George loved to watch Bea from this angle as she lost herself to the intense feeling slowly building.

George loved and hated when Bea went slow. It was frustrating waiting for the orgasm she desperately needed, but she also loved the journey to it.

She had her hands on Bea's hips, pushing deeper inside her wife with every thrust. Bea leaned over, and her long hair brushed George's face, and George immediately sucked one of Bea's nipples into her mouth.

George rolled her tongue around and knew Bea was liking it by the noises she was making and the fact that she started to thrust herself on her cock all the faster.

"Oh yes, Georgie." Bea grasped her hair and looked into George's eyes. "I love you—make me come."

Quickly, George flipped them over, so she was on top. She placed Bea's legs over her shoulders and began a deep thrust.

"It's so deep, yes, like that," Bea groaned.

George could feel her orgasm building up faster now, and she knew she wouldn't last too long. She leaned over so that her cock was thrusting against that special spot inside her.

"Yes, faster, Georgie."

When she felt Bea's legs start to shake, she knew neither of them would last long.

"I need you, Bully." Bea reached out for her in desperation.

She let Bea's legs fall to the side and brought her lips to her wife's. "Jesus, you feel so good, Bea."

Bea wrapped her arms around George's neck. She felt like it was all going to be too much, like she always did when George stroked that place inside her.

George thrust faster and groaned, "I'm coming."

As always, George's thrusts made her drop off the edge into a deep orgasm. As her whole body shook, George cried out and then fell into her arms.

They both lay there trying to get their breath back.

"That was so good, Georgie."

"Yes." George kissed her, then rolled to the side.

Bea lay on her chest and could still feel her heart hammering. "I love you, Bully."

"I love you too, my darling."

Once they had recovered, Bea said, "It's two o'clock in the morning. You have to be up at five."

"I don't care. This is more important than sleep." George put her arms around Bea and squeezed her tightly.

Bea loved this time. Their lives were so busy, and always with people around them. This was the one time they could truly be alone together.

"It's worth being a little tired—you're right, Bully."

After a minute or so, George said, "I need to speak to Katya. The new Vospyan ambassador is coming to be received by me tomorrow. I feel like I'm betraying her, and us, by doing it, but it is my duty."

Bea sighed. "I know. In Vospya men like the ambassador would have women like us tortured or worse."

"The violence against women and gay people is awful. The leader of the freedom fighters is a gay man who was tortured for who he was. Nikola Stam, his name is. Brave, brave man. It's not the prime minister's doing this time. He wouldn't have their government officials on British soil, but if a new ambassador to Britain is sent, I have to officially meet them. It's my job."

"Katya will understand you have no choice, but you should tell her about it," Bea said.

"How do you think Katya's settling in with the children and the staff?"

"She's wonderful with the kids. They love her already. She's quiet and keeps to herself amongst the staff, I think, but I asked Holly to keep an eye on her. Clay didn't seem to take to her at first, but it's difficult learning to work together so closely."

"You weren't terribly keen on working closely with me in the beginning." George grinned.

Bea laughed. "Yes, and then I ended up in your bed and our working relationship improved."

"Very true. Maybe I'll have a word with Clay. Ask her to help Kat settle in. That should hopefully smooth it all out."

"Good idea, Bully," Bea said as she grasped her intelliflesh strap-on and squeezed. "Now give me a kiss."

Bea loved the chance to lavish all her sexual attention on George whenever she got the chance. It made her feel happy and fulfilled a need in her. George was the more dominant partner and always topped Bea, but only by Bea gently leading her.

George had been a sexual novice when she met her, and exploring George's sexual desires and fantasies was one of the joys in Bea's life. Plus one of the good things about a woman using intelliflesh was that they were always ready for round two.

CHAPTER SEVEN

Over the next week, Katya and Clay's prickly relationship settled down to a ceasefire. Giving Clay her time with Teddy really helped with her mood, although Katya didn't think Clay really trusted her.

Katya was tidying up the nursery while Anna slept, and Clay had Teddy in the garden to play. She gathered up pieces of a jigsaw and heard a cry. Anna must be awake. Even though the royal couple weren't officially back to royal duties, the Queen still had her boxes and Queen Beatrice was preparing for the start of her new campaign next week. So she'd had more time alone with the children yesterday and today than previously.

She walked into Anna's bedroom and saw Anna trying to pull herself up by the bars of the cot.

"It's okay, I'm here," Kat said. She lifted a blanket from the cot and then Anna and wrapped her up in it. Anna smiled, gurgled, and grasped at her hair.

"You are a good girl. Come on, let's go into the nursery."

She walked with the baby to the window of the nursery and saw Teddy, Clay, and the gaggle of dogs running on the lawn below.

"Look, Anna. It's Teddy. Wave to Teddy."

Anna came alive when Teddy's name was mentioned. She just loved her big sister. Kat helped her wave her hand, but Teddy and Clay didn't see them.

Kat laughed out loud when she saw the dogs and Teddy bowl Clay over and fall on the ground. Clay got up and chased them. It was no wonder that Teddy came in from playing with Clay exhausted.

Anna chewed on Kat's finger. "Are your gums bothering you, sweetheart?"

Clay and Teddy came closer to the house, and Clay looked up and pointed up, obviously having spotted her with Anna at the window. When Clay smiled and waved to her, Kat felt a wave of excitement, and her stomach fluttered pleasantly. She hadn't experienced that since her crush on the PE teacher at school.

How strange.

Just as she was about to think some more about this feeling, the nursery door opened, and the Queen walked in. Katya curtsied.

"Your Majesty."

Anna immediately reached out for George.

"Come here, my angel." George took Anna in her arms and kissed her. "My precious girl, have you been good?"

"The perfect angel as always, ma'am."

"That's my girl. Is Teddy out with Clay?" George asked.

"Yes, ma'am."

George cleared her throat and said, "Can I have a word with you, Kat?"

"Of course, ma'am." Katya immediately got a bad feeling that something was wrong.

"Let's take a seat." George indicated to the two chairs by the window.

Katya sat down and tapped her fingers nervously on the table.

George sat Anna on her knee. "I wanted to explain to you about something that is going to happen tomorrow."

"What is it, ma'am?"

George sighed. "I feel terrible about this, but the new ambassador to Britain from Vospya is coming to the palace tomorrow, to be received by me."

Katya's heart sank. Anyone who the Vospyan government would make an ambassador would have the blood of many innocent people on their hands. "You don't have to explain yourself to me, ma'am."

"I'm not explaining myself. I just want you to be informed and feel safe," George said.

Katya didn't think she'd ever felt truly safe since the last day her family was together before they were shot.

George continued while Anna pulled at her hair. "The new ambassador must be received by the monarch—this is not the prime minister's doing. He wouldn't have anyone from the oppressive regime anywhere near Britain, but this I must do."

Katya was full of emotions, none of them good. "Thank you for telling me."

"You won't see him. He'll be here, then gone very quickly indeed. In and out, okay?"

"Thank you for being so understanding, ma'am," Katya said.

George took Anna's hand and said, "In a different world my family could be in your position, Teddy or Anna could be in your position, all alone in the world. I would hope they would find help and safety from other cousins across the sea."

Katya thought of her mother and father and how grateful they would be to George and her father before her. "I know my mother and father would like to say thank you for trying to shield me, ma'am."

"Don't mention it. I'm only too happy to have someone who Bea trusts with our children. That is reward enough."

❖

Clay held Teddy up on her shoulders. After running around outside, Teddy's legs were too tired to walk through the palace.

"Giddy up, Clay," Teddy said.

Clay got a few odd looks from the staff as she neighed like a horse, but she didn't care. She was eager to get to the nursery. She had found herself relaxing slightly around Kat over the last few days, ever since Kat recognized the importance of her playtime with Teddy, and she'd heard nothing back from her childhood friend, Rosco.

No news was good news, she told herself. She wanted to like Kat, but she was prickly sometimes, stubborn often, and secretive. Clay would never truly relax until she had some evidence that Kat's secrets didn't affect the princesses.

When she'd been outside and looked up at the window, Clay saw Kat and Anna looking down at them. Kat smiled at her, a genuine smile, and her heart felt the tiniest bit lighter. Clay had excitement dancing around inside her for no reason and couldn't wait to get back to the nursery.

As they approached the door, Teddy said, "Whoa, horsey."

Like a good horsey, she did, then lifted Teddy down from her shoulders. "Let's go and see Kat."

When she opened the door, she didn't find Kat, but the Queen was sitting on the floor, playing with Anna.

"Your Majesty." Clay bowed quickly.

Teddy ran over to her mum and hugged her.

"There's my little tiny terror." George kissed her and stood up, then put Anna in her baby walker. "Go and play for five minutes, Teddy, Mummy will be here soon too."

"Sorry, ma'am, the princess and I were out playing. Has Katya gone somewhere?"

George walked over to her. "I told her to finish for the day. I've finished all my duties, and Queen Beatrice will be back from her office soon. Could I have a quick word with you, Clay?"

"Of course, ma'am."

"You will know Katya is originally from Vospya, from her security file," George said.

That was about all she knew. "Yes, ma'am."

"The new ambassador from Vospya is coming here tomorrow to be received by me, in his new post. I told Katya, so she won't be surprised by it, and she understands it is simply a duty I must do."

"Yes, ma'am," Clay said.

George continued. "I know that Katya still feels pain from her time as a child in Vospya."

Clay was confused. The Queen was taking a special interest in a member of staff who was their nanny?

"I wanted to ask you a particular favour, Clay," George said.

"Anything, ma'am."

George smiled. "Thank you. Please keep an eye on Katya for the Queen Consort and myself. She is an integral part of our royal court here, as a nanny and a person. But I think with her history, and the news that continues coming out of Vospya daily, she may feel distressed, perhaps unsafe sometimes. I would take it as a personal favour if you could keep an eye on her and make her feel safe here."

This was strange. It was like everyone knew more about Katya than she did. There was a story here that she just wasn't getting. No one seemed to care about Katya's missing or unusual history. They just simply trusted her.

"Yes, ma'am. You can count on me," Clay said.

George patted her on the shoulder. "I knew I could count on you."

Clay could discharge her duty to the Queen by looking out for Kat, at the same time trying to find out who she was. After this conversation, that meant even more. She desperately wanted to find out Kat was just a normal woman without any bad intentions, and in fact she was starting to really hope she was.

❖

Clay knocked on Katya's door. Katya opened the door and looked extremely surprised to see Clay. Clay couldn't blame her—she hadn't been the most welcoming—but now that she had a mission to perform for the Queen, she would be laser focused, and might smoke out any bad intentions if Kat had any.

"Clay? Is there something wrong?"

"No, I just never got a chance to say goodbye."

Katya looked at her suspiciously, but Clay just stood there through the awkward silence, knowing Katya's posh politeness would make her ask her in.

"Oh, well. Won't you come in?" Katya said.

Clay was in like a shot. She glanced quickly around the room, trying to take in as much as she could, hoping she might learn something about Katya's background. There was a cup of tea set on the coffee table. On her bedside table she saw a picture of a very big family group, maybe twenty or so, smiling and laughing. Then her gaze caught sight of what she assumed was a young Kat with her school uniform on, and an older woman with her arm around her.

"You have a nice room. It's bigger than mine and you have a sink," Clay said.

"It's nice—yes, I have a kettle and a sink. So…"

Clay wanted to spin this conversation longer, especially since Katya looked like she'd been crying.

"My room suits me. Besides, at Windsor the Queen has given me the chance to rent a small cottage—well, I say cottage, but it's smaller than that. Badger's Hollow."

"Excuse me?" Katya said.

Clay stuffed her hands in her pockets. "Oh, sorry, that's what the cottage is called. Cute, isn't it?"

"Very cute."

Clay just kept talking, not giving Katya a chance to wind up the conversation. "I haven't seen it yet. I heard it needs a lot of decorating, but I'm sure I'm up to that. You'll have to come and see it."

Katya looked hugely perplexed at the whirlwind of chatter coming from her. She sighed. "Clay, is this another attempt to question me about my background? I am not here to bring down the royal family or hurt them."

"I never said otherwise. Why would you say that?" Clay said.

"Oh, I don't know," Katya said sarcastically. "Perhaps because you've been suspicious of me since I've arrived, you think I'm some sort of spy, and you've not been very friendly."

"Hold on—"

There was a beep from Katya's phone on the coffee table. Clay was halted when Katya held up her hand as she read the notification on her phone: *Breaking news from Vospya.*

"TV, news channel 573," Katya said.

"What's wrong?" Clay asked.

A white-haired man in a suit surrounded by security people was standing outside a public building flying the Swiss flag.

"Who is that?" Clay asked.

"Prince Louis, the last surviving member of the Bolotovs," Katya said while taking a seat to watch the live news report.

"Who are the Bolotovs?"

"The royal house of Vospya. They were overthrown and murdered by the current regime. Prince Louis only escaped because he was out of the country at the time. Let me listen," Katya said.

Prince Louis wore a lapel pin with the Liberty Freedom Fighters flag on it, which was the Bolotov coat of arms.

He began, "Ladies and gentlemen, I'd like to make a short statement. Since my family was murdered by the so-called Vospyan Democratic People's party, I have watched with horror as the country of my birth was devastated by the oppressive regime of President Loka. My people tortured, murdered. Ethnic groups and those with different sexual orientations tortured, raped, and killed.

"It has broken my heart to see my homeland turned from a liberal, true democracy to a right-wing oppressive regime. In the years since I left, I have been subject to multiple assassination attempts, but I am still here, and that means the Bolotovs are still here, and we are with the people of Vospya.

"I have watched with admiration the Liberty Freedom Fighters sacrificing themselves for all good thinking people of Vospya, and I'm pleased to say that they have gained strength and drawn people to their cause.

"The leaders of the Liberty Freedom Fighters have asked me to step forward and assume my hereditary role, as my brother the King's rightful heir, and pledge my support for their cause.

"As your King in exile, I appeal to anyone in the Vospyan armed forces who feels lost and disillusioned, anyone who wishes to live in a truly free country, to join with the Liberty Freedom Fighters and bring back the Vospya we all remember. Thank you."

Clay didn't quite know what she had watched there, but she knew it was significant, partly due to the look of shock on Katya's face.

"What just happened there?" Clay asked.

"Prince Louis has never taken the title of King, even though he *was* as soon as his two brothers died. He wanted to leave the crown with his brother in tribute to him. But the freedom fighters have asked him to come out and support their cause, and he has," Katya said.

"Will it help?" Clay asked.

"Those that want democracy will gather under the banner of the royal house because it stood for safeguarding democracy. Vospya was a constitutional democracy, like Britain."

"So he's your King now?" Clay noticed Katya's hands were shaking a little.

"Yes," Katya stood up quickly. "If you don't mind, I'd like to be alone."

Katya walked her back to the door so quickly that Clay was in the hall with the door shut in her face before she knew it.

This was getting even weirder.

Alexander Chak sat at his desk reading the security bulletins that came in overnight. Victor, his private secretary, was sitting on the other side of the desk.

Alexander slammed his fist down and then got up and walked to the window. "Fucking royalist pig."

"Sir?" Victor said.

He turned around and shouted, "Prince *fucking* Louis. I will not call him king. You've seen the reports? People have been flocking to the Liberty Freedom Fighters flag overnight. Not just civilians, military men and women."

Victor nodded. "It does look as if we are heading for all-out civil war, Your Excellency."

"Why do they flock to a banner and a man who represent their former oppressors? President Loka's government gives them safety, with those degenerates of society eliminated for the greater good."

He turned back to the window and looked out over London. This had come at a bad time for him. His position as ambassador in such a country as Britain was the next step in the ladder. A ladder which he planned to end in one way—at the top.

A knock at the office door interrupted his chain of thought.

"Yes."

Anita, his admin, walked in. "The carriage is here, Your Excellency."

Alexander grinned. "Wonderful."

He walked to the steps of the embassy and saw an ornate carriage waiting for him, staffed by men and women in royal livery. When Alexander found out about this little tradition, he was excited and delighted.

A state coach took any new ambassador to an audience with the Queen at Buckingham Palace, to present to her their letter of credence, a letter from his country of origin to the monarch, giving him their seal of approval.

"Oh, Victor, it must make our new friend the Queen sick to send this for me, but I am going to enjoy every moment."

He stepped into the carriage and Victor handed him a large ceremonial pouch with the letter of credence inside.

"When you're taken in to see Her Majesty," Victor said, "hand her this, and then the audience should take about twenty minutes, Your Excellency."

"I'll enjoy every last minute, Victor."

The door was shut, and the carriage set off with a police escort across to Buckingham Palace. People on the pavements stopped and looked, no doubt wondering who this important person was. Alexander loved it. The carriage eventually pulled through the gates of the palace, and Alexander was wowed by the grandeur.

"A lowly rebel fighter in a carriage ride to Buckingham Palace as ambassador. Not bad, Alexander."

❖

"His carriage is here," Bea said.

She and George were in the grandest of the state rooms, the white drawing room, waiting on the Vospya ambassador.

"He'll be here soon. It makes me sick to have him in the palace, but it has to be," George said.

Bea walked over and straightened George's collar. She was wearing her Irish Guards uniform. "You look scrummy," Bea said.

"I don't want to look scrummy—I want to look commanding. I don't want this man under any illusions that he is welcomed by me. This is all strictly business."

"Good, we'll have him out of here in no time. Just do your queening and bish, bash, bosh, he'll be gone," Bea said.

George raised an eyebrow. "Queening?"

"Yes, queening." Bea noticed something new on the uniform. "This wasn't here last time."

George brushed her arm where the new badge was. "It's the emblem for the former Vospyan Royal Engineers. My grandfather was an honorary colonel-in-chief. I had Cammy sew it on. Show a bit of solidarity with my Vospyan royal cousins."

"You are good, Bully. I hope he recognizes it. I hope King Louis can gather the courage of the people to return Vospya to its glory."

"My papers from the ministry of defence say that the country is now in a state of open civil war, but to win, the Liberty Freedom Fighters need some help from the military. If they start switching sides in decent numbers, then they have a chance. Our prime minister is trying to encourage the UN to send peacekeeping forces, which may be necessary."

Bea kissed George on the lips. "I better go. Good luck."

"Five minutes, remember," George said to Bea.

She nodded and left the room by the side door, just in time for the knock at the main doors.

Major Fairfax walked in with the new ambassador and bowed, but Alexander Chak did not. He kept staring ahead to her.

George's anger boiled in her stomach. Not because he didn't bow—she never cared about that—but he was clearly doing it to make a point.

Again, not following protocol, he walked forward, held out his hand, and spoke first. "Queen Georgina. So nice to meet you."

George stared at his hand like it was a snake, but she took it briefly and got it over with. "Ambassador, you brought your letters of credence?"

He handed them to her. "Such a strange ritual."

George took the letter and set it on the table, ignoring his comments. "Please sit down."

They sat and George adjusted her uniform. In a completely neutral voice she said, "How are you enjoying living in London?"

"It's very different from Vospya. Very cosmopolitan," Alexander said.

George knew what he meant. The freedom to be who you truly are. "That is what we love about it, about our whole country."

"Clearly."

George heard a disdain in his voice.

"This is a beautiful, grand palace. Shame it only houses one family."

Alexander seemed to be baiting her, but George didn't bat an eyelid. "Tell me? Where does President Loka live?"

Alexander was struggling to hide his anger. George knew exactly where he lived. Gorndam Palace.

"He lives in the former royal palace, but he was chosen by the people to rule them."

The sham elections in Vospya only had one party on the ballot sheet, so that meant nothing. Loka was a dictator, one who enjoyed all the trappings of royalty without giving back to the people.

George had had enough of this man and was saved when Bea walked into the room. George stood politely at her entrance, but Alexander didn't. Instead his eyes lit up, and he looked up and down Bea's body, openly appraising her.

George tried to keep her cool and wished she had just asked Cammy or Major Fairfax to interrupt them. Then she wouldn't have to suffer her wife being ogled in this way. "Darling? Is something wrong?"

"Yes, there's an urgent call from the prime minister."

George turned back to Alexander. "We'll have to cut this audience short, Ambassador." She touched the hidden buzzer under the side table to alert Major Fairfax. George could tell he knew she was basically kicking him out.

He finally stood, and then his gaze landed on the military patch on her arm with the royal coat of arms.

"The Vospyan Royal Engineers?"

"Yes, my grandfather, the King, was colonel-in-chief. He was a great friend to the late King of Vospya and cousin two or three times removed."

"Hmm," Alexander said, "lucky the times of kings is over." Major Fairfax entered to escort him out. "Goodbye, Georgina." He turned his back on her in disrespect and walked out at top speed.

Bea hurried to her. "What a slimy, horrible man. He called you Georgina."

George opened her arms to Bea and kissed her head. "He's gone now, and hopefully we won't see him again."

❖

Clay walked into the packed security room and took a seat beside Cammy. Everyone was here for a special meeting of the security team. From next week, the royal schedule was going to be packed, and Quincy wanted to make sure everyone knew their jobs.

Quincy liked to be thorough, and organized them in a military fashion, which made sense, given her background. Quincy stood beside a holographic smart screen to talk them through the battle plans, as she called them.

"Settle down, everyone. I wanted to make sure everyone is clear about their duties for the upcoming month. We will have detailed meetings every week for the program of events, but this will be an overview of what's to come."

Clay thought about her promise to the Queen, that she would stay for two months before making her decision to leave. Could she leave when the Queen needed her most in these next few months?

When she was working during the day, playing with the children, having lunch with her friends, sparring verbally with Kat, she didn't feel the pain of her grief so severely, but when she was alone in bed, lying in the dark, things were so different.

At night, Clay felt a deep sadness and loneliness in her heart, and nothing would distract her from it. She couldn't wait for the oblivion of sleep and a new busy day to start.

Quincy continued, "Shortly, Major Ravn from the Denbourg secret service will be joining via video link. First things first—the State Opening of Parliament on Monday. As you know, this is one of the biggest events of the year. MI6 and the police have the route planned and coordinated. Marksmen on all the major buildings, and secret service officers posing as police constables along the route. Clayton, Driver?"

"Yes, ma'am?" Clayton and Jack replied.

"After you escort Princess Edwina to nursery school first thing, you won't be needed again till the afternoon, so I want you both with the main team at parliament."

"Yes, ma'am," Clay said. She loved being part of these big events. It was such a buzz, and Clay knew Quincy liked her in and around the royal couple during these high-profile appearances, as she was the sharpest, deadliest shot on the team.

This was another thing she would miss if she left. She genuinely cared for the royal family, and she knew it would be a very different kind of job guarding a high-ranking British official.

"Next up is the documentary on the royal family, and I'll bring in Major Ravn at this point. Major, are you there?"

Major Ravn's face appeared on-screen. Clay had met her during various visits between the families, both in Britain and in Denbourg. She was strong and commanding, and Clay wouldn't like to get into a fight with her.

"Yes, I'm here, Inspector Quincy."

Clay knew how seriously the whole Denbourg secret service took their job after the assassinations of Queen Rozala's father and brother. They did not take even the smallest of risks with the Queen's safety.

"Would you like to say a few words to the team?" Quincy said.

"Yes, thank you. The Queen and the Crown Consort will be flying in next Friday, and we will be staying for a month. Normally security would be tight, but even more so now because the Queen is in the last few months of pregnancy. Crown Consort Lennox is very concerned that we take no chances with the Queen's safety, so I know I don't need to ask for your cooperation. Both of our teams have worked so well in the past, but for this trip there is more than the Queen's safety to consider."

Quincy nodded. "I can assure you, Ravn, that our protection squad will be happy to work closely with you on this trip as always. Now…" Quincy started to give details of the royal Denbourg flight and what would happen on arrival.

Clay liked Queen Rozala. She always brought a lot of laughter whenever she visited, but she truly admired the quiet strength behind her that was Crown Consort Lennox. She'd given up her career, her personal life just to be with Queen Rozala and walk behind her, giving her confidence to be the Queen she was.

The Queen had come a long way since she was that party girl falling out of nightclubs, owing in no small measure to the calming, loving influence of Lennox, Clay was sure.

The meeting finished, and she wandered back to her room. She went in, got changed out of her suit, and flopped on the bed. It was a really comfortable room, and her mum would have been proud that she lived at Buckingham Palace. Then her thoughts turned to Katya and her unusual behaviour.

Katya had gone from smiling and waving at the window to pushing her out of her room. Clay could understand Kat's worry about the news from her homeland and its King in exile, but she seemed to go into a complete panic.

Clay's phone started to ring. "Answer call."

"Clay?" It was her old friend Rosco.

"Rosco? Have you got something for me?" Clay asked.

"Yes and no," Rosco said.

Clay sat up on the side of her bed. She was nervous about what he might have found. Things had changed since she'd first contacted him for information. Now she truly hoped there was nothing untoward in Kat's past. She wanted everything about her to be above board. It surprised her how her feelings had changed.

"What does yes and no mean?"

Rosco sighed. "Your woman—"

"She's not my woman," Clay corrected him.

"All right, touchy. *The* woman you asked me to find out about, she has security systems around her like I've never seen before. My computer guy said the job was really challenging, so your favour is well and truly paid."

"Okay, okay, just tell me." Clay's heart was pounding. *Please don't be anything other than a nanny.*

"Katya Kovach did not exist before she arrived here in the UK at ten years old. Her history before that time has been wiped, similar to what you would see happen with a secret service new recruit, but not a child."

"Why would they hide a ten-year-old's history?" Clay asked.

"I don't know. It's weird, but that's something you'll need to find out," Rosco said.

"Wait, that's everything?"

"Yeah, I did say yes and no. You're lucky we even got into her file."

"Okay, thanks, Rosco."

Katya just got more mysterious by the day. The Queen wanted her to keep an eye on Katya, and Quincy was satisfied with a security report with virtually no information on it. Something just wasn't right, and she was going to find out what.

CHAPTER EIGHT

On Monday morning, Buckingham Palace was barely controlled chaos. It was the State Opening of Parliament today, the biggest event of the year for the Queen. It was also Teddy's first day back at nursery, but she wasn't pleased she was going to be missing all the excitement.

Bea sat at her dressing table, dressed in an ivory dressing gown, as Holly finished her make-up. Lali sat on an armchair in the dressing room with Teddy on her lap. Teddy was full of excitement and couldn't keep still.

"There you go, Your Maj," Holly said.

Bea looked closely at herself in the mirror. "I think it gets harder and harder to make me look presentable with each passing month, Holls."

"Oh, shut up," Holly said. "You're super gorgeous. Isn't she, Lali?"

"Beautiful. Isn't Mummy beautiful, Teddy?"

Teddy climbed down from Lali's lap and ran over to her mother. "So pretty, Mummy."

Bea hugged her. "Thank you, sweetie." She looked to the crystal-encrusted white dress hanging on the door, and the diadem sitting in its box on the table. "I feel like the fairy on top of the Christmas tree with that on. Plus, two kids later, it gets tighter every time I wear it."

There was a knock at the dressing room door. "Your Majesty, it's Katya."

"Come in."

Katya came in with Anna all ready to go out. "It's time for nursery, Teddy."

Teddy screwed up her face. "Come with you in the carriage, Mummy?"

Bea gave Teddy a kiss. "No, you go and have fun at nursery. Miss Tanya said she will show Mum doing her queening on the TV for the children." She took her hand and walked Teddy over to Katya. She gave Anna a kiss and said, "Look after them, Katya."

"Always." Katya smiled.

Once they left Bea turned around and sighed. "Okay, girls, time to get me into my fancy-dress costume."

The bomb- and bullet-proof Land Rover was waiting for Katya and the children at the private door of Buckingham Palace. Katya walked out of the door carrying Anna in her car seat and holding Teddy's hand.

Clay approached and said, "Can I help?"

"Yes, if you could get Teddy strapped in, I'll get Anna's car seat fitted in."

"No problem. Come on, Teddy."

The car door was opened by Jack, and Katya fitted the car seat in securely. She kissed Anna's chubby little cheek and said, "Let's get your sister to nursery."

Katya was looking forward to work this week. The kids' two mums were back to full-time engagements after the Christmas break, so she would be able to implement her timetable of teaching through play with the children.

Jack slipped in the car next to the two princesses. She shut the door and saw Clay standing at the driver's side door. Katya walked around the car and said, "What are you doing?"

"Driving. I always drive Teddy to nursery. Inspector Quincy doesn't believe we should rely on the self-drive function. It's much safer to have full control."

"I know the protocol, Sergeant Clayton, but it's my job to drive. I'm the nanny—you are the protection officer."

Clay narrowed her eyes. "And how are you going to cope if we engage in a security incident?"

Kat pushed past Clay and sat in the driver's seat. "I'm fully trained in defensive driving and self-defence."

Clay gave a sarcastic laugh. "And who taught you that? Nanny school?"

Without missing a beat, Katya replied, "Yes. Now get in the passenger's seat."

Clay sighed and walked around the car. She got in and said, "I don't like this."

"Buckle up and concentrate on your protection of the princesses."

"We'll talk about this for next time. No nanny school self-defence class is going to cut it in the real world."

Katya gave her a look that could kill. She hated anyone underestimating her. She put her anger to one side and pulled away from the front door and then out of the gates of the palace. The roads leading from the palace had barriers on the sides, and armed police milled around the area as it was secured.

"Security out in force already?"

"Yeah, some of them will be MI6, posing as a police officers. Since the King and Prince of Denbourg were assassinated, protection and security was pumped up. It could easily have been our royal family."

"Horrifying." Katya had a flash of her father and mother being shot through the head. She gasped and held the steering wheel tightly.

"Are you all right, Kat?" Clay asked.

"I'm fine. We will never let that happen, Clay. We have to make sure they're safe." Katya looked in her rear-view mirror to see baby Anna holding Jack's finger.

Clay looked slightly confused. "Yeah, we won't let that happen."

She believed Clay and trusted her. She knew if it came to it, Clay would die for those girls, just like her own nanny had done. Now Teddy and Anna had two people who would die for them and keep them safe from the world.

❖

George waved her white-gloved hand towards the crowd who lined the route to the Palace of Westminster. She and Bea were in the Irish State Coach, pulled by four horses. In front of them a carriage carrying the royal regalia led them down the mall.

George looked over at her wife, who looked regal and beautiful all at once. She was so proud of Bea and how well she had embodied the role as consort at the same time as making it her own.

"What are you looking at, Bully?" Bea said.

"How beautifully you wave. Your royal wave has come on leaps and bounds since I married you."

"It's been a hard apprenticeship, but I think I've finally nailed it," Bea joked. The carriage jolted as it rolled over a stone. "Oh, these carriages weren't built for comfort, were they," Bea said.

"Not at all. It's lucky we don't have to travel this way all the time," George said.

The carriage slowed, and George looked out up ahead. "Class of school children up ahead, Bea."

George instructed that, whether she was in her car or carriage, they slow down when passing groups of youngsters, so the children could see them better.

Bea leaned over and along with George waved to the children waving flags along the side of the road.

"So sweet, they're all in school uniform. They must have gotten out of class for a few hours."

Bea leaned back and looked her up and down slowly. "You look so delectable in your navy uniform. All these gold tassels—if only we were in here alone."

Bea softly stroked her fingers along the hilt of George's gold sword, and George was immediately turned on.

"Jesus Christ. Don't do that now, my darling, or I'll give the TV cameras a glimpse of too much."

Bea gave her a cheeky smile. "You sure?"

"Bloody wave, woman."

Bea laughed and went back to waving to the crowds. "If you're sure."

❖

"Are you all right, my darling?" George asked.

Bea's stomach was turning over with nerves. Both she and George were being prepared with the royal regalia in the robing room in the House of Lords. Around her Holly was trying to make the purple royal robe sit properly.

"I'm nervous, that's all."

Cammy used a brush on George's uniform. All that was left to put on were the crowns. George's was very heavy, so she liked to leave it to the last moment to put on.

"I think that's you all done," Holly said.

"Ready, Cammy?" George asked.

"Yes, ma'am."

Cammy and Holly went to the two boxes on the table and took out the respective crowns and placed them on George's and Bea's heads. The jewels and pearls sparkled in the light.

"How do we look?" Bea asked.

"Beautiful and regal," Holly said.

Cammy started to walk to the door and said, "I'll just check that they are ready for you."

George held out her hand for Bea to take. "Shall we?"

Bea laughed and took her hand. They had a little tradition every time they opened parliament.

A long time ago parliament put a painting of Charles I in the robing room. It was meant to remind any monarch that came to open parliament that they were only there by the will of the people. If they had ideas of taking more power than a constitutional monarch should, the King or Queen could end up beheaded like Charles I did.

The barbed joke by members of parliament was light-hearted but full of symbolism. It was George and Bea's little tradition to ask Charles for luck before they went out.

"Wish us luck, Charles."

Cammy came back and said, "They are ready."

"Right." George adjusted her crown. "Let's go."

Four young boys dressed in royal regalia carried the hems of their robes. George and Bea walked arm in arm to the main chamber of the House of Lords. All the peers of the realm stood waiting for them, in their own robes and coronets.

The grand royal thrones sat right next to the door through which they entered. They walked up the steps to the throne, and Bea waited for George to sit first. Bea then followed her, and the young boys adjusted the trains of their robes and laid them cascading down two or three steps from the throne platform.

When both of them were settled, George said, "My Lords, pray be seated."

Everyone sat, and the sound of low murmuring filled the chamber. George signalled for the members of parliament to be called to her presence.

No matter how many times Bea took part in this, she could never get over the grand splendour of it all. The gold braid and the sparkling diamonds everywhere. Back in her anti-monarchy days, she hated this. But now she understood it better.

It wasn't about George exalting her power—it was about parliament reminding her and the country that they lived in a constitutional monarchy. Parliament and the people called the shots, not the monarchy and the aristocracy.

❖

Later that evening Clay walked to the cafe downstairs to see if she could find Katya. She hadn't seen her since they had picked up Teddy from nursery and come home. She had been really quiet, and Clay took the task the Queen had given her seriously—she had to keep an eye on Kat.

She spotted Cammy and Lali sharing a piece of chocolate cake.

"Clay," Cammy said, "take a seat and distract my wife from stealing my cake."

"Sorry, I was looking for Katya. Has she been in?" Clay asked.

"Aye, she said she thought she'd use the gym. How long ago was that, lassie?" Cammy looked at Lali.

"Half an hour ago, I'd say."

"Thanks, I just need to tell her something."

Clay ran to her room and got changed into shorts and T-shirt. The palace had a gym and swimming pool that the staff could use. The rule was that if a member of the royal family came to use it, you had to leave, but the two Queens were always really relaxed about it.

She took the lift down to the gym. The doors opened, and she saw only Katya in the gym, over on the other side on some mats, doing yoga poses by the look of it.

She walked over but didn't say anything as she didn't want to disturb her in the zone. As she got nearer, Katya moved so quickly, and the next thing she knew, she was flat on her back, with Katya straddling her.

"Jesus. What did you do that for?" Clay said.

"You shouldn't sneak up on people." Katya lowered her face closer to Clay's and grinned. "A royal protection officer downed by a nanny?" She tutted. "Not good, Sergeant."

Clay suddenly felt the closeness of their positions, and heat travelled to her groin. She slipped her hand onto Katya's thigh, and as she looked into Katya's eyes, she knew she felt it too.

She could just imagine pulling Katya close to her and bringing their lips together. She spotted Katya's lips parting, and her breathing shortened. She decided to take her chance and quickly flipped Katya onto her back and held her hands above her head.

Katya struggled to get away but Clay lowered her face inches from Katya's. "A protection officer never gives up, and I never like to be on my back."

Clay was caught up in Katya's beautiful green eyes. Heat rushed all over her body. *I need to kiss her.* Katya's lips were parted, and she wetted them with her tongue. Clay lowered her lips. They were going to kiss.

Then Katya moved her head to the side and said in a soft voice, "Let me up, now."

Clay didn't need to be asked twice. She stood up and gave Katya her hand. There was an awkwardness between them now, and Clay didn't know what to say. The heat from being so close to Katya was still coursing through her body. They'd nearly kissed, and her body wanted nothing more in the world than to touch her lips to Katya's.

"I'm going to get some water," Clay said.

She walked over to the side of the gym and got a bottle of water out of the fridge. She took a long, cool drink, and then some deep breaths. Clay couldn't believe what she'd nearly done.

A woman had never made her feel that hot, so hot that she nearly didn't control herself. A woman she didn't a hundred percent trust.

Get a grip.

When she turned around, Katya was back on the mats doing her yoga poses. She had to go back over and talk to Kat, or it would just seem weird.

She sat on the mat beside her. "You do yoga a lot?"

Katya sighed and moved out of her pose. She had hoped Clay would go and use the equipment and leave her alone to cool down and get a hold of herself.

She had nearly let Clay kiss her. She wanted Clay to kiss her. Katya wanted to put her arms around Clay's neck and pull her to her own lips, but at the last second she had managed to overcome her hormones.

Being that near to Clay's tight, muscular body set her on fire. Clay had on a sleeveless T-shirt, and she imagined running her fingers over her muscular shoulders and down her strong arms.

From the first moment she had seen Clay, she had been attracted to her. She was butch, strong, but had a youthful, boyish charm that was different from Cammy, Quincy, or the Queen herself.

That had been dampened by Clay's mistrust of her and rudeness, but she had started to warm up to her more recently.

"Yes, I enjoy it. It clears my mind." Katya leaned forward and whispered, "Are you still trying to find out if I'm a spy, Sergeant?"

Clay smiled and shrugged. "Even if I was, does it matter if you have nothing to hide?"

"I suppose not," Katya replied.

Then Clay's face turned serious. "I'm kind of a straight up and down person, so I'll be straight with you. I truly hope you're not a spy and don't have any ulterior motives because I like you."

Katya smiled. Clay had an innocence about her that was unbearably sweet. She could see how the last nanny took advantage of her.

"I don't know how you got to be a police officer, Clay. You're too nice and too honest for any police interrogation."

Clay leaned back on her hands, making the muscles in her shoulders and arms more pronounced.

God, she is gorgeous.

"I can be hard when I need to be, Kat."

Kat's heart started to pound as it had when she was on the floor. She wanted Clay's sculpted body over her, and inside her. She grabbed for the bottle of water beside her and took a big drink.

Clay continued, "Besides, we can't be good at everything. I'm a good shot—that's my thing. I can shoot the wings off a fly."

"Where did you learn you had that skill?" Kat asked.

Clay took a breath to answer, then hesitated. "It's a long story. So, did you watch the opening of parliament today?"

"Yes, Lali and I watched it on the TV in the cafe. Where were you?"

"You know the place where the two Queens got out of the carriage?"

Katya nodded.

"Just there, and I waited until they came out and got back to the palace safely. Inspector Quincy likes me to be anywhere a shooter might have a clear shot. I keep my eyes on the crowd, the sides of the buildings, the roofs, and if anything happens—"

"You shoot the wings off a fly?" Katya finished for her.

"Exactly. What goes on inside, I've never quite understood. It's like a weird ritual."

"It's very important," Katya said seriously.

"Why?"

Katya knew the symbolism of the ritual and had been emotional as she watched it on TV today. She remembered as a little girl watching her uncle, the King, doing something similar at the Vospyan parliament.

"Even though you see the crowns, the sparkling jewels, the pageantry, it's about a constitutional democracy."

"How can strutting around with crowns on be about democracy?" Clay asked.

"It's all symbolism. The procession to the parliament is about military power, to show the monarch is symbolically top of the tree. The Queen and Queen Beatrice sitting in the Lords surrounded by the peers is a nod to their historical power, but then when the Queen commands the Commons to attend her, they saunter through to the Lords, chattering to each other. It's a tradition to not be formal, and somewhat blasé, because they know they have the power really. It's the government that writes the Queen's speech, not her, but they know she will defend their democracy no matter what."

"Wow," Clay said, "I was born here, and you know more than me."

"That's an English boarding school education for you."

"You talk about it with a lot of passion," Clay said.

"Democracy means a lot to me. That's why Prince Louis claiming his crown meant so much yesterday. He was becoming a symbol for the democracy Vospya once had, and the people can gather around his banner and hopefully one day we will prevail."

"Do you feel British or Vospyan?" Clay asked.

"A mixture of both, I suppose. I was born there, but Britain gave me a home, a safe place to live, and a good education, so I owe it my life."

"Doesn't sound like something a spy would say," Clay said hopefully.

"Unless I was a very good spy." Katya teased.

She winked and Clay's heart thudded.

Jesus. I'm sunk if she is not who she appears to be.

Clay cleared her throat and said, "Listen, do you want to meet a few times a week and practice your hand-to-hand combat? You can practise the skills you said you learned at nanny school, and I can hopefully give you some pointers."

"Or I could give you pointers?" Katya said with a smile.

"Well, yeah, if you think you can. How about it?"

Katya sighed and stood up. "Well, all right, but I don't do friends or anything else. I'm a private person."

What a weird thing to say, Clay thought. She jumped to her feet and replied, "That's good because I don't want a friend. I'm investigating you, remember?"

Katya laughed. "Of course you are, Sergeant."

Clay watched her walk away, and her heart felt light for the first time since her mum died. *I want to know who you really are, Kat.*

CHAPTER NINE

Katya was one month on the job now and starting to settle into the rhythm of the court's working week. On Fridays the royal court decamped from Buckingham Palace to Windsor, the Queen's weekend home.

This weekend was going to be more special because Queen Rozala and her partner were arriving to take part in Queen Beatrice's new project.

Teddy was overexcited about her aunt, as she called Roza, coming, so Katya and Clay offered to take both children out for a walk in the grounds.

Katya had Princess Anna in a carrier and Teddy was holding Clay's hand as they walked across the grounds. Katya was beginning to like Clay's company. She was uncomplicated, what you saw was what you got, despite her attempts to smoke her out as a spy. Clay just had the best interests of the people she cared about at heart, and she appeared to really care about the royal children and their parents.

"Horsey," Teddy said as they saw a rider up ahead.

"So it is. A nice one too," Katya said.

Clay smiled at Katya. "Teddy loves her horses, just like her mum."

"The Queen is a very good horsewoman."

"I've never been on a horse in my life. It would terrify me," Clay said.

"Horses are wonderful animals. You should try riding."

Clay gave a mock shiver. "No thanks, I'll leave that to all you toffs."

"I'm not a toff. I'm a nanny, for goodness' sake."

"Likely story. You went to boarding school and Cambridge. That's a toff where I come from. Hey, do you want to see the cottage the Queen is letting me rent?"

"Yes, if you'd like," Katya said.

"I would." Clay rubbed the back of her head bashfully. "I'd like your opinion. I've never had to make decorating decisions before, and it needs to be decorated."

Oh God, Katya thought. Why did she have to be so adorably bashful? "Let's go, then."

They walked down to a wooded area, and just through the trees was a small cottage that looked like it came from a fairy tale.

"It looks like it should be in *Little Red Riding Hood*. It's so sweet, Clay."

Teddy jumped up and down. "This Clay's house?"

Clay lifted Teddy up in her arms. "Yeah, so I can be here to play with you at weekends."

Just then Katya's phone rang. She took it out of her pocket and the caller flashed up on the screen: *Auntie Victoria*. A code for her MI6 contact. A nod to the shared ancestry of the Bolotovs, the Buckinghams, and many other European royal houses through Queen Victoria's many sons and daughters.

She answered and said, "Hold on, Auntie." She looked up to Clay and said, "I'll catch you up. I need to take this."

"Okay, come on, Teddy," Clay said.

Katya waited until Clay and the princess were inside. She bounced on the balls of her feet to keep Anna content while she spoke.

"I'm here."

"How are you, Katya? Settling into your new role?" the female voice said.

This voice had always made her feel less alone, even though she couldn't put a face to it. It was warm, caring, and understanding. Sometimes she wished she could meet the person the voice belonged to.

"Very well, thank you, and yes, I'm extremely well-settled. My role here with the children is hugely rewarding," Katya said.

"Excellent. Hiding in plain sight has always been our watchword since you arrived in this country, and this is certainly hiding in plain sight. Especially with the royal documentary starting next week."

That was something that worried her slightly. Queen Beatrice would need her to attend events that the children were going to with her, and her face would be on national and international screens. But who would remember her face? No one.

"I hope this will go well, because I'm happy here," Katya said.

"That makes me happy to hear. On to business, the first being an update on your uncle Louis. His actions have made a huge difference to the cause of the Liberty Freedom Fighters, and the new British government is delighted by that, unlike previous administrations. People are flocking to their cause."

Katya closed her eyes in silent prayer, that those who fought would win the day. She kissed Princess Anna's soft hair and then said, "It's wonderful to hear that."

Katya was actually starting to feel optimistic for her country of birth. Never in all her years in Britain had the prospect of overthrowing Loka's dictatorship seemed possible.

Her contact continued, "There are those within our number who believe your uncle should be told of your existence."

This made Katya's stomach swirl with a mixture of fear and excitement. Her only family left in the world, an uncle who she remembered as a kind, generous man, and she couldn't even talk to him. It had been calculated that he should continue to think she perished with the rest of her family, so that information couldn't be gotten out of him under duress.

They were the only two members left of the Bolotovs, and Prince Louis was under constant threat of assassination. In the early days, it had been thought that he might indeed be captured, and the threat to Katya by association was huge.

"Really? I would love him to know, but would it be safe? It might expose me," Katya said.

"You're right. That's the conclusion we have come to so far, but we'll keep it under review. Now for the main reason for my call. There has been new activity trying to access your secret files but, we have ascertained, not from anyone connected to Vospya. Strangely from someone connected to a London business group with a slightly shady criminal association. Have you had anything unusual happen lately or know anything about this?"

Katya looked up to the cottage and felt a smile start to form. Her little detective.

"I might have an idea. Leave it to me."

❖

Clay was chasing Teddy around her new living room when Katya walked in the door. Clay quickly stopped running and said, "Be careful, Teddy," in a vain attempt to sound responsible. "Everything okay?"

Katya had a small grin on her face and Clay felt like she was missing something.

"Yes, perfectly."

Clay glanced to the side and saw Teddy was playing with her toy plane on the stairs. "Well, come in. What do you think? I know it needs decorating but—"

Princess Anna started babbling in her adorable baby talk.

"I think Anna likes it," Katya said. "It's a great space. Looks like it will be a cosy little home when it's finished."

"Yeah, I hope so." Clay pointed to the kitchen door. "The Queen put a new kitchen in this week, and there's a new bathroom going in. It's been really nice of the Queen to do that for me."

Katya walked over to Clay, and Anna reached out for Clay's hand.

"It doesn't surprise me. Queen Georgina is a very kind person," Katya said.

"I think part of it was trying to get me to stay." Clay realized that sounded bad. "I mean, to make me feel more included in the royal court."

"Why? Where are you going?" Katya asked.

Clay hesitated. If she explained to Katya that she had requested a transfer, the next question would be why. She didn't want to talk about her feelings to anyone, but before she could stop herself it just came out.

"The others probably told you that my mum died before Christmas."

Katya nodded. "Yes, I'm really sorry, Clay."

"Thanks, well after the short leave I had recently, I asked for a transfer abroad. I just wanted to get away. I've got nothing else here."

"But the princesses love you, and your friends do too," Katya said.

"But as you told me, the princesses aren't my real family."

"I'm sorry, Clay. I shouldn't have said that."

"No, you were right, they aren't, but they do care. The Queen asked me to give it a few months before deciding. I think the cottage and the apartment at the palace are to make me feel less alone," Clay said.

Katya was silent for a moment and took another step towards her.

She looked in Clay's eyes and Clay couldn't tear her gaze away from Katya.

"Do you feel alone, Clay?"

Clay stopped breathing and her heart thudded. She felt caught in Katya's beauty, her tenderness, and forgot everything that concerned her about Katya's secretive, suspicious past.

"Sometimes—a lot," Clay admitted.

Katya raised her hand close to her cheek, and Clay shivered in anticipation of her touch, but a squeal from Anna interrupted them, and Katya pulled her hand away.

The moment was lost. Katya stepped back quickly and there was an awkward silence.

Clay felt obliged to fill it. "Do you want to help me choose a colour for the walls? I've got some tester pots."

"Yes, let's do that."

It sounded as if Katya was so happy they could manoeuvre past that close moment between them.

Clay gathered the pots from the top box in the corner and brought them over. "Teddy, do you want to help me paint?"

Teddy clapped her hands together and ran over. "I help."

"This might not be the best idea." Katya laughed as Clay handed over a small tester brush to Teddy.

"It'll be fine. You'll be so good at painting, won't you, Teddy."

Teddy jumped up and down. "Yes!"

George was in her Windsor office, catching up on some work, while waiting for Roza and Lennox to arrive. They would both be staying at an apartment in St. James's Palace during the week of their stay and spending the weekends with them at Windsor.

The phone on her desk buzzed, and Bea's face popped up on the screen.

"Georgie, they're just a few minutes away."

"Okay, I'll be right down."

She grabbed her suit jacket from the back of the chair and slipped it on. Bea liked her to dress more casually at the weekend, but she couldn't greet her cousin in a pair of jeans and her old cricket jumper. It wouldn't be polite.

George hurried down the stairs and saw Bea waiting for her at the bottom. She took her hand and kissed her cheek.

"Are the girls still out walking?" George asked.

"Yes, I asked Kat to keep them out until after Roza and Lennox arrived, or we'd hardly get a chance to say hello."

They walked out onto the steps at the entrance and saw the Denbourg royal car coming up the road.

"It's going to be so nice to have them visit, Georgie."

Unusually the car screeched to a halt, as if the driver had been instructed to stop at once. Then the back door was flung open, and Roza struggled to get out of the car, which wasn't easy at seven months pregnant.

Major Ravn was out of the car and helping her in moments.

"No," Roza shouted as she got out.

George and Bea looked at each other questioningly.

Lennox was out next from the other side of the car. "Roza, please, listen."

"Just leave me alone, Lex," Roza said. "I've nothing more to say to you—ever!"

"Bloody hell," Lex said with exasperation.

George went down to take Roza's hand, and like a switch had been turned in Roza's head, she smiled and said, "It's so good to see you, George."

They kissed on both cheeks, and George led her up to Bea. They greeted each other, and Bea said, "Let me help you in."

After they went in George looked to Lex, who was standing by the car shaking her head.

"You look like you need a drink, Lex. All is not well in the House of Ximeno-Bogdanna-de Albert-King?"

Lennox sighed and then said, "I need a drink most days now. My wife always was high-maintenance, but now she's pregnant and even more challenging."

She walked up to George, bowed her head, and they shook hands.

"You love it, though?"

Lex smiled. "It makes life interesting."

"Pregnancy can be a difficult time," George said.

"It's good to be here. Maybe talking with Queen Beatrice and your mother will help her. I think she is thinking about her late mother recently."

George immediately understood. Roza's mother had died giving birth to her and left a huge hole in the family, and especially in Roza's life.

"Let's get you a drink, then." George patted Lex on the shoulder, and they walked in.

❖

"It's so good to see you, Roza. How are you feeling?"

Bea had guided Roza to the drawing room and gotten her comfortable on the couch. George and Lex were standing by the fireplace, giving their wives a bit of space to chat.

"Like a pregnant whale. Lex will tell you I'm being impossible, apparently. I will tell you the truth—she's getting on my last nerve, micromanaging everything and being bloody annoying. Anyone would think *she* was the Queen." Roza gave Lex a look that could kill.

Bea remembered those feelings she had in late pregnancy, when George's very presence could annoy her and fuel a deep fury inside her.

"I remember those times I wanted to kill George, but now looking back, I see how difficult pregnancy is for the partner not carrying the baby. They feel helpless, sometimes, and guilty when we are going through discomfort and pain. And they make it worse, fussing around you just to feel like they are helping."

Roza furrowed her eyebrows. "Whose side are you on, Bea?"

Bea smiled. "You know what I mean."

Roza sighed. "I suppose you're right. It's not just Lex—it's the whole bloody Denbourg court. They hover around me like Lex, and you've no idea how hard I had to push to be able to come over and work with you on our project."

"You know I told you we could do this later in the year, after the baby was born," Bea said.

"I know, and I told you, Lex, and all my officials that I had to be here at the launch. It's important to me. I think the whole court is worried something might happen, like it did when I was born," Roza said softly.

Bea could now see the extra worry and stress that Roza was dealing with. Losing a mother in childbirth would bring a whole host of worries when you had a baby yourself, and no mother to share experiences with would make things even worse.

"Your officials and ministers care about you, Roza. They're bound to worry," Bea said.

Roza rubbed her hand over her large baby bump. "Do they? Or do they just care about the heir being safely delivered?"

"You know that's not true. Roza, your country loves you. When your father and brother died, Denbourg was in chaos, and everyone was worried you wouldn't take your throne, and your second cousin, Prince Bernard, would step in—and you know the extreme right wing views he has. But you didn't let them down. You stepped in to your role as Queen and head of state like a dream and brought calm to the chaos. They just want to protect you."

Roza nodded. "I suppose. I wish my mama was here, Bea. I have Perri, who has been like a mother to me, but still."

Lady Perri was Roza's lady-in-waiting and had been that to Roza's mother before she died.

Bea squeezed her hand. "Nothing will substitute for your mother, but you have us all behind you, loving you, supporting you."

"You're right." Roza looked over to Lex. "Lex is good to me. In fact, I don't know how she puts up with me."

Bea watched as Lex met Roza's gaze. Then a smile broke out on Lex's face when Roza extended her hand to her.

Lex hurried over and kissed her hand and then her lips. Just then a page arrived with a tray full of drinks and handed them out.

"Sit down, Lex. Bea was just going to tell us about this evening, weren't you?" Roza said.

Bea wasn't sure what she meant at first, but then it clicked. "Oh yes, tonight's presentation."

Lex and George sat on the couch opposite.

All the family and some of the staff who would be involved in the filming of the documentary were to be given a demonstration of what to expect from the filming.

Each member of the family would have footage shot at various events to coincide with Bea's project, the Year of the Family, including their oldest member, the Dowager Queen Adrianna.

"The filmmaker, Aziza Bouzid, is coming here tonight. Every one in the family will be here."

"Aziza is a very well-respected filmmaker," Lex said. "I've seen most of her work, I think."

"Yes, she's usually doing a lot more hard-hitting stuff than this. I met her when I was working at Timmy's. She was brought in to make a short film for the charity. We hit it off really well," Bea said.

"Not too well, I hope?" George joked.

"Hardly. She's very straight, and very beautiful. Half of Hollywood chase after her."

Before anyone could reply, Teddy burst through the door and ran in shouting, "Auntie Roza!"

Roza opened up her arms straight away to her goddaughter, and then all of them burst into laughter when they saw Teddy's face and hands were covered in paint.

"What happened to you, Teddy?" Bea asked.

"Your Majesty, I'm so sorry," Katya said. Kat couldn't believe this. What would Queen Bea and Queen Rozala think of her?

She had warned Clay to be careful with the tester pots of paint, but she had gotten distracted. They both had, and the next time they turned around, there were paint handprints all over the wall, and then Teddy rubbed her face with her paint-covered hands.

Clay was now lurking outside the drawing room like a coward while Katya faced the music, holding little Anna in her carrier.

"We—I was helping Sergeant Clayton choose a paint colour for her new cottage, and things got out of hand."

"Don't worry about it. It gave us all a good laugh. Roza, Lex, let me introduce our wonderful new nanny."

Katya had wondered how it would be to see Rozala again. They'd enjoyed playing together one summer when the Denbourg royal family came to Vospya on a state visit.

Teddy was now sitting on Roza's knee. When Roza looked up at her, Katya's heart thudded. Roza's smile fell away, and she appeared to recognize something in her.

They were only young children when they met, but something in Queen Rozala's face told Katya she was trying to place her.

Bea continued, "Katya Kovach, may I present Queen Rozala and Crown Consort Lennox."

Katya curtsied to them both, and Crown Consort Lennox said, "It's nice to meet you, Katya. You've taken on a big job with these two princesses."

"Do bring over Anna, Nanny Katya," Roza said.

She walked over to Roza, and Bea helped take Anna from the carrier. While she did, Katya could feel Roza's eyes on her, presumably trying to work out who she was. Teddy ran over to Lex, and Bea handed

Anna to Roza. Now that she had Anna in her hands, she forgot about her examination of Katya.

"Oh, isn't she adorable," Roza said, "and grown so big since we last saw her. Look, Lex."

"She is beautiful. Just like this big girl," Lex said as she tickled Teddy.

Bea looked up at Katya and said, "Why don't you leave them with us just now. I'll get Teddy washed up in a little while."

"Yes, ma'am." Katya curtsied and then walked out of the room.

❖

A nervous looking Clay waited outside for her. "Was everything okay?" Katya ignored her and walked past her to the stairs. Clay followed close behind. "Kat? Was Queen Beatrice okay with everything?"

"I'm not speaking to you," Katya said.

Clay caught up with her on the first landing and said, "Oh, come on."

"You stood out there like a coward, Sergeant Clayton, while I faced the music."

"I was too nervous with Queen Rozala being there. She makes me nervous. You're more used to these kinds of formal things."

They got to the children's Windsor nursery, and Clay followed her in. At the cottage Clay had been too busy lapping up Katya's attention that she didn't realize that Teddy had carried on painting herself and everything around her.

Katya turned around and said, "Don't tell me, you have a crush on Queen Rozala."

Clay gulped. How could Katya read her so well?

"What? No—well, maybe. I have a thing for unattainable women."

Katya tidied up the toys on the floor. "So it seems. I've seen the way you blush around Queen Bea and Holly sometimes."

But was Katya unattainable? Clay thought. Her growing affection and attraction for Katya made her ask that question. Katya wasn't a queen, a royal, or a friend who was in love with her boss, like Holly was, but she was an unknown. Hopefully not a spy or someone who would leak stories to the press like their last nanny.

The evidence and her gut instinct made her relax and dare to trust Katya, but in the past, her gut hadn't been that trustworthy. Could she afford to fall for a woman like Katya, and could she even stop herself?

"I looked like a fool in front of Queen Rozala, Clay."

"Hey, you were distracted too."

It had been nice in the cottage. The normally very guarded Kat had laughed and talked with great enthusiasm about the decorating. It had been fun.

"I suppose I was," Katya admitted and gave her a slight smile.

That glint in Kat's eye made her stomach flip. There was silence while Kat carried on tidying and, strictly speaking, Clay should leave. She had protected the princesses out on their walk, and that was over now. She didn't really have much excuse to stay in the nursery. She probably should go and check in with Quincy, Jack, and the rest of the team, but she didn't want to leave Kat. Clay was enjoying her company too much.

"How was Queen Rozala when you met her?" Clay asked.

"You mean your crush?" Katya grinned.

"She's not really, not any more anyway." No, now Clay had someone else to dream about, Katya. She had been, ever since that night in the gym.

When Katya pinned her to the floor, she was caught up in her beauty and lost a bit of her heart, she was sure. She thought about Kat pinning her to the floor every night since. Every time she closed her eyes.

Since her mum died, grief, pain, and running away had been the things that had floated across her mind in bed. Now, thoughts of Katya were taking over. She was desperate to find out what kind of woman Kat liked.

"So, we've established *I* like unattainable women," Clay said. "What about you?"

Kat looked at her for a few seconds, then said, "It's not really appropriate work conversation."

Clay walked over and began to help her pick up the stray toys and books. "I thought we were friends? It's just a friendly conversation."

Kat gave her a look and said, "Do friends check up on each other?"

What did she mean by that? Kat couldn't know about the enquiries she'd made about her. "What does that mean?"

"Oh, nothing." Kat sighed. "I don't have a type."

"Everyone has a type. Butch, femme, androgynous, dapper, lipstick lesbian—" Clay was praying she'd pick *butch*.

Instead Kat stood up and leaned against the window with her arms folded. "Being awfully presumptuous there, Sergeant. What if I said a tall, muscular man?"

Kat was playing with her, she knew. She'd seen the look of lust in Kat's eyes when they'd shared that moment in the gym.

Clay walked up to Kat and said, "Then I wouldn't believe you."

"You are that certain in your gaydar?" Kat said.

"Yeah, it's pretty good, I'd say," Clay replied.

"It's not important, Clay. I don't date."

Clay could feel a sadness in that answer.

"Why would you say that? Everyone wants somebody."

"Not me. I don't want a relationship," Kat said firmly.

"Why?" Clay asked.

Kat waited a moment or two and then said, "You have to share too much of yourself, and I don't want to do that."

Kat was becoming more unattainable by the second. It was no wonder she had a crush on her.

"I always thought relationships were about sharing your burdens, not giving up anything. Loving is part of life—don't you want to do that, Kat?"

"I need to get back to work. Aren't you needed downstairs?" Kat said.

With that, Clay was pushed away. But little did Kat know she'd made Clay all the more determined to find out what was holding Kat back, what she was hiding.

That evening, one of the rooms in Windsor Castle had been set up as a cinema by the documentary maker Aziza Bouzid, to show some clips of her work. Some of the main staff involved with the documentary filming—Kat, Clay, Quincy, Holly, Cammy, Lali, and Jack—were invited to the presentation and were sitting in the back row.

One of the Queen's most trusted housemaids was watching over Teddy and Anna, as they slept, to allow Kat to attend. The rest of the royal family involved in the project had arrived earlier, and now Kat and the rest of the staff were waiting on the royals who would join them here.

There was one royal already in the room. Prince Theo was eagerly trying to engage Ms. Bouzid in conversation as she set up her presentation, but she didn't appear to be giving him the attention he craved.

Holly leaned over and whispered, "I think Prince Theo might like Aziza."

They all chuckled, and Cammy added, "Aye, but she doesn't seem to be impressed with royal status. He's having to work hard."

The door opened, and a page said, "Her Majesty the Queen."

They all stood immediately, and Queen Georgina walked in with Queen Adrianna on her arm, followed by the rest of the party. Once the Queen and Queen Rozala were seated in the front row, everyone else followed suit.

Queen Rozala turned around and looked back at Kat quizzically. Kat was sure Roza was on to her. She should have known taking this job would compromise her quiet life and anonymity, but she hadn't had the heart to let the Queen down, or the princesses. It was her job to be the safe, loyal, protective person that her nanny had been.

Theo took a seat in the front row beside his sister, George. Kat couldn't help but smile. He was so obviously smitten at first glance, and who could blame him. Aziza was stunning, and in a completely natural way.

She had long dark hair and light brown skin, feminine but not frilly in any way. She wore a black turtleneck sweater and a pair of snug jeans. She gave off the vibe of an alpha female, and that was intoxicating. She was strong, passionate, knew what she wanted, and, Kat imagined, usually got it.

Katya had watched her documentary on Vospya. It had been fascinating, and heartbreaking. There were testimonies of people who were tortured in state police custody, which had been too awful for Kat to listen to the first time she saw it, but the second time she made herself listen to every word. She wanted to be a witness to this brutality. They were her people, and she had to bear this pain along with them.

Her thoughts were interrupted by Ms. Bouzid.

"With Your Majesties' permission, I'll start my presentation."

George nodded to her.

"Good evening, Your Majesties, Your Royal Highnesses, and members of the royal household. My name is Aziza Bouzid, but I'd like you to call me Azi. Queen Beatrice has given me the honour of making a documentary about her new campaign, the Year of the Family. First, I want to let you know how I work."

Azi picked up a tiny earpiece and placed it in her ear. "You won't have to worry about having lots of crew around you. There will just be me."

Seemingly out of nowhere a buzzing could be heard, and something whooshed around the room. Queen Adrianna raised her stick to bat it away, apparently thinking it was an insect.

"No, Granny," Theo said, "it's a camera."

"A camera?" Adrianna said in disbelief.

The assembled audience chuckled.

"Quite right, Prince Theo," Azi said. She held out her hand and a tiny black item landed on her palm. "This is the drone camera I use. I direct from the ground with a remote team controlling the drone from our production office in Central London. I like my documentaries to be intimate and real, and you can't do that with lots of crew hanging around. Please be yourselves, and don't worry about saying too much or something too personal—Their Majesties will have full control on what is in the final cut, rest assured."

Clay whispered, "Wow, she's amazing, isn't she?"

Kat was astonished to feel a knot of jealousy for the first time in her life. That was a total surprise. She sighed. "She's very good at what she does."

Clay furrowed her eyebrows. "Is there something wrong?"

"No," Kat said sharply. Why was this bothering her? She was disappointed in herself.

After the presentation Azi mingled with the guests, Theo hanging on her every word.

Kat was standing with Clay, enjoying a drink. "Are you sure you're okay, Kat? The clips of Vospya—"

"I'm okay."

Azi had shown clips of the Vospya documentary, and Kat was so tense that Clay noticed and took her hand. Clay's touch did calm her.

"I'm okay. I think maybe I should go back upstairs to the children," Kat said.

Clay shook her head. "Wait, the Queen asked you to hang back and meet Azi."

Kat didn't want to watch Clay develop another crush on another woman who was not her. She could have kicked herself for even thinking that.

"I suppose."

"I've never seen Prince Theo so nervous. He really is hot for Azi."

"Are you?" Kat said pointedly.

Clay screwed up her face. "What? No. Azi isn't my type."

Kat took a step towards her and said in a low voice, "What is your type?"

They gazed into each other's eyes, and Clay gulped hard. "Um…"

Then Azi interrupted their small moment. "Ms. Kovach?"

"Yes, hi. This is Sergeant Clayton."

"Please to meet you both. Katya, you are from Vospya, I heard."

"I am, and I wanted to thank you for the frank documentary you did. It opened a lot of people's eyes."

"Thank you. Here's hoping that peace will soon come to Vospya," Azi said.

"I'm praying for it every day. Hopefully you'll be able to do a follow-up documentary when things get better."

"The only place I couldn't film was Gorndam Palace. It looks beautiful. I would really have liked to see inside," Azi said.

"It is beautiful. It's one of the oldest palaces in Europe. The red room, the Japanese room—" Kat caught herself when Azi looked quizzically at her. It might sound like she knew a little too much.

"You know the palace very well. Not many people know about the Japanese room. At what age did you leave Vospya?" Azi asked.

Azi was right, the name of the Japanese room had changed after it was bombed during the Second World War, when most of the collection of Japanese antiques were destroyed. It then officially became the portrait room, but the family always still called it the Japanese room.

"Ten. My mother was always really interested in the royal buildings, and she told me endless stories about the palace's history."

Azi pursed her lips as if she didn't quite believe her. She couldn't afford slips like that.

CHAPTER TEN

The next morning Lex accompanied George for her morning run in Windsor Great Park. In front and behind were protection officers from both Britain and Denbourg. Cammy was just off to George's side, and Lex's main protection officer, Bohr, ran beside her.

They had been going for around twenty minutes and just getting into their stride.

"So, how are things really going in the Denbourg court?" George asked.

"Much better than they were when we first got married. After we came back from our honeymoon, I soon got a taste of Denbourg officialdom in action, as I've told you before. It was wasteful, slow, and inefficient. Roza gave me free rein to make reforms, and they're finally beginning to bear fruit."

"You don't need to tell me the slow pace at which royal courts can move. Your professional business and charity experience must be a great asset," George said as they ran along.

"I've tried to change the way Roza's charitable work is done and set up the Crown Consort's Trust, so that I can focus on causes that I find important—drug and other addiction charities. I'm enjoying that side of things."

"I'm glad to hear it. I feel so much happier now that Roza has you. I don't know how she would have coped becoming Queen, without you."

"She'll always have me, George. Roza is my life's work, and I'll be beside her until my last breath. Now we have our little one on the way, and I have even more reason to protect them both," Lex said.

"You will be a wonderful parent, Lex. How is Roza this morning?"

"She's okay. Still talking to me, which is a bonus, but she was very distracted last night. I don't know why. Oh, Roza did ask if she could talk to you this morning."

"Of course. As soon as we get back, and I get cleaned up. Now, let's see if we can outrun our guards."

"Yes." Lex grinned, and they were both off like a shot, the guards struggling to keep up, apart from Cammy, who was as fit as anyone could be.

❖

Princess Anna sat in her high chair in the nursery while Kat was trying to spoon porridge into her mouth with not a great deal of success.

Normally she was very good at eating, but this morning she was out of her routine. Queen Bea usually fed her breakfast, but this morning Bea was in her office, preparing for the launch.

Clay and Jack had taken Princess Teddy out for a walk with the dogs, giving Kat a chance to concentrate on getting Anna to eat.

"Come on, big girl. One mouthful. It's yummy."

Anna did take a spoonful this time, then smacked the spoon she held on the tray of the high chair repeatedly. She had to have her own spoon to play with or nothing would get eaten.

Kat wasn't looking forward to the week ahead, or the months ahead. Not because of her job or the people she worked with—no, it was because she would be seen in the public eye. For a guarded, extremely private person like her, the crowds of people, the media, the photographers, not to mention the documentary filming would be difficult.

Last night at Azi's presentation, it was brought home to her what she was facing. The documentary would be up close and personal with them all, not just the family. Azi wanted to show the world that the family encompassed the staff and all the royal court.

But Kat just wanted to fade into the background. She shivered when she remembered the clips from the documentary Azi had made inside Vospya, detailing the human rights abuses and torment her people endured.

Clay had sensed she was tense and upset by it. There in the darkness as they watched, Clay took her hand and squeezed it, a simple gesture that gave her the strength to get through the rest of the film clip.

It was so hard not to like Clay. She was sweet but strong, tough but saddened by grief, and she had an open heart. Clay's distrust of her was waning, unless it was some complicated plot to make Kat open up to her and expose her for the spy Clay thought she was at the beginning.

But she didn't think Clay was capable of being that calculating. She was too friendly, too caring. No, asking someone to hack into her full security file was about as far as she thought Clay had gotten.

The nursery door opened, and Teddy bounded in with Clay, Jack, and the dogs.

"Hi, did you have a nice time, Teddy?"

"Yes, we picked flowers for you." Teddy handed her over a handful of daisies.

"Thank you very much," Kat said.

She looked up at Clay and found she was smiling warmly. "We thought you'd like flowers, Kat."

"I do. Thanks very much."

Clay's smile was making her heart pound that little bit faster.

They were interrupted by Queen Bea walking into the nursery. They all bowed or curtsied quickly, and Teddy ran to her mummy, while Anna excitedly shouted in her own baby talk.

"Everyone relax," Bea said, "I'll take over with Anna, Kat. The Queen would like a word with you in her office."

Kat was immediately worried. Something must have happened in Vospya. "Now, ma'am?"

"Yes, if you could."

Bea took the spoon from Kat, and Kat brushed down her uniform. She looked at Clay, who also appeared worried.

"Jack and I will walk you downstairs, Kat."

Somehow that show of support from Clay made her feel better. They left the nursery, and soon she was at the door of the Queen's office.

Jack walked away, but Clay touched her arm and said, "I hope everything is okay. I'll be around if you need me."

She nodded and said, "Thanks."

Once Clay had gone, she knocked at the door.

"Come in," Queen Georgina said.

When she walked in, Kat was surprised to find Roza sitting there too. Kat had that nervous sinking feeling.

Kat curtsied to them both and said, "You wanted to see me, Your Majesty."

"Yes, we both did actually. Queen Rozala came to me this morning, asking me who you were, because she was sure she recognized you."

Kat knew it. Roza had seen the little girl in her from the start.

"Yesterday," Roza said, "it kept bugging me. I know you—I truly believe I do."

George said, "But I told Roza that it was not my secret to tell. It's up to you, Katya, but you know Queen Roza's position means that she will keep our classified information to herself. You can trust her on that."

What could she do? There wasn't much choice now. She should have taken a nice boring job with a banker's family or something. There would have been safety in that. But given the choice of job again, Kat was certain she would pick this job every time. It was her duty to the Queen's family.

The Queen's father had protected her and paid for her schooling and her expenses at university. Being able to pay that kindness forward was her calling.

She turned to Roza and said, "I will tell you the truth, ma'am. We have met before, a long, long time ago."

"I knew it. Where did I meet you, and who are you, Katya?" Roza asked.

"My real name is Princess Olga Bolotov of Vospya and Marchioness Romka."

Roza's jaw fell open in shock. "Olga? You're joking…George, this can't be real. Olga died at the hands of Loka's rebels with the rest of the family. I remember my parents grieved for them."

"Do you want to tell her, Kat?"

Kat gulped and nodded. "I remember your visit with your family most fondly, ma'am."

"So do I, Olga. Normally my father's overseas trips were so boring, but having you to play with was fantastic. I loved it. Tell me, what happened to you?"

"When the rebels took the palace, I was out walking in the forest behind the palace with my nanny. On our way back we heard screams and shouting. We hid in the trees beside the gardens at the back, and I had to watch my family—"

Tears came to Kat's eyes and George quickly gave her a tissue.

"If this is too hard…" Roza said.

"No." Kat wiped her tears away. "I want to tell you." Kat gathered herself and continued, "I saw my family shot. One of the soldiers who shot them looked up and saw us in the undergrowth. Nanny told me to run, and we did, but they soon caught up with us. A royal guard retreating from the palace tried to defend us, but Nanny told him just to take me and run. As we ran I heard the shot that killed my nanny. She died for me."

Katya had drifted off into her dreadful memories but was brought back by Roza standing up slowly. She was in tears.

Roza pulled her into a hug and said, "I'm so glad you're alive, Olga, and I'm so sorry about your family. I know how hard it is to lose those closest to you."

Roza really was the only one who could understand losing your family through violence. "Thank you, ma'am."

"So how did you end up in Britain?" Roza asked.

Kat helped Roza sit back down. "The soldier got me to the coast and secured a place on a ship leaving for the UK. The government was informed when we docked at Plymouth, and George's father, King Edward, was told about me. He arranged for me to go to school, paid all my fees and anything else I needed. He was very kind."

"I didn't know anything about Olga being alive," George said. "My father and the government felt it would make her a target if the Vospyan rebels knew she was here. The information was on a need-to-know basis."

"What about Prince Louis?" Roza asked.

Kat shook her head. "MI6 believed it safer for me to remain dead in my uncle's eyes. It would put us both at risk. It's been hard, but I'm so proud of him for coming out and taking his rightful position as King."

"Yes," Roza said, "my government tells me that more civilians and military personnel flock to his banner every day."

"I pray every day that Vospya will be free again," Kat said.

Roza turned to George. "When did you find out about Olga?"

"Only over the Christmas break. We've been looking for a good nanny, as you know, and my private secretary had been tipped off about her by a friend in the security services."

"Why did you want to be a nanny, Olga?" Roza asked.

"After Cambridge, I felt a need to be that person that my nanny was to me, and I just wanted to live a very normal life. Royal life killed my family—I just wanted to fade into the background. Plus, I love children."

"I did tell Kat that I would help her be or do whatever she wanted, but she chose to be with us, hiding in plain sight," George said.

"Wow," Roza said, "it's remarkable. You're a brave woman, Olga, braver than I would have been."

George leaned forward on her desk and said, "Look at us. The three highest ranked female royals in Europe, and nobody would ever guess."

Kat prayed that no one would ever know.

Today was the launch of the Queen Consort's Year of the Family, and Bea was taking both princesses to a children's play-day at her former charity, Timmy's.

Timmy's also meant a lot to Queen Rozala. She had worked there with Lex during her stay with her cousins, before she became Queen.

The playroom of Timmy's was like a huge gym hall, and it rang loudly with the happy sounds of children's laughter. There were games set up, clowns, play equipment of all kinds, and sensory equipment, as some of the children had special needs.

Queen Bea, Queen Rozala, and Lennox were making their way around all the parents and children. Azi was keeping her distance and directing the little drone camera that buzzed around the room.

Bea had Anna in her arms, but Teddy had run over to Clay and Kat, who were standing on the perimeter of the room.

"What's wrong, Teddy?" Kat asked. "You don't want to play with the other children?"

Normally Teddy was a very confident child, so her shyness was unusual.

"Everyone is looking at me," Teddy said bashfully.

Clay crouched and said, "You want me to take you over to the clown?"

Teddy shook her head.

Queen Rozala approached them with a blond-haired little girl. "Teddy, I'd like you to meet my friend Summer."

Summer gave Teddy the most beautiful smile. "Hi, Teddy, you want to come and see the clown with me?"

Teddy took her hand immediately, and the pair ran off together.

"Aww," Kat said. "That's sweet."

"I met Summer when I worked here with Lex. She's a wonderful girl. I thought she'd help Teddy relax. Adults were bowing to her, and it was making Teddy uncomfortable," Rozala said.

"She's a lovely little girl," Clay said. "Is she ill or…?"

"She's much better since she started a new treatment. Hopefully it'll make a huge difference in her life. I better get back to the queening. Can you keep an eye on them?"

"Of course," Kat said.

Once Rozala left, Clay felt an awkward silence descend. Just when Clay thought Kat was warming up to her, and they were building a friendship, Kat pulled away from her. Ever since the private meeting Kat'd had with Queen Roza, she'd changed, going back into her shell and giving one-word answers to any conversation Clay attempted. There was something going on, and she just wished she could find out what.

"Is everything okay, Kat?" Clay asked.

"Yes, why wouldn't it be?"

"Ever since you had that meeting with Queen Rozala, you've been different. Stressed, even."

"Stressed? Of course I'm stressed. I'm watching my homeland be destroyed by civil war every day," Kat snapped.

Clay said nothing. She didn't want to make matters worse.

"I'm sorry for snapping at you. I didn't mean it."

"That's okay. There is something wrong, though, isn't there? You can tell me."

Kat looked at her, and Clay felt she wanted to tell her, but then she turned her attention back to the scene in front of them.

"I can't," Kat said. Just as Clay was about to reply, Queen Bea signalled for Kat. "Sorry, looks like it's time for the Queen's speech."

What is going on inside your head?

"Are you not hungry, Clay?" Holly asked.

Sunday was their day off, but Clay's mind had been occupied with thoughts of Kat. She'd been so quiet today at breakfast, and Clay was more sure than ever that she was hiding something, something that was causing her pain.

After a day of trying and failing to shop for her new cottage, Clay had joined Quincy and Holly in the dining room. Cammy and Lali were usually there for dinner too but had gone to Lali's parents for the evening.

"No not really. I was worried about Kat. She's usually here by now," Clay said.

Holly grinned and nudged Quincy. "I think maybe Clay likes our new nanny, Quin."

Clay felt burning embarrassment in her cheeks. "No…no, nothing like that."

"Holly," Quincy said, "you're embarrassing Clay."

"Oh, okay. Honestly, are all you police protection people so repressed?" Holly joked.

Clay said nothing. She wasn't repressed, in fact she cared too easily, but she was embarrassed talking about women with Holly.

Yesterday kept going round in her head. What had changed after Kat's meeting with Queen Rozala? She had to know.

"Quin?" Clay said.

"Yes?"

"Yesterday, Kat was asked to meet Queen Georgina and Queen Roza, and ever since she's been quiet. Sad, even. Do you know anything about it, and are you sure there isn't any more information about her background?"

Quincy put down her cutlery and dabbed her mouth with a napkin. "Clay, I know it's difficult sometimes, but we all have our place in the chain of command, and there are secrets that are on a need-to-know basis. As I told you before, I did question the lack of information on Katya's file, and the Queen herself told me it was top secret, that I was to dig no further, and to trust her. I trust the Queen's word, and I respect when a superior officer gives me an order."

"That's what I don't understand. How could a nanny be top secret?" Clay said. "Do you think she's a secret service agent? I mean, on our side, not the other side."

"Kat's not a secret agent," Holly said. "She's just a normal woman."

"It doesn't really matter what we all think," Quincy said firmly. "We need to trust the Queen."

Holly saluted Quincy. "Yes, sir."

"Very funny." Quincy sighed. "Clay, remember Azi is shooting some footage of the princesses leaving for nursery tomorrow morning."

"Yeah, I remember," Clay said.

Quincy gave Holly a kiss and stood up. "I'm just going to meet with Major Ravn and go over the week."

"But this is our day off," Holly said.

Quin hesitated for a second. "Well, you know…this job…"

"I know, I know. An inspector's work is never done. You're never off duty," Holly said.

Once Quincy had gone, Holly said, "I don't know how anyone in the protection squad has long term relationships with people outside the royal court. They'd never understand the all-consuming hours."

That thought had often popped into Clay's head. This wasn't so much a job, but a way of life.

"I pushed it too far, didn't I?" Clay said.

"No—you know how yes sir, no sir Quin is. In my book, it's good to question things that make no sense."

"It's not that I don't trust Kat—I do. But the last time I did that, I made mistakes."

A smile crept up on Holly's face. "You do like her, don't you?"

Clay was super embarrassed, and all she could think of to say was, "Shut up."

Holly nudged her with her elbow. "Tell the truth."

"Okay, fine. Yes, I like her, but I just don't get her."

Holly clapped her hands together excitedly. "Yes, yes, I knew it. I told Lali, but she wasn't sure. Wait, what do you mean, you don't get her?"

"Just that she confuses me," Clay said.

Holly laughed. "I confuse Quin most days. What in particular?"

Clay let out a sigh. "Well, one minute we're getting on really well, and I think things are going fantastically, and the next, she just brings down this cold, icy shield and doesn't even want to talk. Like, since she had a private talk with Queen Rozala."

"Give her a break, Clay. She's in a whole new world with us here, plus her home country is in turmoil. It's got to be hard to watch that."

"You think it's safe to follow my gut and trust her?" Clay asked.

"I don't know any more about her than you, but I know Queen Bea. She doesn't trust easily, and she's trusted this woman from the first. That tells me that she knows everything about her and doesn't have a problem with anything. So relax, and get to know her better. You'd make a cute couple."

"Holls, stop it," Clay protested, but she felt a little bit of pressure lifting from her shoulders. Maybe she could try to get to know Kat better?

❖

Kat was meant to be reading, but really she was just holding a book. Her eyes kept flicking up and down to the TV news playing in the background. Even though the sound was down, the flashing images of fighting still caught her attention.

Vospya was in all-out civil war now, and the Liberty Freedom Fighters were gaining ground every day, but the cost was high. Death, destruction, children orphaned by war. It broke her heart, and her anxiety was rising.

She shouldn't watch, logically Kat knew she shouldn't, but she couldn't tear her gaze away from it. In one way Kat felt she had to live through every horror, even as only a witness, because her people had to live through much worse.

It wasn't as if there was anything new on the news channel. It just kept looping through the same scenes, interspersed with images of her uncle Louis, now King. She was very proud of him for putting his head above the parapet, shining a light on the atrocities, making speeches as a rallying cry. His involvement was working.

More people from the armed forces joined the freedom fighters every day. She only felt anger that so many people had to die for the cause of good. Tears started to spill from her eyes, and she wiped them away quickly.

"TV off."

She couldn't take any more sadness for tonight. She jumped when she heard the rustle of paper at her door. She got up and walked over to find an envelope with *To Kat* written on the front.

She opened it and found a small bunch of daises taped to a note: *Since you liked them so much when Teddy gave you a bunch, I thought I would too. Hope you're okay, superspy. Ronnie (Clay)*

Katya laughed and felt the tension in her body lift. "Oh my God. She's so silly. Silly and sweet."

Kat hurried over to her bed and flopped onto her back. She read and reread the message again, and before she could think logically, she dictated a text. "*Is that Clay or Ronnie?* Send."

As she waited on a reply, she pulled the note to her chest and closed her eyes. She could see Clay's face over hers as they lay on the mat that night at the palace gym.

Her phone beeped and Kat's heart started to beat faster. She hadn't felt anticipation of a simple text before.

It's both. Mum called me Ronnie, so whatever you'd prefer. Did you like your flowers?

Yes, I loved them, thank you. They cheered up my night. So, what did you do with your day off, Ronnie?

Kat flipped onto her stomach and played with the petals of the daisies. "God, I'm like a twelve-year-old girl."

Spent the day online looking for furniture for the cottage. Well, I say the day, I got bored after an hour and then went for a run, then played some games.

Games? What kind of games?

Virtual games.

Kat rolled her eyes. *Seriously?*

Well what else is there to do? My friends are spending their days off together.

Kat wondered why Clay didn't have friends outside their royal circle. Surely there must have been someone, at least from school or childhood? Not that she had friends like those, but she was a special case. It wasn't safe for her to have friends, apart from Artie. And he'd just decided they were going to be friends and wouldn't let her push him away.

She felt sad that Clay didn't seem to have a social life outside the palace walls. Clay, it appeared to her, was someone who needed human contact. Kat was used to loneliness. It had been her life, and essential for her safety.

She got up and picked up the family picture she always kept close. She touched her finger to them all, a way of connecting to them in some small way. She got to Uncle Louis. The decision to remain a secret from him was made for her, but she dreamed of knowing him and was scared of it at the same time.

She feared the grief of loss would come tumbling out if they met again. Two lonely last members of a dying family dynasty that stretched back centuries. Kat put the picture down when she heard her phone beep. She had gotten caught up in her worries and forgotten her conversation with Clay.

She sensed Clay craved that human interaction that a friend, family, or lover could bring. She saw that when she gazed into her deep brown eyes. Maybe she could be that friend? A friendship, as far as it went, was all she could muster or commit to.

As much as she was attracted to Clay, and how her heart felt lighter in her company, being anything more than friends was impossible. How could you have a relationship with someone you didn't truly know? It would be dishonest.

Clay's text read, *I'll say goodnight if you're busy.*

There was sadness in those words. She did need a friend. Someone to care for her.

Do you want to bake with us on Wednesday? We're making pizza.

Oh, wow. Pizza? My favourite. Yeah, if Quincy doesn't need me for anything, I'd love that.

Great, well I'll say goodnight. Sleep well, Ronnie.

You too, superspy.

Kat chuckled at Clay's nickname for her. Clay made her feel lighter, happier, and dissipated her sadness for a time. Maybe she needed a friend like Clay in her life.

CHAPTER ELEVEN

Clay sang with the song playing in her bedroom as she got ready for work. She woke up this morning not with sadness, like she usually did, but with an excited energy. She checked her hair one last time in the mirror.

"Perfect."

Then she slipped on her shoulder holster, which held the tools of her trade—two handguns—and finally her navy-blue suit jacket.

"Let's go."

Clay was excited to go downstairs and spend more time with Kat. Their text message conversation was different. They had crossed some invisible line between work colleagues and a true friendship. In fact, to Clay's mind, they were teetering on the line between friendship and more.

Holly's words of wisdom about trusting Kat had really helped Clay let go, and let herself trust, and embrace her attraction for Kat. Kat was still a mystery and had her secrets, but Clay had been convinced that was for people above her pay grade to worry about.

All Clay wanted to do was get to know her better. This week was going to be good. She had one event to accompany the princesses to, with Queen Bea, and then hopefully she'd get to make pizza with Kat and the girls. Then next week Kat had promised to help paint Badger's Hollow, along with her other friends.

"Maybe we could make a night of it?" Clay said to herself. "I'll get pizzas, drinks—it could be brilliant fun."

Clay was all set and half walked, half ran out her bedroom door and down the corridor of the staff quarters. She couldn't wait to see Kat. On Monday mornings, the royals left from Windsor Castle in the morning directly to whatever appointments or business they had, and later went home to Buckingham Palace. The Queen felt staying over Sunday nights stretched out the weekends at their favourite place.

So Clay's first job on Monday morning was to escort Princess Teddy to nursery school, and that meant sharing the car with Kat. She bounced down the main staircase and to the front door. The car was already there waiting, along with Jack.

"Morning, Jack. Everything ready?"

"Yes, ma'am."

Every time Jack called her *ma'am*, Clay felt like looking behind her to see who he was talking to. She still thought of herself as the young, raw police officer who'd joined the protection squad just a few years ago.

"Good."

Clay looked at her watch. Kat would be coming down soon. She heard a small burr of noise in the air and looked up to see a tiny drone camera. Azi walked round the corner, talking to her camera crew via earpiece and microphone.

"I want a shot from above as the car pulls away, Mike. Slowly drawing away so you see the full majesty of the castle."

"Morning, Azi," Clay said.

"Good morning, Clay. All ready for your big scene?"

"You're making me nervous." She didn't like being the centre of attention. As officers they were meant to merge into the background, not be the main interest of the scene.

"Don't worry. Just pretend the camera isn't here," Azi said.

Clay liked Azi. She was a beautiful woman with a strong, super confident personality. She supposed that Azi would have needed that in some of the unstable and scary places she had filmed her documentaries.

She heard footsteps behind them and expected it to be Kat, but instead, to Clay's surprise, she heard Theo's voice.

"Good morning, everyone. How are you all today?"

That was odd. Theo normally left after Sunday dinner and didn't stay till Monday morning.

Azi rolled her eyes at his sudden appearance, but both Clay and Jack bowed.

"Good morning, Your Royal Highness," Clay and Jack said together.

Azi didn't bow but finally looked at him and said, "Morning."

Theo seemed really nervous to Clay, and she realized then that he had a huge crush on Azi, but Azi was going about her business, not giving him any attention.

Must have been unusual for a prince not to get attention from a woman.

Theo clapped his hands together and said, "Thought I would come and wave my beautiful niece off to nursery school."

Theo had never done this before. He walked down the steps and followed Azi around the car. He definitely liked her.

"So, tell me how you go about setting up the scene," Theo asked.

It was funny to watch Prince Theo working hard for a woman's attention. From what she heard and saw in the media, that was not normally needed. He was good-looking, but when you added the royal title on top of that, he was quite the catch.

Azi, however, did not look impressed.

Clay heard Teddy's voice and got her own case of nervous excitement when Kat walked out with the children. "Morning, Kat. Morning, Princess," Clay said.

Teddy hugged her legs. "We're going to nursery, Clay."

"We sure are."

"Good morning, Ronnie," Kat said with a smile.

Clay's stomach flipped at the use of her family name. But she saw Kat's smile falter when she noticed Azi and the tiny camera buzzing around.

"I forgot this was happening this morning," Kat said.

"Don't worry, it's only to get a shot of us leaving."

Azi walked up to them and said, "Hi, Kat. Whenever you're ready, put the princesses in the car. Don't even think about the camera."

Theo came bounding up to them. "Kisses before you go, Teddy."

Teddy gave Theo a hug and a kiss, then kissed Anna, who was in Kat's arms.

"See you later, sweet girl," Theo said.

Kat was tense. She hated the thought of being on camera. Since she was ten years old, life had been about fading into the background, but now in this high-profile job, she was stepping more and more into the light.

Theo took a few steps back and said, "Pretend I'm not here."

Azi stood off to the side and nodded to them. Kat tried to turn her face away from the camera, but it was buzzing around all over them, so her position didn't make much difference.

Jack opened the back door, and Kat put Anna into her car seat while Clay took Teddy around to the other side and strapped her in.

Once Anna was secure, Kat got in the front seat quickly, and then Clay joined her. Kat breathed a sigh of relief.

"Are you okay?" Clay asked.

"I just hate being on camera. Let's get going."

Kat told the computer where they were going, and the self-drive car started moving. Royal protocol meant the human driver kept their hands on the wheel, in case they needed to take control quickly.

Kat looked in the rear-view mirror and saw Jack in the car behind them, keeping a safe distance. Once they were out of the grounds, Kat breathed a sigh of relief.

"I don't know why we need to be filmed," Kat said.

"Something to do with the staff being like family," Clay said. "It's all done now. Hey, what did you think of Prince Theo? He has a major crush on Azi."

Kat smiled. "I'm still surprised you don't have a crush."

"Hey, she's straight, and besides, she's got a bit too much of a top energy for me," Clay said.

Kat felt her skin heat up at the thought of Clay topping her. "Stop it," she whispered to herself.

"What?" Clay asked.

"Oh, nothing really," Kat said.

They drove on through the London streets, Teddy singing in the back to some children's music that Kat had put on. Anna sweetly joined in with her adorable burbling.

After arriving at the nursery, Kat took Teddy in while Clay stayed with Anna. Kat quickly returned to the car.

"Okay, Anna," Kat said, "it's just us now. Let's go home and play." Kat clapped her hands together, making Anna do the same.

Clay laughed.

"What is it?" Kat asked.

"You're just so sweet with the children."

"Don't, you'll make me blush."

The car drove off, and they began chatting about the week ahead. Then Kat's phone signalled a notification and her heart sank.

"What's wrong?" Clay asked.

"Why?"

"You just shivered. I've seen you do that before when your phone beeps."

"It's a news notification. Every notification seems to be about Vospya these days, and it makes me feel worried and sad."

"Then switch off the notifications, and the news won't upset you."

"I can't do that," Kat snapped.

"Why?"

"Because I need to share in what's happening with my people. They can't switch off the daily terror, torture, and murder of the civil war, so the least I can do is share in the pain in this very small way."

Clay reached over and squeezed Kat's hand. "I'm sorry. You do what you feel you need to do."

Kat nodded and said, "Computer, read notification."

"As the Liberty Freedom Fighters gain ground in their push towards the capital city of Viermart, Vospya, government troops step up reprisals against innocent members of the public and call for them to give up the names of the prominent freedom fighters. King Louis sends a message of support and asks the world to do more to intervene in the toxic civil war."

Kat gulped to try to stop the tears that were forming. "It's okay. Let's go home."

❖

That evening Queen Georgina and Queen Bea hosted a drinks meet-and-greet at Buckingham Palace, with Queen Rozala and Crown Consort Lennox. It was to celebrate Britain's close relationship with Denbourg, the Denbourg officials, dignitaries, artists, actors, celebrities, and even footballers who made Britain their home.

So Kat was taking care of the princesses. She was sitting in her armchair watching the baby monitor screen. Both girls were sleeping, but she had a door straight through to their bedrooms, from her sitting room, if she was needed.

Since Kat had some time to kill, she called her friend Artie.

"Hi, Artie, it's Kat."

"My lady? At last. I thought the royals had you under house arrest," Artie joked.

"Sorry I've taken so long to call, but everything's been so busy. New routines, huge palace to get used to. How's your job going?"

"It's okay. Kids are great, but the parents"—Artie began to whisper—"a bit full of their own importance. Own their own building company. Not exactly royalty, although they think they are."

Kat chuckled. "Well I'm not giving away any secrets by saying my family are very nice, and very down to earth."

"You're so lucky. Was it Miss Dorcas who recommended you for the job?" Artie asked.

"Yes, she'd heard on the grapevine they were having trouble finding someone."

"I won't ask for any state secrets, but what about the staff? Are they nice?"

"Really welcoming. Like a big family really. I wasn't expecting that," Kat said.

"Anyone who sets your heart aflutter?"

Kat immediately thought of the daisy chain that Clay had given her, which sat on her bedside table. "Don't be silly. You know I'm not interested in relationships," Kat said.

"Who mentioned relationships? I'm talking about some hot and heavy sex."

The evocative image of lying under Clay with her arms clasped around Clay's neck burst into her mind. She closed her eyes and could almost taste Clay's lips and see the beads of sweat on Clay's brow as she thrust her fingers inside her.

"Kat? Kat? Are you with me?"

Kat was jolted from her lustful thoughts and found herself sucking on her finger, and her heart was pounding hard. "What? Sorry, I was miles away."

"There is someone, isn't there."

"Sort of someone I like, but nothing will come of it," Kat said.

"Wow, that's the first time you've ever admitted liking anyone. So, spill."

"The young princesses' police protection officer. She's really attractive, but it's not going anywhere, so don't get excited."

"Hmm," Artie said, "sounds like she gets you excited, though."

❖

Clay had been looking forward to Wednesday afternoon all week, but she wasn't sure if she was going to make it. The security meeting had gone on longer than planned, but as soon as it was finished, she ran through the palace and downstairs to the kitchens.

The kitchen was empty of staff, but Princess Teddy and Kat were there with aprons on.

"Clay!" Teddy said.

"Hi, Princess."

Kat looked really happy to see her. "I thought you weren't going to make it, Ronnie."

"The meeting dragged on. Where's Anna?" Clay asked.

"Queen Bea and Queen Rozala are spending a few hours with her. Get your apron on, Sergeant," Kat said and threw an apron to Clay.

"Can't wait." Clay slipped off her jacket and put on the apron. She clapped her hands together and said, "Where do we start?"

"Christophe the chef was kind enough to have some dough prepared for us. So we're going to roll that out and then put on our toppings. First, hands washed, Sergeant."

"Yes, ma'am." Clay grinned.

Clay rolled up her shirt sleeves to her elbows, washed her hands quickly, and got back to the kitchen table.

"This is going to be great fun, Teddy," Clay said.

"And a teachable moment. Queen Beatrice is keen to show Teddy food doesn't just appear by magic on a tray a page brings."

"Yeah, I never thought of that. Most kids are in homes where they are in the kitchen all the time, but not Teddy. So what's first?" Clay asked.

Kat said to Teddy, "You tell her."

Teddy, who was standing on a step so she was high enough, said, "Roll the dough, Clay."

"Got it." Kat had placed a bowl with a lump of dough beside her. She lifted the dough and whacked it down on the table.

"I'm just going to the fridge to get some of the toppings," Kat said as she walked off. "Put some flour down before you roll, both of you."

Both Clay and Teddy put their hands in the bowl with flour at the same time, and when they pulled their hands out a puff of flour went over both of them.

Teddy giggled. "It's like snow, Clay."

Clay grinned and threw some more flour at Teddy. "I got you, Teddy."

They were both shrieking with laughter when Kat returned with some bowls full of toppings.

"Clay? I might have known I couldn't trust you."

"Uh-oh, she's caught us, Teddy."

"We're having a flour snow fight, Kat."

"So I see." Kat gave her a hard stare, but then it softened into a smile. "You are impossible, Ronnie."

Clay loved Kat's smiles, especially when they were given to her. Every smile she got made her heart hurt less and feel less lonely. Did Kat feel the same?

❖

Kat finished packing the dishwasher and walked back to the kitchen table, where Teddy was sitting eating her finished pizza, and Clay was standing munching her own.

"If Chef Christophe saw the mess you two left, he would have banned us from his kitchen."

"We had fun, and fun can be messy." Clay winked.

That wink set off fireworks inside Kat. Why did she have to be so, so, sexy—and sweet. A deadly combination.

Kat cleared her throat and rubbed little Teddy's back. "Is it tasty, Teddy?"

"Yum!"

Kat moved closer to Clay and leaned against the table. Clay was munching on her own pizza.

"What about you, Ronnie?"

"Yum," Clay said with her mouth full.

"How can jalapenos, green chillies, spicy pepperoni, and pineapple be tasty? It would blow my head off."

Clay licked her fingers after finishing her slice of pizza, and Kat couldn't take her eyes off them. There was something about Clay's lips that drew her in. She imagined sucking on her upper lip and then slipping her tongue between those lips.

Clay wiped at her mouth with a napkin. "Is there something on my face?"

Kat desperately wanted to touch Clay, and she spotted a smudge of flour on Clay's cheek.

"You have some flour here."

Kat stepped closer and gently brushed the smudge from Clay's cheek, but then it turned into a caress. She was caught in Clay's eyes, those warm brown eyes, which just pulled her in.

Clay put her hand on her hip and pulled her closer. "Kat? I—"

Teddy shrieked and they jumped apart. "I finish my pizza."

Kat closed her eyes and tried to control her breathing. That was totally unprofessional.

When she opened them, Clay was trying not to look at her. The awkwardness in the room was uncomfortable.

Eventually Kat said, "I better get Teddy cleaned up and back to the nursery."

Clay lifted her jacket. "Yeah, and I should go back up to the security office, I suppose. Thanks for inviting me. I had a great time."

"You're welcome, Ronnie."

Clay smiled and said, "See you later, Teddy."

"Bye, Clay."

Once Clay was gone, some of the kitchen staff started to appear to prepare for tonight's dinner.

"Better get you cleaned up, Teddy."

Kat sat Teddy up on the table and went to get a paper towel to wipe her face. She got some and wet it under the tap. She started to think about Clay again, and her heart sped up. She could still feel Clay's soft skin under her fingertips.

Stop thinking about her. It's not going to happen.

Kat went back to Teddy and began cleaning her up. She heard a beep from her phone and she shuddered. It was probably some bad news from back home. She took out her phone and it wasn't bad news from home. It was a news article that Artie had emailed her.

It read, *Who is the Buckinghams' unusual new nanny?*

Oh no. Kat started to panic. She couldn't afford to make the news.

After Clay had finished work, she went in search of Kat. All the staff had been talking about a news story that hit this afternoon. Holly said that Kat had been upset by it. Clay looked it up and the headline read, *Who is the Buckinghams' unusual new nanny?"*

She tried Kat's room, but she wasn't there, so Clay went down to the gym. Clay knew she liked to lose her emotions in exercise. Sure enough, there she was, beating the living daylights out of the punching bag.

Clay didn't make the mistake of walking up unannounced this time. "Kat?"

Kat turned around. She was sweaty, breathing heavily, and her eyes were red. Clay walked over to her and said, "I saw what was written about you. Are you okay?"

"I should have known taking this job would put me under the microscope, but this? I'm not a celebrity—I'm a normal nobody. Why do they care?"

Clay took her hand. "You're not a nobody, and they care because they love something to write about the royals' private life."

"I can't get this sort of publicity, Ronnie," Kat said.

It wasn't nice to have your privacy breached, but Clay couldn't understand why she was so distressed.

"Why? I know there's something else. Why is this upsetting you so much?"

"I like it here," Kat said. "I've never really had a lot of friends. But now I have Holly, Quincy, Cammy, and Lali, and you. I don't want to have to leave here."

Now Clay was worried. She didn't want Kat to go anywhere. "Why would you have to do that?"

"It wouldn't be safe," Kat said.

"Why? I don't get it."

Kat looked down to the floor. "I can't tell you. I'm not allowed to tell you."

As much as Clay hated not knowing, she said, "Okay, but one thing"—she gently lifted Kat's head and saw tears in her eyes—"you will always be safe here with me, and you'll always have a friend."

Kat wiped away the tears and looked puzzled. "You're just accepting that I can't tell you? Normally you're trying to find out everything about me. I know you asked someone to look into my security files."

Oh, shit. How could that have gotten back to her?

"I was suspicious. I felt protective about the only people I cared about. I didn't have my mum any more, but my friends and Teddy and Anna, I had them to care about."

Kat took a step closer towards Clay and searched her eyes. "Then what's different now?"

Clay smiled and said softly, "I trust you, superspy."

Kat placed her hand on Clay's chest and whispered, "Thank you, Ronnie."

Clay cupped Kat's cheek and they moved slowly together. Their lips came together, gently, softly. Clay felt like she was melting. She opened her mouth slightly and ran the tip of her tongue along Kat's bottom lip.

Kat moaned and opened her mouth to her. Kat's moan set Clay on fire, and just as she was about to deepen the kiss, voices could be heard coming downstairs to the gym.

Kat took a big step back and said, "No, I can't do this."

"Why? I care about you, Kat."

Kat picked up her towel and said, "You don't know me."

A group of five men came into the gym, and their moment was most definitely gone. Kat hurried away up the stairs, leaving Clay elated and confused. Kissing anyone else had never felt like that. She decided in that moment that she would do whatever it took to know who Kat truly was.

Not because she was suspicious any more—she trusted her superiors—but because she wanted to know who Kat the woman truly was. The woman who was stealing her heart.

Alexander Chak rolled off the warm body underneath him and said, "Get me a drink."

Anita, his secretary, sat up and pulled on her discarded dressing gown.

"Hurry up, whiskey and soda."

"Yes, Alexander."

Alexander was very much enjoying his new role and his new secretary. The only thing he wasn't enjoying was the news from Vospya. The civil war was becoming ever more serious. He thought that the terrorists would be dealt with swiftly, but instead their numbers and determination were growing since the so-called King threw his weight behind them.

The president was losing a tight grip on the country. He knew there was discontent growing amongst his government, and rumours were mounting that Loka was going to be replaced. Alexander agreed and wanted to back the winning horse. He had worked too long and too hard to lose the power he had. One day, he knew, Vospya would be his. That was his ambition.

The TV on the wall was playing some stupid entertainment programme. He grabbed the remote control to put on the news. But before he did, video of the Queen, her wife, and her children played. "Disgusting."

Anita came back with his drink and handed it to him. "Who is disgusting?"

"The two lesbian queens."

The video moved on to a blond woman holding the young princess's hand. She was beautiful. The report said that it was the new royal nanny.

"The new nanny, eh?" Alexander said. "Queen Georgina knows how to pick her women."

"I read about her. She's from Vospya," Anita said.

"What? The royal nanny is from Vospya?" Alexander was surprised.

Anita slipped back into the bed. "Yes, I read about her online. She is a refugee, been in Britain most of her life, it said."

Alexander paused the TV on the nanny's face. "You're one of us, are you? Then why did you run away?" There was something that niggled at him. Something he thought he recognized. "Tomorrow, I want our security people to find out everything they can about that nanny. Okay?"

"Yes, Alexander."

He took a long drink of his whiskey. He had gotten where he was from lowly poor rebel soldier to Vospyan ambassador by trusting his gut, and his gut told him he had to know this woman's story.

CHAPTER TWELVE

Holly walked along the palace corridor and smiled as she saw Clay outside the nursery door. Clay had been a bit down over the last few days, she had noticed, which wasn't good. Clay had been much brighter since moving to the palace and spending time with Kat.

More than anything, she had hoped that the distraction of a beautiful woman might help distract Clay from her grief, but not so far this week.

"Good morning, Clay. Where's Jack?"

"Morning, Holly. He's having a review with Inspector Quincy," Clay replied.

"That's just what you need first thing in the morning," Holly joked. "So, what's on the agenda today for the princesses?"

Clay sighed. "Nursery run, then the usual timetable."

Kat came out of the royal bedroom holding Princess Anna. Holly noticed Clay tensed up immediately. Holly remembered how tense Quin would get whenever she was near. Clay definitely had the hots for Kat.

"Good morning, Kat, and hello to you, sweet girl." Holly took Anna's little chubby hand and kissed it. "How is she today?" Holly asked.

"She's fine. Anna's always a happy girl," Kat said.

"Are you three going to have a walk today or go to the park?"

Holly watched as Kat quickly glanced at Clay, who was trying her best to stare ahead impassively. She could almost feel the tension between the two.

"I think I'll take Anna for a walk in the gardens. There were photographers at the park the last time."

Holly knew being splashed across the celebrity gossip columns had upset Kat. She prized her privacy, and the little she knew, it was for good reasons. She had tried asking Quin, but she took her oath of secrecy extremely seriously, and besides she didn't know the full story.

"They're always going to be around, Kat. It used to drive me mad, but you learn to block them out, or you're always paranoid. Clay will keep you safe anyway. Won't you, Clay?"

Clay turned and looked straight at Kat as if Holly wasn't there. "Always."

Uh-huh. Super sexual tension.

"Okay, well, I'll see you guys later. Queen Bea's make-up won't get done on its own."

"They're still in the breakfast room, Holly," Kat said.

"Thanks, I'll get set up, then."

Holly walked into Bea's dressing room and opened her make-up box. She laid out all her brushes and checked on Queen Bea's outfit, which was hanging up in the wardrobe covered by a clothes bag. Once everything was ready, she walked through the interconnecting door to the family sitting room and knocked on the door of the breakfast room. It was really their dining room, since George and Bea preferred to eat all their meals here in the smaller room, unless the extended family was coming to dinner.

"Come in," Bea said.

She opened the door and walked into the room. George had Teddy on her knee and Anna's empty high chair sat by Bea.

Holly curtsied and said, "Morning, Your Majesties. Just to let you know, I'm ready when you are, Bea."

"I'm just coming, Holls."

George said, "You go ahead. I'll pop this terror into the nursery, darling."

"If you're sure," Bea said.

George got up and both she and Teddy gave Bea a kiss. "Have a good day with Roza."

"Bye, Mama," Teddy said.

Bea gave Teddy the biggest hug. It was so sweet to see Bea with children. Being a mum really suited her.

Bea stood and tightened the tie of her silk dressing gown and followed her through to the dressing room. "How is Quin this morning?"

"Oh, her usual, a hundred mile run before breakfast, then pulling poor Jack in for a review first thing. Sometimes I think she'd like to give me a job review."

Bea smiled and sat down at her dressing table. "Oh? And what would your score say?"

"Nine out of ten, losing a mark for my untidiness and not turning off lights when I leave a room. That drives her crazy."

Bea laughed. "A nine from someone with Quin's high standards is as good as a ten."

"I think so," Holly said. "So, ready for the camouflage?"

"Yes, let's do this."

"Quin said you and Queen Roza are going to the maternity unit today."

"Yes, I'm glad Clay isn't with us today. Hospitals could stir up a lot of emotions for her."

"Yeah, that's true." Of course, it was Kat who was stirring up her emotions at the moment.

"What are you and Quin doing for the weekend? Anything special planned?" Bea asked.

Holly started to dab moisturizer onto Bea's face. "We're helping Clay paint the cottage. Me, Quin, Lali, Cammy, Kat hopefully. A painting party. You know the kind of thing, bring a few drinks and help the owner paint in double-quick time."

"Oh, that's right. George said Quin, Cammy, and Clay were having Saturday off. So we were to have a quiet day at Windsor," Bea said.

"Azi said she might pop in. I think she thought she might get a feel for the family atmosphere we have together. She's become a friend too. A really nice woman. Intense, but really nice."

"I think Theo agrees," Bea joked.

"I thought he had a bit of a crush on her." Holly dabbed the make-up primer on her friend's face.

"She's all he can talk about, but she thinks he's the party prince who spends all his time with rich heiresses. Which is sometimes true, but that's only one side of him. He's knuckled down to his charity work since I first met him."

Holly dabbed foundation onto Bea's cheeks with a sponge, carefully giving it an even spread. "I'll make sure to tell Azi that when I can. Prince Theo is a lovely, kind, and generous man."

Bea furrowed her eyebrows. She remembered something that Holly had said earlier. "Wait, did I hear you say *probably* Kat? I thought she was fitting in well, one of the gang now. I told her we would look after the kids ourselves over the weekend."

"She is fitting in, and she was coming, but things have turned slightly frosty between Clay and Kat."

"What?" Bea said. "Clay's still not suspicious, is she? George made it clear that she was trusted. Did you not tell her that?"

"I did, and it's not suspicion. Our Clay is falling for Kat, and the sexual tension is just pinging. I don't know what's happened in the past few days, but Kat seems a bit frosty to her now."

"Oh no." Bea sighed.

"What? What's wrong with Clay being into Kat?"

God, there were so many complications Bea could think of. Most worryingly, seeing Clay hurt. How could she explain that loving Kat, one of the two last members of a dying royal house, could be difficult, without giving away state secrets?

"Nothing is wrong, just complicated."

Holly put her make-up sponge down and leaned against the dressing room table. "You know, don't you? There is a secret about Kat—Clay was right."

She hated keeping secrets from her friends. Bea always had been an open book to them, but this was different. These secrets saved lives.

"I can't tell you, Holls. I hope you can understand and trust me that it is for a very good reason. But Clay loving Kat could cause her to be hurt, emotionally. I don't know if Kat can give Clay what she's looking for, especially just now."

Holly folded her arms. "I understand. Wait a minute. She's from Vospya. They're in civil war. It's something to do with that, isn't it?"

Bea couldn't lie and struggled not to be open to her friends. She took Holly's hand and said, "Please don't ask me, Holls."

Holly smiled. "It's okay. I live with Quin, remember? I'm used to secrets. You think I shouldn't encourage them?"

"How can we discourage love, if it's there? Complications can't stop love—I should know that. We'll just need to be there for them if and when we need to be."

"It might be a moot point, anyway, going by Kat this morning."

"She did seem a bit distracted, but with everything going on in Vospya, it's hardly surprising."

"I knew Vospya was important." Holly winked.

❖

Clay looked in the rear-view mirror and checked on Princess Anna. She was happily chewing away at a toy while the only other sound in the car was the news playing on the radio.

They were in the private car park of Teddy's nursery school, with Jack in a car beside them, waiting for home time. The silence between her and Kat since they'd kissed had been growing with every passing day, but today was particularly frosty.

Clay had tried conversation, but she got nothing back, except for yes, no, maybe. Kat was so shut down, as if she was lost in her own mind. Every time the news mentioned something about some battle in Vospya or the death toll for the day, she saw Kat flinching.

She wanted to comfort Kat, but if all Kat could manage was anger or frustration, then Clay would take that, but she hated the silence, always had. If she pissed off her mother, or had a teenage strop, five minutes later she was begging for forgiveness. This felt so similar.

Clay cared about Kat. She couldn't hide from it any more. The kiss they had shared opened up a part of her heart she didn't know existed. She assumed after their kiss they would explore that, or at least talk it through, even if Kat was scared—but nothing.

Her ears pricked up at the news report: "As the Liberty Freedom Fighters gain ground, making their way towards the country's capital, government forces raided a village suspected of harbouring freedom fighters. There are unconfirmed reports that over fifty villagers were shot and killed."

Clay glanced at Kat and she saw her hold the steering wheel so tight, her knuckles were white.

"Kat—"

Kat unbuckled her seat belt and said, "I'm going in for Teddy now."

Clay grasped her hand. "Wait, you're upset. I'll go in, and you can wait with Anna."

"No, I'll get her." Kat opened her driver's door. "But you can drive us home."

Before she could say anything, Kat was off and out of the car.

Clay watched her walk away and got out of the car. Kat never let her drive. There was so much going on in Kat's head, and she was worried Kat was becoming overwhelmed. If only Kat would open up to her. Jack joined her from the car behind.

"Is everything okay, Sergeant? Ms. Kat looked upset."

"She just heard some bad news about her country on the news."

"It's crazy over there, isn't it?" Jack said. "I saw there were rumours the leader, Nikola, had been captured. I hope that's not true because he's driving this revolution," Jack said.

Clay hadn't seen that, and she hoped Kat hadn't. "It's hard to think about how those people are suffering. But we can hope."

Clay knew if she was over there, she'd be rounded up and tortured or worse. Gay women and men were top of President Loka's death list.

"Sorry I can't come to your painting party," Jack said. "It's my mum's birthday, and I can't pass up the chance of having the day off."

Normally they would have to stagger days off at the weekend, because the royal family would need them. But the Queen, knowing Clay wanted her friends' help on Saturday, gave them all the weekend off, insisting the family wouldn't venture out this weekend.

Clay had forgotten her painting party was tomorrow. Would Kat even come to it now? She was hoping to spend some time with her and have some fun.

"Don't worry about it, Jack. Spending time with your family is more important." The back door to the nursery opened and Teddy came running out to her.

"Clay, I painted a picture," Teddy said.

Clay lifted her up in her arms and gave her a kiss on the cheek. "Good girl, Princess Teddy."

Kat came walking behind, holding Teddy's backpack and her painting.

"Everything okay today?" Clay asked.

"Yes, fine," Kat said.

Clay felt waves of tension coming from Kat, like she was teetering on the edge of breaking down. In an ideal world she'd wrap her arms around her and make it all better, but she couldn't.

She understood the impulse to shut down emotionally. It's what she had done when her mum died, but what had helped was Holly and her friends, gathering her up and comforting her. Clay didn't know if Kat would ever accept that kind of help.

"Are you sure you want me to drive?"

"Yes, I'm too distracted. I'll put Teddy in her seat," Kat said.

Clay had to help her. She couldn't stand Kat being in pain. There was no doubt about it. Clay was falling for Kat big time, even more so now that Kat was showing her this vulnerability.

❖

Bea watched Roza hold the newborn baby boy they had both just met, with pride. What a difference there was since the party girl princess first came to stay with her and George. Today Bea and Roza were visiting a newly opened state-of-the-art maternity unit in St. Wilfred's Hospital, London, as part of their joint Year of the Family project.

The tiny cameras buzzed around them like insects, while the hospital room door was kept shut from onlookers. Azi directed the cameras via her remote team from outside, where both security teams kept guard on the doors.

"He's beautiful," Roza said. "What time was he born, Jenna?"

The young mother, Jenna, had been chosen to meet the two Queens as her partner, Dena, a corporal in the army, was serving in a British military base in Denbourg.

"Half past eleven last night, ma'am," Jenna said nervously.

Bea wanted to put Jenna more at ease. She walked to the side of the bed and said, "I think you might have to fight Queen Rozala to get your son back."

The three women laughed and Jenna seemed to relax.

"How long do you have left, ma'am," Jenna said to Roza.

"Two months. It can't come quick enough now," Roza said. "The backache is getting too much."

"Just don't talk about the birth, Jenna," Bea said.

Jenna laughed. "I won't, ma'am."

Bea had meant it as a joke, but she saw Roza stiffen and she didn't laugh. Strange.

She turned back to Jenna. "Your partner is serving in Denbourg, I understand. It must be really hard for her to miss the birth of your son."

Jenna gulped down a few tears. "It is, ma'am. I miss her, and I'm sad for what she's missed out on, but duty is everything to Dena. In fact, when I told her you were both coming to visit me, she asked me to pass on her and her regiment's thanks to you and Queen Georgina for your support of the armed forces. They all really appreciate it, and when Dena is far away from me, it's sad, but it makes me proud that she is serving her Queen and country."

It never failed to amaze Bea how the armed forces held George in high regard. It never occurred to her before she met George that the monarch was the buffer between the forces and the government of the day and kept politics out of military matters.

Even if an officer, soldier, sailor, or airman disagreed with their government, they knew they were serving the Queen, not the prime minister.

"That's very kind of her to say, and please tell Dena that I'll convey her message to the Queen tonight. I know it will mean a lot to her."

Jenna's face lit up. "Thank you, ma'am."

"I hope Dena is enjoying Denbourg," Roza said.

"Oh yes, ma'am. She says it is a very beautiful country."

"I must visit the base in Strander." Then Roza looked up at Bea. "If Queen Georgina will allow me and Crown Consort Lennox to visit her troops?"

"I'm sure she'd be delighted," Bea said with a smile.

Jenna's son started to fuss.

"I better hand him back to you, Jenna," Roza said.

Bea took the little boy in her arms and carefully handed him back to his mum. Then she gave Roza her arm to help her up.

"It was so nice to meet you, Jenna," Bea said.

"Good luck with the baby," Roza said.

"And with yours, ma'am. I hope everything goes well for you and Crown Consort Lennox."

Again Bea saw something in Roza. Was it worry?

After leaving the hospital room followed by the cameras, Bea nodded to Azi, who stopped filming and walked ahead to get some shots of them coming out of the hospital.

That was the great thing about insisting Azi direct the documentary. Bea could trust her to be discreet with the filming and cut any sensitive material.

The staff from the hospital lined up outside to wave them off, along with a group of children from a local school who were waving the flags of Britain and Denbourg.

She and Roza thanked the hospital staff and waved to the children as they made their way to the car. Both Quincy and Ravn opened up the car doors for them, and they got inside. As soon as the doors were shut, Roza asked for the cold air to be turned on.

"Are you okay, Roza?" Bea said.

"Yes." Roza rubbed her baby bump. "Just a bit hot."

Once the car had moved off and they'd waved to the children, Bea got a bottle of water from the car fridge and handed it to Roza.

"Thanks." Roza took a sip and gasped. "That's better."

"Are you sure you're okay?"

Roza scrunched up her face. "Backache, and my ankles are sore.

I can't believe I have two more months of this, but it'll be worth it in the end."

"I'm sure Lex will be happy to rub your back and your feet this evening."

"Not likely." Roza snorted. "I'm not telling her."

Now Bea was confused. "Why?"

"Because if I tell her, she'll say I told you so. We had so many arguments before coming for this trip. If I complain now, it'll be"—Roza put on a low, comic voice—"I told you so, Roza. I know everything, Roza. I know best, Roza."

Bea chuckled. "She wouldn't say that."

"She would, I'm telling you. She thinks because she's older, she knows best about everything. Sometimes I feel like a little girl in her eyes."

"Lex loves you. She gave up everything to come and marry you. She's not that bad, is she?"

Roza sighed. "No, I suppose not. It's just Lex loves me so much, and she cares so much, that sometimes she can be a tad overbearing. But I shouldn't be complaining, should I? I love her." Then Roza started to cry.

Bea grasped her hand and said, "Hey, hey, what's wrong?"

"I just love her so much."

Hormones.

Bea gave her a tissue. "Are you're sure there's nothing else? You seemed a bit tense in the hospital room when the birth was mentioned."

Roza wiped her tears. "I keep worrying about the birth. What if something goes wrong? Like it did with my mama? What if my baby boy or girl has to grow up without me?"

Bea pulled Roza into her arms. "It won't. What happened to your mother was a one-in-a-million thing. Besides, medicine has moved on."

"Perri says I haven't to worry, but I feel Lex worries, and if she's worried, I should be."

Bea shook her head. "She's just worried the way any other partner would be. George fussed about constantly when I was pregnant. The one who isn't carrying the child can feel helpless, and guilty at the discomfort and pain you're going through. She's just trying to protect and make sure you're safe."

"I suppose." Roza sighed.

"Tell her how you feel, tonight. It'll be worth it," Bea said.

"Okay, I will." Roza rubbed her stomach. "I know I'm supposed to provide an heir and a spare, but I don't know if I can go through this again."

"I thought that, and then I held Teddy and Anna in my arms, and the pain and discomfort vanished from my mind."

"Wait," Roza said with surprise, "are you planning to have a third?"

"We've talked about it. I know George would love to have a big family, and I know as soon as I see you holding your little bundle, I'll want to get pregnant again. I love being a mum."

"Three little ones? You're a braver woman than I," Roza said.

"Maybe I'm a bit crazy, but your little one needs lots of cousins to play with."

"Thanks, Bea. It really helps to talk to you about these kinds of things, and I will talk to Lex tonight. I promise."

Bea smiled. "Good, it'll be worth it."

"This is all you have?" Alexander said with disbelief.

His official, Victor, nodded. "There's nothing more, sir. I didn't believe it myself, and when I checked, I got the same results. This woman has no history before arriving in Britain aged ten."

Alexander peered at the blown-up picture of the blond woman. "Katya Kovach. Who are you?"

There was something about her that chimed with him. What was it?

"I want one of our people on her. There must be a way to find out more about her."

"Yes, sir," Victor said.

"Is there anything else?" Alexander asked.

Victor shifted uncomfortably. "The UN is building support to intervene in our civil war. There is talk of a resolution being made by Denbourg to send a peacekeeping force into the country."

Alexander threw the picture aside angrily. "They can't do that. We are a sovereign country. They can't meddle in another country's affairs."

"They seem determined on humanitarian grounds."

Alexander snorted. "Liberal dogs. We are the best run country in Eastern Europe. What does President Loka have to say?"

"President Loka's attention doesn't appear to be on these pressing matters. He's arrested the head of the army. He wishes to put him on trial for the many soldiers that have joined the freedom fighters."

"Jesus Christ. That man is losing his mind. They weren't at first, but now they are. He's paranoid that all of his ministers and advisors are out to get him, and they're going to be if he keeps turning on his own," Alexander said.

Loka was on his way out, he was sure of that, but Alexander couldn't show his hand until he was sure which of the government heavyweights was going to win the fight for power. Only then could he secure his position.

"That'll be all, Victor." He remembered the security file. "And remember to get someone on this woman, Victor."

"Yes, sir."

One day he would be the one vying for the leadership, but for today he would keep his powder dry.

CHAPTER THIRTEEN

Kat was finally back to her room after a long day with the children. As always on Friday, the family and the royal court had decamped to Windsor. Kat much preferred living at the castle at weekends to the impersonal Buckingham Palace. She made a cup of tea and sat down in her armchair. She'd had a hard day of trying to be happy and smiley for the children when she felt nothing approaching happy.

Her head was a mess of confusion and anxiety. The troubles back in her home country, her growing feelings for Clay, and the piece of so-called journalism on her had tipped her over the edge. It was just too much to cope with.

If there continued to be public interest in who she was, she might have to leave her post here. If anyone from the Vospyan authorities got wind of who she was, not only would she be in danger, but the British government and secret service would deem her a risk, by association, to the princesses.

Kat took a sip of tea and said, "It's only a matter of time."

That was her fear. She was living on borrowed time here when it was just starting to feel like home. She had friends, a community, something she had never had before. And then there was Clay.

Why did I have to make things even more complicated?

The kiss she'd shared with Clay had awakened a part of her that she didn't know existed. A needing, wanting part of her. Every time she'd closed her eyes since they kissed, it was all she could think about.

Kat knew Clay was hurt that she was pushing her away. She had pushed people who she had begun to become close to since she was a girl, her only way of coping, but Clay was different.

Never before in Kat's life had she been in danger of losing her heart—until now. Just being in Clay's company made her body ache for her. If only Clay was still distrusting of her, it would make things easier, but she did trust her now and was willing not to ask any more questions.

She heard a knock on the door and got up to open it. Her heart fluttered at the sight of Clay in her gym shorts and T-shirt.

"Hi," Clay said brightly, "are you coming down to the gym to spar tonight?"

Clay was obviously just going to pretend everything was all right between them and hope that she would come around.

"Not tonight. I'd rather just be on my own. I've got a lot on my mind."

"All the more reason to exercise and spar. It clears your head and gets all your frustrations out."

That was the thing. Sparring with Clay made more frustrations than it helped. It felt like foreplay to Kat, and she couldn't afford to go down that path. Having Clay that close, especially pinning her to the floor, got her hotter than she could handle and fuelled her fantasies.

"No, I just want to be on my own."

Clay looked crestfallen and Kat felt guilty.

"Okay, um…are you coming to the cottage tomorrow, with all the rest of our friends?" Clay asked.

"No, okay?" Kat said with exasperation. She immediately regretted it. "I'm sorry, that didn't come out right. I—"

Clay interrupted her and couldn't hide the wounded look on her face. "No, you don't need to explain. I've got the message loud and clear." Clay turned and hurriedly walked away.

"Ronnie? Stop, listen."

But Clay didn't stop. She walked away hurt and angry.

Kat shut her door. She slapped herself on the forehead. "Bloody idiot. What did you say that for?" She walked over to her armchair, flopped down on it, and covered her face with her hands.

Clay deserved so much more than she could give her. This was so hard. If the first job she'd been offered hadn't fallen through, she wouldn't be in this type of emotional mess.

Someone knocked on the door. Maybe it was Clay coming back?

She jumped up and opened the door and found Holly there. "Hi, Holly."

"Hi, I wanted to check you were okay. You didn't come to dinner in the dining hall," Holly said.

"I didn't feel like it. Um…come in."

"Thanks."

Kat wanted to be alone, but she felt obliged to offer Holly a cup of tea. "Would you like tea?"

Holly reached into her bag and pulled out a bottle of wine. She grinned and said, "How about some wine?"

Kat smiled. "Yes, I could do with a drink." She got glasses and they sat down. "Sorry, I don't have any wine glasses."

Holly poured into two big tumblers. "That's okay. We can fit more wine in these. So how's things?"

"Fine," Kat said a bit too quickly.

Holly furrowed her eyebrows. "Truth, Kat. I know the splash in the media upset you."

Kat took a drink of wine. It was nice and cold. Holly must have brought it straight from the fridge.

"Yes, it did. I don't ever want to be the centre of attention."

"It happened to me when I started working for Bea. It wasn't nice, but George and Bea knew it wasn't of my doing. The press would do anything for a royal story. You just need to learn to ignore it."

"I know, but I can't be the centre of attention, Holly. I can't, and I can't explain," Kat said.

"Oh, the secret thing? Don't worry, Bea didn't tell me, but she did tell me you did have some difficult things to deal with."

Kat rubbed her forehead. "Everything is piling on top of me just now, it feels like. The civil war in Vospya, watching my people die every day, the press trying to poke around and see what they find out about me, and then there's Clay—"

"Whoa, whoa, back up," Holly said.

Kat squeezed her eyes closed. What did she mention Clay for?

"What about you and Clay?" Holly grinned.

Kat sighed. She'd never had a female friend she'd shared secrets with growing up. It felt strange. "Clay and I have gotten closer since I arrived here, and…"

"And?"

"And we kissed the other night, after the splash about me in the press. I didn't plan it. I would never have planned it to happen."

"I knew it. I knew this morning there was sexy tension. You couldn't meet a nicer woman than Clay," Holly said.

"It was a mistake, Holly. I can't let anything happen between us."

"Why? Clay is just adorable."

Kat clasped her hands in front of her and stared at them, not wanting to make contact with Holly. "I know she is, but I can't, not with my situation. We haven't talked about the kiss since it happened," Kat said.

"Oh no. Kat, I know she's falling for you. She's told me."

Kat looked up. "She's falling for me?"

Holly nodded. "You're going to have to talk about it, one way or another. Maybe at the painting party tomorrow? You could take some time, go off on your own, and talk to her."

"I'm not going tomorrow. She came to my door just before you to ask if I was still coming—I told her no. She was upset, and I hated upsetting her, but I just can't be what she wants."

Holly poured out some more wine. "I'm not going to lie, Kat. She really likes you, and I don't know what's holding you back, but if you truly believe that you can't explore what you have with her, you have to be straight. She's a sweet, caring person, and she's just lost her mum. Don't hurt her any more than you need to."

Kat thought about looking into Clay's soulful brown eyes and wanted to gather her up in her arms. "I won't. I promise."

Later that night when Kat was lying in bed, all she could see and think about was Clay. More than a few times she'd composed a text to send her to apologize for today, but she chickened out.

She closed her eyes and allowed her mind to conjure up a picture of how her life could have been different. A world where she wasn't constantly looking over her shoulder, or worried about people finding out who she was.

Kat saw herself meeting Clay in a pub or club, or at a party, and falling for her, as she knew she would. They would date, have so much fun together, and fall in love.

A beautiful dream.

❖

Clay threw old sheets around the floor of her new cottage in preparation for her friends coming to paint. The Queen had had a new bathroom and kitchen fitted and new wooden floors laid throughout, so all she had to worry about was painting and furniture.

She had some essentials, her bed and fridge-freezer from her flat, but she needed so much more. Most of the furniture at her old flat was worn out and not worth moving, so this was going to be a new start.

Clay had picked up a whole bunch of beanbags at a shop and scattered them around the living room, so her guests had somewhere to sit in-between painting.

She walked to the kitchen and opened the fridge. It was packed with bottles of lager and wine, to help her guests enjoy the day. She thought about Kat and wished she was coming. It had really hurt the previous night when she said she wasn't. Clay didn't know the story of her life that was holding her back, but what could be so bad that she couldn't explore what they had together?

Clay might not have had much experience with serious relationships, but she did know that they had something special together. When they kissed, her body was set on fire, and Clay wanted to feel that again and again. Whatever problems Kat had, they could work through them.

She picked up a cold bottle of lager and opened it with the bottle opener, then took a long drink. There was a small part of Clay that hoped Kat would change her mind and turn up with the rest of their friends. She could only hope.

Clay sighed and said the words that were burning inside her. "I'm falling for you, Kat."

Her melancholy thoughts were interrupted by the doorbell. She hurried to the door and her heart started to pound at the thought of Kat being there. Clay opened the door to find Holly, Quincy, Cammy, and Lali, but no Kat.

Clay's heart sank but she put a smile on her face, "Thanks for coming, everyone. Come in."

Holly threw her arms around her. "Are you okay, Clay?"

"Yeah, uh…I'm fine."

Did Holly know something about her and Kat?

Cammy held a pack of lager and a bottle of whiskey. "I thought I'd bring a wee dram in case we start to flag later."

"Thanks for coming guys, really."

Quincy smacked her on the shoulder. "No need to thank us. We'll get this place shipshape in no time."

Finally Lali kissed her on the cheek. "We'll help you make this place a home, Clay."

Clay felt so privileged to have such amazing friends, but she couldn't help feeling disappointed and sad that Kat didn't come.

❖

Kat stood by the window of her room and watched people coming and going from the castle. Earlier she had watched her friends walking to Clay's cottage. They laughed and joked as they walked, and Katya wished she was with them.

She woke up on Saturday morning having had a disturbed night's sleep. She had nightmares about running away from the murderers that killed her family, mixed up with dreams of trying to find Clay.

Her mind was so mixed up, and her feelings were so out of control. Normally she would distract herself by getting involved in her work, but the personal staff had an unexpected day off. George and Bea were having a family day at home, watching films and playing games, just to let them all help Clay with her new cottage. But she wasn't helping. She was stuck here moping around, thinking about Clay, instead of being with her, helping her.

"What am I doing?"

She was so worried about losing her place here, away from the new friends she had come to value so much, and she wasn't even spending time with them.

"To hell with this."

Before she could change her mind, she got her jacket and handbag and made her way out of the castle. Then she walked into the town of Windsor, just outside the castle, and headed to the supermarket.

She took a basket and walked around picking up snacks for her friends, and some wine. Kat stopped to study the wine, and after a few seconds felt like someone was watching her. She turned around quickly, but only saw a couple across from her, studying something else on the shelf.

Strange.

She chose two bottles of wine and paid for them and the snacks. As she walked back to the Windsor Estate, she wondered if Clay would be pleased to see her or if she had burned her bridges.

More than twice during her walk back, she almost went straight home to the castle but eventually found her way to the front door of Badger's Hollow.

Kat was nervous, and butterflies fluttered around her stomach. She hesitated with her hand on the doorbell, but then took a breath and used all her courage.

A few seconds after ringing, the door was opened by Lali. "Kat, you made it. Kat's here, everyone."

Everyone was busy painting or mixing paint or having a drink.

Her eyes immediately sought out Clay. There she was at the other end of the living room area, crouching down with a paintbrush in her hand.

Clay looked up at her, then stood up slowly. Kat was hit with a thud in the chest. Clay looked gorgeous in a pair of old, ripped jeans streaked with paint, a sleeveless T-shirt that showed off her strong arms, and bare feet that made her look deliciously undone.

The rest of her friends in the room faded to the edges as she met Clay's eyes. She held her breath to see what Clay's reaction would be. Then the most wonderful thing happened—Clay gave her the biggest smile.

She isn't annoyed with me, even after all I said.

❖

Clay couldn't have been happier. Kat had come to her, despite trying to push her away. She couldn't have been more excited. She led her to the kitchen and poured her a glass of wine.

"I'm so glad you came, Kat," Clay said.

"Me too. I'm sorry for what I said to you yesterday. I was stressed, and I took it out on you. That wasn't fair."

"Forget about it. I already have."

Kat reached out and clasped her hand. "You're too understanding, Ronnie."

Clay squeezed her fingers. The smallest of touches made Clay feel like she had no oxygen in her lungs. Like she wouldn't breathe properly until Kat kissed her again.

"What would you like me to paint?"

Clay's head was full of mush. She shook it and said, "Me, I mean, come and paint with me."

Kat smiled and nodded. "Lead the way."

Clay gave her a brush. "Here."

"Thanks."

They both started painting and kept bumping into each other. Every time they smiled, and soon Kat was pushing her back, playfully.

"You stay in your own area, Sergeant."

Clay bumped her with her shoulder. "It's you that's in mine."

The sexual tension was ramping up by the second. Especially since Kat was getting an up-close-and-personal view of Clay's muscular shoulders and arms, as she stretched to paint.

Holly shouted over to them, "Hey, behave, you two, or I'll send the inspector here over to separate you."

Everyone laughed, and Kat felt her cheeks redden. Being with Clay was so exciting and fun. She hadn't thought for one minute about all her worries since she got there.

They were interrupted by a knock at the door.

"Who could that be?" Clay said. She found Azi holding bottles of wine and behind her was Prince Theo.

"We're not too late, are we?" Azi said.

"No, no, there's plenty still to do," Clay replied.

Azi walked in and said, "Look who I found. You don't mind me bringing a guest?"

Prince Theo walked in and everyone stopped what they were doing and bowed.

"Relax, everyone. I'm just Theo here, okay? Forget the prince bit."

"Yeah," Azi said, "I always forget the prince bit. Come on, you."

Clay looked over, floundering over what to say.

Kat jumped in and said, "Of course you're not too late. Come in, get a drink, and we'll set you to work."

Clay smiled and Kat winked at her. She led Azi into the kitchen, leaving Theo to talk with the others. Kat poured her a glass of wine.

"It was really nice of you to come, Azi," Kat said.

"I had nothing planned, and I thought this might give me an insight into the family feeling amongst the staff. Plus, princey boy out there kept bugging me for a date. I thought I'd give him some real work to do."

Kat laughed. "Theo is really nice. He's not the party prince any more."

Azi sighed. "Yes, I'm beginning to see that, and he's awfully good-looking, just like his sister."

Kat thought she'd take this chance to put in a good word for him. "Has he told you about his charity foundations? He takes a lot of pride in the work he does with them."

"Yes, he's invited me to take my cameras to a homelessness project he works for. I'm eager to learn about that side of him."

Kat smiled and refilled her own glass, then picked up some bags of crisps to take back through. "We'd better get going, or we'll be accused of slacking," she said, leading the way back to the living room.

CHAPTER FOURTEEN

After a long day of laughter, fun, and hard work, Kat and Clay were the only ones left that evening. The rest had gone home to get cleaned up. The paint did seem to get everywhere. Perhaps the amount of lager and wine had something to do with it, Clay thought.

They reclined against beanbags, side by side, elbows touching, which neither of them commented on. Clay was loving the closeness they were sharing. Having Kat so close and so relaxed was a joy.

It felt like a great privilege to be allowed to see this relaxed side of her. Kat was so guarded and careful under normal circumstances, and to actually get Kat to trust her thus far was a great achievement, Clay realized.

"Everyone's done a great job. Although I don't know about my wall," Kat said.

Kat pointed to the wall she'd been working on, and there were perhaps a few streaks, but Clay was happy. It would remind her of a brilliant day spent with Kat.

"Nah, it's perfect," Clay said.

"You're biased."

Clay gave her a look of mock incredulity. "Me? I don't think so. I'm hurt that you'd think that."

Kat play-hit her on the arm and laughed. "Stop it. It's been a nice day, though, hasn't it?"

Kat's hand moved down to hers and loosely held her fingertips. Clay was frightened to move in case she spooked her.

"It's been a really nice day, good friends and you. I'm so happy you came."

"I'm sorry about this week. It's been stressful," Kat said.

"Hey, you've already apologized. It's fine—God knows what I'd be like if I was in your position, watching my country tear itself apart."

"I shouldn't take it out on the people I care about," Kat said.

She does care about me.

There was an excited tension building between them, and Clay was frightened Kat would retreat, so she tried to make conversation.

"My mum would have loved this house."

Kat smiled. "And been proud of you, I bet."

Clay smiled. "I hope so."

Kat squeezed her fingers and said, "Would you tell me about your mum?"

"Yeah. Her name was Trinity, and she was a strong woman. My brother and I never knew my dad."

"You had a brother?" Kat said with surprise.

Clay nodded and looked down at their clasped hands. She nodded and said, "He died—was killed when I was younger."

"Oh God. I'm so sorry, Ronnie. What happened?"

"He was shot, and I saw it happen."

Kat was shocked. She was not expecting Clay to say that. She saw Clay flinch as she closed her eyes and appeared as if she was reliving the moment. Kat recognized the movie that would be playing in Clay's head.

She squeezed her hand tightly. "Ronnie?"

Clay shook her head. "Sorry, I can still see it so clearly. You know?"

"I do know. You don't have to talk about it."

Clay cleared her throat and gulped hard. She was still clearly affected by it. "No, I'd like to tell you. I'd like you to know me better."

"Okay, well, I'm good at listening," Kat said.

"Remember I told you that I'm such a good shot?"

Kat nodded.

"I first found that out when my brother taught me to shoot. He was ten years older than me, and I looked up to him so much."

"He taught you to shoot? What, at like a shooting range?" Kat asked.

Clay laughed. "No, he took me to the VR centre—"

"VR?" Kat interrupted.

"Virtual reality. We shared a love of gaming. It was our thing. He taught me to shoot, and when he realized how good I was, we took part in team events, storming alien worlds, playing World War Two battles, things like that."

Kat rolled her eyes, "Really?"

"Kai, that's my brother, he was great too. I idolized him, and I wanted to be like him."

She ran her hand up to Clay's bicep and softly stroked her. Clay shivered, and Kat saw goosebumps erupt on her skin. Clay reached across and put her hand on Kat's hip.

Kat didn't protest. It felt right.

"So, what happened?" Kat asked.

"On our way home one night, my brother was shot."

Kat gasped. "How? How did that happen?"

"Wrong place at the wrong time, the police said. He had sent me across the road to get him a drink from a shop, and he was down. He got in between a gang hit. I saw this big, muscular guy, who I looked up to and thought was invincible, crumple and fall. He was shot in the chest."

Kat could see Clay was living her memories again and inched closer so she could comfort her.

"I ran to him. I was holding his hand when he slipped away."

"I'm so sorry, Ronnie."

Kat didn't think of anything except comforting her. She stroked her cheek tenderly, and Clay came back from her memories. "Thanks. I never really got to talk about this before. Mum never wanted to talk. It was too painful."

"You can talk to me," Kat said.

Clay smiled, then pulled her onto her shoulder. Kat hugged into the side of her neck and placed her palm on Clay's chest. She could smell her cologne and feel her heart beat under her palm.

It felt so right to be lying here, so safe. "What happened next?"

"After Kai died, I didn't care about school, and I got in with a bad crowd," Clay said. "Mum wanted to get me away from London, from everything. She wanted me to live somewhere quiet and safe."

"Where did you go?"

"A tiny village in the country. Drysford in Devon."

"How did you feel about that?" Kat asked.

"I hated it at first. We were the only Black family in our tiny village, not that the people made us feel different—they really welcomed us. I missed my friends and way of life in London, but that's what Mum wanted me to get away from," Clay said as she placed both arms around her.

"You settled in, then?"

"Eventually. There was a branch of Army Cadets in the next village over. One of the officers there knew my story and took me under his wing. I loved Army Cadets. I got to shoot and practise shooting in the real world, not the virtual one. It was great."

"So how did you get to the police?" Kat asked.

"Well, when I came to the end of school and made it clear university wasn't for me, a chief constable friend of my commanding officer suggested I join the police. He was impressed with my shooting skills. It was weird—I never saw myself as the type of person the police would want, but I was excited by it, and I've never seen my mum as proud as she was the day I passed out of police training college. I vowed from then on never to let my mum down, and to make her proud."

"I can just imagine how proud she was of you, especially when you began to work with the royal family," Kat said.

"Oh yeah. She loved that. Mum was a big royalist. Loved all the pomp and parades. After college I got fast-tracked from the firearms unit to police protection. My life could have been so different if she hadn't gotten me out of London. Caught up in my grief, I might have taken a wrong path."

Kat sat up and cupped her cheek. "You don't give yourself credit, Ronnie. You're a good, honest person. I think you would have found your way in life."

Clay slipped her hand into Kat's blond hair. "You maybe have too much faith in me."

"No, you're a loving person. The way you are with the princesses just shows it."

"I'm loyal to those I care about. I care about you, Kat. I care more and more every day."

Kat's heart started to pound. She'd never wanted anyone more than in this one moment.

"You don't know me, Ronnie. How can you care about someone if you don't truly know who they are?"

Clay leaned her forehead against Kat's. "I know who you are in here"—she placed her hand on Kat's chest—"and I'm falling for you. Everything else is just details."

Kat forgot everything that was holding her back and said, "I'm falling for you too, and it terrifies me."

❖

Clay didn't want to do the wrong thing or spook Kat, like she had after their first kiss, so she held back and let Kat make the first move.

"I'm falling for you, Ronnie, but I'm frightened to explore it. I'm happy here, and I'm frightened it will all be taken away from me."

"How could it be taken away from you?" Clay asked.

Their lips were now inches apart. "I can't—"

Clay caressed her face. "I'm here now, in this moment, and that's all we can live for. Who knows what the future will bring?"

"No." Kat pressed her lips to Clay's and she moaned.

Clay let her set the pace so that she felt comfortable, but comfort soon became the last thing on Clay's mind as she felt Kat's tongue trace her lips. Clay shivered when Kat lightly scratched her nails over her shoulders and biceps. Clay wanted her so much that it was so hard to take this slow.

Kat pulled back from the kiss and looked deeply into her eyes.

"You have beautiful eyes," Clay said.

"No, I don't. I've always been embarrassed by them—one eye half green, half blue. The girls made fun of me at school for that."

"They're unique, you are unique, and I think that makes you the most beautiful woman I've ever met."

Clay caressed Kat's face with her fingertips. Kat appeared to be thinking hard, and Clay sensed that they were standing on a precipice. Either they were going to take it further or back off, but that had to be entirely Kat's decision.

After silently gazing for a few seconds, Kat said, seemingly randomly, "I love it when we spar—in the gym, I mean."

"Yeah, so do I. You're quite good, for a nanny."

Kat gave her a pinch for that joke. "No, I mean I think about it a lot, especially the last time."

Clay remembered the last time. They'd ended up on the floor kissing. Was this Kat's way of telling her what she wanted? "Oh yeah? Show me why."

"I can't. Not here, anyway." Kat got up from her beanbag and extended her hand to Clay.

Wow, did she really mean—was this really happening? Clay got up, and Kat led her upstairs to Clay's bedroom. Clay was glad she'd tidied up.

They stopped by the bed, and Kat grasped her sleeveless T-shirt and pulled Clay close, so their lips were inches apart.

Kat whispered, "When the lights are off, and I'm all alone, I think about sparring and you pinning me to the floor. I've never had thoughts like that before."

"Yeah?" Clay said breathily.

She was so turned on. Kat had actually fantasized about them being together.

"Yes."

All worry about pushing Kat too far disappeared when their lips came together again. Their kisses were frantic this time, and Kat started to pull at Clay's T-shirt. After Kat pulled it off, along with Clay's sports bra, she slowly peeled off her shirt, revealing a beautiful lacy ivory bra.

All Clay could think about was putting her mouth on that lace and teasing what was underneath.

"You want to spar?" Clay said.

Kat gave her a small smile, and in an instant she'd swept Kat's legs and pinned her to the bed.

"Like this?"

"Yes."

Kat trailed her fingers over her shoulders and down her chest. Clay could hardly breathe. She placed her hand on Kat's lace-covered breast and squeezed.

"Ronnie, take it off."

Clay unclipped her bra, and her mouth watered at the sight of Kat's generous breasts. "Is this what you thought about?"

Kat pulled her face down to her breast. Clay blew on her hardening nipple, just to tease, and Kat moaned.

"Yes, in your mouth."

Clay used the tip of her tongue to trace around Kat's nipple. Kat arched her back in pleasure, and maybe to try to encourage her to use her mouth.

"Please, Ronnie."

Clay didn't need to be asked twice. She drew Kat's nipple into her mouth, sucking, licking, making her lover squirm beneath her. Then she became aware of Kat pulling at her jeans, so they both shrugged out of their jeans and underwear.

Clay let Kat's nipple pop from her mouth, then pushed her thigh between her lover's legs. When she felt Kat's wet heat, she said, "Fuck, you're so wet."

Kat cupped her face. "I always am when I think of you."

Clay thought her heart might explode out of her chest, she was feeling so much. "When you think of me, on your own, show me what you do."

Kat hesitated, then moved her hand down to her sex, but just held it there. She was unsure of herself. This was revealing too much.

Just as she was about to remove her hand, Clay put hers on top and said, "Show me?"

In that moment Kat lost a huge piece of her heart. She trusted Clay and knew she would be safe with her.

Clay had gone so carefully with her, never pushing or going too fast. She pressed her fingers into her own wetness and groaned when Clay's fingers grazed her clit. That was her fantasy, and it was really happening. Slowly she let Clay's fingers take the lead, then removed her own.

Clay rested her forehead against Kat's and whispered, "Is this what you want?"

"Yes," Kat breathed.

Clay's fingers stroked both sides of her clit and pushed down to her entrance, but never dipped in. Each time she did, the ache for her to go inside increased until she couldn't keep her want to herself.

"Ronnie, go inside."

Clay kissed her lips and then said, "Is that what you want?"

"Yes."

Clay stroked around her clit a few more times, then kissed her deeply. Clay pushed her two fingers inside Kat. Kat moaned out loud and wrapped her arms around Clay's neck.

"Yes, Ronnie."

Clay thrust gently at first and slowly built up a rhythm of stroking around the sides of her clit and then pushing inside her.

Kat thrust her hips, and as her orgasm built, she got more confident.

"Faster, Ronnie. I need it."

Clay kept her fingers inside Kat and hastened her thrusts. "What do you need, baby?"

Kat felt heat sweep over her body, and her nerves were on fire. All normal polite restraint was leaving her fast.

"I need…"

Clay grazed her neck with her teeth and said, "You need what? Tell me what you say in your fantasy."

"I say, fuck me, Ronnie."

Clay stopped thrusting and lifted her head to smile down at her. "You do?"

"Yes."

Kat's body was so out of control, so needing to come, that she would have said anything at that moment.

Clay positioned her own sex against Kat's thigh and whispered, "Tell me again?"

"Fuck me, make me come."

Clay answered her by pushing her fingers inside her again and starting to thrust against her thigh. The feeling in her sex coupled with Clay's own moans of pleasure were making her orgasm come closer and closer.

"Oh yeah."

"I want you to come, I want you to come with me, Ronnie."

Kat looked up at Clay. She was thrusting fast, and her eyes were closed, concentrating on the pleasure she was feeling.

I'm doing that. I'm making her feel like that.

That was it for Kat. She threw her arms around Clay as the pressure in her sex exploded, and pleasure and heat and love waved over her, to the ends of her fingertips.

She was overwhelmed and shocked at the intensity. Then Clay started to thrust erratically against her thigh.

"Yeah, yeah, fuck, fuck."

Kat was surprised when she followed her instincts, wrapped her legs around Clay, and squeezed, and she started to come again. Her orgasm was smaller, but deeper.

Clay kissed her hard and then rested her head on Kat's shoulder. "Oh my God, that was amazing. Are you okay?"

"I'm so okay. I came twice."

Clay lifted her head and grinned, looking pleased with herself. "Twice, huh?"

"Yes, it was so much better than my fantasy."

❖

Sometime later Clay lay on her side and gazed into Kat's unusual green eyes. Kat looked as if she was thinking hard. Clay stroked a lock of her blond hair behind her ear, and said, "What are you thinking? You're not regretting this, are you?"

"I'm thinking that I don't feel every worry, every stressful thought, when I'm with you. You make me feel safe."

"Do you feel unsafe normally?" Clay didn't like that thought one bit.

She watched as tears came to Kat's eyes. "Yes, it's been my way of life since I was ten."

Clay pulled her closer and wiped her tears. "I wish you could tell me why, but I won't push you. As long as being with me makes you feel safe, then that makes me happy."

"Do you have any plans for today? I'd like to spend more time with you," Kat said.

"I did think about going to shop for some furniture for this place, since my online shopping was such a disaster, but if you want to do something together, I'd love that."

"I usually go and visit my old headmistress on Sunday, she's like a mother to me, and I wondered if you'd like to come. Maybe we could go and look at some furniture first, then go to Dora's house?"

Wow. Kat was being so open. She wasn't running away. She wanted her to meet the only family she had.

"I'd love that."

Kat smiled. "I think she'll like you."

Suddenly Clay felt nervous. What if she didn't?

After a trip to the furniture store in an out-of-town retail park, they travelled by taxi to Dora's retirement flat. Kat had called her in advance, and she had been very excited about the idea of Kat bringing a friend, something she had never done before.

Since leaving the furniture store, Clay had become quiet. "Are you okay, Ronnie?"

"Just a bit nervous about meeting someone who is like a mum to you, and she's a posh private girls' school headmistress. She might think, who's this pleb you've brought home?"

Kat laughed and smacked Clay on the arm. "Don't be silly. She's not snobby. Dora's got a heart of gold. Don't worry."

The taxi pulled up at the retirement flats, and they got out. Kat reached out and took Clay's hand. "Come on, Ronnie."

Kat almost felt like skipping, she was so happy. Today had given her insight into a normal relationship. Waking up in each other's arms, going out shopping, walking around hand in hand.

Opening up to Clay sexually had opened up the need, the desire, to share herself emotionally. Could she have a normal relationship? Clay said she was falling for her, but she didn't know who she was falling for. Was it fair? Why did she always think the worst? She'd denied herself a normal love life, never letting anyone close, and she was sick of it.

They walked into the lift, and it took them to Dora's front door. She was already waiting for them.

"Kitty Kat, you're here at last," Dora said.

Clay snorted at her nickname, and Kat dug her elbow into her ribs. "We are, and I've brought a friend."

Dora kissed her hand as usual and ushered her in. Kat smiled when she saw Dora had laid out sandwiches for them and little cakes.

"You didn't have to go to all this trouble, Dora," Kat said.

"It's not often you bring a friend home. Introduce me, then."

"Dora, let me introduce Sergeant Veronica Clayton, who works with me at the palace. Clay, this is Dora."

Dora shook Clay's hand with gusto. "I'm so pleased to meet you, Veronica. My, what a strapping police officer you are."

Kat giggled when she saw Clay's embarrassment.

"It's really nice to meet you, Miss Dorcas," Clay said nervously.

"Dora, please. Well, come in, come in. Let's get you a cup of tea."

When Dora went to get the teapot, Clay said, "Kitty Kat?"

"Oh, shut up and sit down, Veronica," Kat said.

Clay had only seen cakes on cake stands in posh film and TV dramas before, and the sandwiches were tiny and delicate. Kat really was from a different world.

Dora came back and poured the tea. "So, tell me about yourself, Veronica. Are you part of the security team at the palace?"

Kat handed her a tiny plate, then used tongs to add some sandwiches to her plate. Thank God she hadn't just dived in with her fingers.

"Yeah, I'm the protection officer for the princesses. That's how Kat and I got to know each other."

"Marvellous, have you had a nice day off together?" Dora asked.

Clay had just popped one of the tiny sandwiches whole into her mouth, so Kat answered for them.

"We went furniture shopping for Clay. The Queen has given her a small cottage on the Windsor Estate, so she has a whole cottage to furnish."

"How wonderful. Windsor is such a beautiful area."

Clay needn't have been worried. Dora was a lovely woman, and she was glad Kat had invited her. After a nice few hours, they travelled back by train to Windsor Castle.

Clay kept a hold of Kat's hand, greedily taking every opportunity to be close to her. Clay wanted to ask what last night and today meant. She wanted to know if this was real, if they were together as Clay really wanted them to be, but she kept putting it off, frightened of the answer Kat would give.

When they entered the Windsor Estate, Clay knew she had to address this soon, before they parted ways, and Kat got a chance to think this was maybe a bad idea. They passed a wooded area, and Clay pulled Kat off the path into it.

"What are you doing, Ronnie?"

Clay manoeuvred Kat up against a tree and smiled. "I wanted a kiss before we got back."

Kat giggled and pressed her lips against Clay's.

After a few seconds Clay pulled back. "Kat? I wanted to ask you something."

"What?"

Clay held Kat's hands but looked down at the ground. She had a knot of worry about what Kat's answer to this question would be.

"Last night and today, it's been amazing. I just want to know what…Oh, this is so hard. What it means for us. Are we together now?"

Clay watched Kat's face go from smiling to tense and feared the worst. "I love being with you, Ronnie. I've never been in a relationship before, so I don't know what to do, what to expect. Why don't we just see how things go, no pressure or anything?"

That was as positive an answer Clay could hope to get from the very careful Kat. It was up to Clay now to show Kat that they were meant for each other, and she would.

CHAPTER FIFTEEN

Queen Georgina waited for the prime minister to arrive for their weekly meeting. She had seen his car pull into the palace a few minutes ago. Baxter the boxer came to her side. She ruffled his ears, then heard a knock at the door.

"Lie down, Baxter. Good boy."

The door opened and Raj Shah entered the room.

Major Fairfax said, "The prime minister, Your Majesty."

"Prime Minister, come in."

Raj Shah bowed and waited for her to sit.

"Please, sit down."

"Thank you, Your Majesty," Raj said.

"I saw you were busy in the House of Commons this week with your new environmental bill?" George said.

"Yes, ma'am. We are hoping to have cross-party support for it. Our children's future depends on it."

"Indeed."

Raj cleared his throat. "Before we talk about some pressing government business matters, there is an issue I would like to bring up."

"Of course, Prime Minister."

"This week I received an MI6 briefing on a matter codenamed Operation Dover."

Operation Dover was the secret service code for Katya.

"I see, yes. I only found out about it at Christmastime. My father didn't wish me to know unless it appeared necessary," George said.

"Obviously I'm delighted Princess Olga survived and is thriving here in the UK—"

"I hear a but coming, Prime Minister."

Raj crossed his legs. "I wonder at the wisdom of making her nanny to the young princesses. She could bring extra danger to them."

"We believed it was an excellent idea. My wife was so affected by our previous nannying choice, she didn't trust anyone until she met Katya. She was brought up in this world, so she understands it, and she is a distant relation. I felt we could trust her. Besides, no one knows she exists, not even her uncle."

"For the moment people don't know she exists, ma'am. Which brings me to my second point. We and our close allies in the UN Security Council feel we will soon have enough support for a peacekeeping mission in Vospya. We and other friendly governments have been having unofficial talks with the Liberty Freedom Fighters. We don't want a situation where the revolutionaries take control and forget about democracy."

"You believe the freedom fighters have a chance of winning the day?"

"Very much so. Our intelligence is that the Vospyan government is descending into infighting, and more members of the military are deserting every day. President Loka has imprisoned the head of the army and is going to execute him."

George was cautious about becoming involved in another country's affairs, but the wilful mistreatment of the people of Vospya was grievous.

"What is the plan, Prime Minister?"

"The freedom fighters have agreed to democratic elections as soon as they win back the country. Elections overseen by the UN to ensure democracy is completely observed. As you know, the freedom fighters have gathered around the former Vospyan monarchy, the Bolotovs, and particularly King Louis. They wish the monarchy to be restored, a constitutional monarchy, as it was in the past. The feeling is the citizens will feel secure that the King is safeguarding their new-found freedom."

As good an idea as this was, George could see the problems, ten steps ahead. "That would make sense."

"To that end, King Louis has been told of Princess Olga's existence. He was overwhelmed with joy, I am told, but we advised him not to contact her at the moment for security's sake. This has to be handled carefully."

George rubbed her temple. "The people will have to be told of Olga's survival eventually."

"Yes. As you must be aware, this will create problems," Raj said.

George got up and walked to the window. "Bloody hell." They were going to lose Katya. Bea would be devastated. Not to mention Katya herself. "Ms. Kovach will be unhappy to lose her anonymity."

"Yes, but it's inevitable. I understand from her contact at MI6 that she doesn't like the limelight," Raj said.

George walked back over to the chair and sighed as she sat. "She also understands duty. I know that. Talk me through the plans."

"King Louis is sixty-five years old, still with many, many years ahead of him, but he is unmarried, and I understand unlikely to marry and have children, which means—"

"She is next in the line of succession, if she accepts it." As George had said, Katya understood duty, but she would be stepping back into a role that got her family shot dead. "It's a big ask to have someone commit to royal life after living out of the public life for so long," George said.

"If and when we are able to secure Vospya, people will need to see future security, beyond King Louis's lifetime."

"I agree. It will just be difficult for her," George said.

"Of course." Raj picked up a folder and handed it to George. "These are my recommendations, ma'am."

George opened up the folder and saw the first item was her replacement as nanny.

"Replace Katya as nanny? I can't agree to that. The princesses love her."

"Ma'am, whatever way this plays out, Ms. Kovach will be a target for disgruntled Vospyan government forces. Her presence will be a danger to your daughters," Raj said.

George would never risk her children's safety, but she appreciated how important this job was to Kat.

"As long as she remains anonymous, they won't be in danger. Katya is happy here. Besides she is rarely in public with the children, and even then she is surrounded by protection officers."

"We recommend further on in the report that Ms. Kovach becomes a protected person. To be frank, ma'am, she will need her own police protection. She is a vital piece in the game to bring stability to the region of Vospya," Raj said.

George would have to be careful. She didn't want to act against the advice of her government, but she also wanted to let Katya live as normal a life as she could, for as long as she could.

"How about a compromise, Prime Minister. Katya stays in her

post for as long as no one has any intelligence as to who she is, and we have another protection officer put on the princesses' security team. Katya will have one officer to keep her safe too, plus we'll control any outside events she is taking part in," George said.

The Prime Minster appeared to consider her proposal carefully.

"If that is your wish, ma'am, but it won't be for long. The young princesses and Princess Olga's safety must take precedence."

"Of course. This isn't something we need to tell her about just now, is it? When that heavy burden falls on her, life will become difficult. I know how much she is enjoying her new friends in the royal court."

"For the moment, ma'am, if that's what you wish. Her uncle is very keen to meet her again, especially before he returns to Vospya," Raj said.

"He's going back to Vospya? Soon?"

Raj sighed. "Yes, he insists. He feels he needs to join his people in this uprising, just to be able to look them in the eye, rather than hide in safety in Switzerland, as he puts it."

"Brave, honourable man." George stood. "Thank you for bringing this to my attention, Prime Minister."

"Ma'am." Raj bowed and left the room.

George had bought Katya some more time, but that's all it was. The secret they had all safeguarded for so long would soon be known to the world.

In the days since Katya and Clay had made love at the cottage, they had been inseparable. When they arrived back at the palace, Clay had spent her nights in Katya's apartment since it was bigger than Clay's room.

Clay pulled Kat to her, so that her head was lying on her chest.

"I never thought I'd be doing this with you," Kat said.

"Why?"

Kat traced her fingers over Clay's stomach. Clay loved the intimacy, something she hadn't shared with a lover before. All of her sexual encounters had been about sex, but this was a whole lot more.

"Lots of reasons. One, when you arrived back to work and found me as the new nanny, you were a pig."

"I was not," Clay said with mock indignation.

Kat smacked her stomach softly. "You were. You thought I was sent here to bring down the monarchy or something."

"Well, you could have been, superspy."

Kat laughed. "I suppose."

"What were your other reasons?" Clay asked.

Clay felt Kat stiffen slightly. "I haven't had lovers before. This is all new to me."

"Seriously? No one?"

Clay couldn't believe such a beautiful woman could get to this age and not find someone to love her body the way she did.

"Seriously. Well, there was a girl at boarding school who I experimented with in all innocence, but my situation is such that I could never let anyone close. I've barely had a friendship, far less a lover."

Clay kissed her and stroked her blond hair with her hand. "Then now, have both, and I'm lucky that you have let me in and shared this with me."

"I trust you, Ronnie," Kat said.

It did cross Clay's mind that if she did trust her, then Kat would tell her the truth, but she hoped it would come in time.

"That means a lot to me, Kitty Kat."

"Oh, don't. That name makes me feel like a little girl."

"I think it's sweet."

"Shut up. I don't want you to think of me as sweet," Kat said with a cheeky grin on her face.

"What do you want me to think of you?"

"The woman who makes you hot under the collar, Sergeant."

"Oh, you do that."

They kissed, and just as it was getting more serious, they were interrupted by the alarm clock ringing. "Shit," Clay said as she attempted to swat at the snooze button.

Kat stretched and said, "What time is it?"

"Half past five."

"I better start to get ready," Kat said.

Clay yawned. "What's on the timetable today?"

"Apart from you? Tuesday is language day."

Kat got up and slipped her dressing gown on. "God, you are beautiful, Kat."

Kat picked up a pillow and threw it at Clay. "Hardly."

"Why do you never accept compliments?" Clay asked.

Kat shrugged her shoulders. "I never liked to stand out, but I did because of my eyes. One green, one half green and half blue. Kids used to make fun of me, and I never considered myself anything but odd looking."

"Your eyes are beautiful—don't ever think otherwise."

"Hmm," was all Kat said in return.

How could someone like Kat not believe she was beautiful?

"What's language day?" Clay asked.

Kat gathered her clothes from the wardrobe. "Some French, some German songs and games."

"But Teddy's not even at school. Isn't it a bit young?" Clay said.

"Children are never too young for learning. They are like sponges at that age. It's only simple words and phrases, not French and German grammar or anything. Teddy is going to be Queen one day, so she'll need to converse in many languages just like her mum."

"It's funny to imagine little Teddy as Queen, isn't it?"

"If she's anything like her two mums, she'll be a great Queen," Kat replied.

"True."

"What's on your timetable, apart from the nursery school run?" Kat asked.

Clay sat up on the side of the bed and rubbed the sleep from her eyes. "I've a briefing at eight with Quincy and the Queen."

"What's that about?" Kat asked.

Clay shrugged. "I don't know. Something to do with the princesses, I'm sure." She picked up the moving photo by the side of the bed. "Is this your family?"

Kat said, "Yes, it was the last time we were all together."

"Which are your mum and dad?" Clay asked.

Kat walked over and pointed to a man and woman. "That's my father, Igor, Iggy they called him, and my mama, Eliana Katya."

Clay smiled. "Your name?"

Kat nodded.

"They look like nice people."

"Yes, they were. I still talk to them every day." Kat's voice cracked.

Clay put the picture down and opened her arms. Kat stood between her legs and wrapped her arms around Clay's neck.

"I'm sorry," Kat said. "It still hurts."

"I know. I understand. I miss my mum every second of every

day. But maybe we can be there for each other and make us both feel better."

"Thanks, Ronnie."

❖

Clay made her way to the Queen's office. She saw Quincy waiting outside the door.

"Morning, Inspector."

"Good morning, Clay."

"What's this about, do you know?"

"Let's go in," Quincy said.

That was weird. Why not give her a straight answer?

Quincy knocked, and they were invited in. Clay bowed, then stood with her hands behind her back.

"Good morning, Clay," Queen Georgina said.

It was clear that the inspector had already been briefed.

"Morning, Your Majesty."

Queen Georgina leaned forward and clasped her hands together. "This briefing is top secret, and on a need-to-know basis. Do you understand?"

"Of course, ma'am," Clay answered.

The Queen continued, "I only found out myself at Christmastime."

What was the Queen about to tell her? From Quincy's neutral expression, she definitely already knew.

"You will have seen news of the civil war in Vospya and Prince Louis taking on his title of King in support of the freedom fighters?"

She couldn't avoid the terrible suffering shown on the news, as Kat insisted on listening to every upsetting event. "Yes, ma'am."

"Well, the UN is preparing to go into the country and help set up democratic elections and a government. To that end, the freedom fighters have requested the monarchy be reinstated in the country."

Clay remembered Kat explaining to her how important she thought a constitutional monarchy was, when they watched Queen Georgina open parliament. But why was the Queen telling her this?

"Have you heard of the Bolotovs?" George asked.

"Yes, ma'am. Kat told me when we watched King Louis on the TV. She said the family had been killed, and he was the last surviving member."

George and Quincy exchanged a look.

"Is that all she told you?" Quincy asked her.

"Yes, ma'am." Weird question.

"There is one more member of the Bolotovs, and as part of the line of succession she will be so important to the fragile peace in the country. The King is in his sixties and unlikely to produce an heir."

"This other Bolotov is living in secret?" Clay asked.

Quincy chimed in to the conversation. "Yes, since she was a child, and kept secret for her own protection."

A bad feeling started to creep up on Clay. "And who she is, that's a need-to-know thing."

"That's right," the Queen said, "and you need to know, Clay. Princess Olga of Vospya came to Britain, aged ten."

Oh my God, no.

"Olga is Katya Kovach."

Clay felt like a huge pile of bricks had been dropped on her chest. "Kat? That was her secret?"

"Yes," Quincy said, "and as you can imagine, that creates significant security concerns."

Jesus. Katya was a princess? Clay just couldn't wrap her head around it.

Queen Georgina said, "Katya has lived under an assumed name and identity since she came here, aged ten, to protect her from Vospyans who would wish to finish off the royal family."

"Was her dad the king?" Clay asked. She was so confused and worried. What would they think if they knew she had come from Kat's bed this morning?

"No, her uncle was King. King Louis is the other brother."

Clay was so shocked and her head was going a million miles an hour.

The Queen continued, "We knew who she was when we hired Kat as nanny, but Kat had always lived a quiet life. She had no need or desire to live as a royal, she wished to be a simple nanny, and she is a distant relation, so I knew we could trust her with the children."

A princess working as a nanny? It sounded so silly, but as she thought of her time with Kat, some things started to make sense. Her extremely emotional response to the news from Vospya. The Liberty Freedom Fighters were standing against the people who murdered her family.

"The prime minister wished her to be relieved of her post—"

"Her job means everything to her, ma'am. She's made really good friends and—"

The Queen held up her hand. "Hang on, I know that, Clay."

Everything was starting to crumble around Clay. She was going to lose Kat.

"I have negotiated a solution. She will stay in her post until her identity is made known, and she will have a dedicated protection officer for times she is out with the children. Inspector Quincy is adding another officer to your small team. It will be your job to lead that team and be Kat's protection officer. Jack and the new officer will concentrate on the girls, and I want most of your focus on Katya. You have to keep her safe. A lot depends on her, for her country, for her people, and for the rest of Europe."

Clay's millions of rushing thoughts were starting to make sense, most of them ending with her broken heart. The one time she'd fallen properly for a woman, and it turned out she was royal.

Shit.

Clay wanted to get out of here. She could hardly breathe.

"Are you all right, Clay? You look quite shocked," the Queen said.

"We are good friends, so it's a shock to find out who she really is," Clay said.

The Queen looked at Quincy and said, "Quincy?"

"Yes, ma'am. Clay, the other part of this is that the Queen wants Kat to have as normal a life as she can, for as long as she can. Once she realizes this great responsibility, she will be quite stressed."

"What do you want me to do?" Clay asked.

Quincy replied, "Don't tell her about the plan to reinstate the monarchy, just that you are keeping her safe. I and my wife will have a word with her. Allow her to live her normal life, before her life doesn't become her own."

I've fucking lost her. "Yes, Inspector." Clay felt sick.

"Good, well, I'll let you two get on with it," Queen Georgina said. "Thank you both for understanding."

Both Clay and Quincy bowed and left the Queen's study. Clay took a deep breath and closed her eyes.

"What's wrong, Clay? You looked really upset in there, I know you two are friends. Holly said you were getting close."

Clay looked at Quincy and said, "We are lovers."

"Jesus Christ."

"It only just happened at the weekend. She was a normal girl then, but now she's a fucking princess."

"Holly said you liked each other, and I saw how close you were getting when we painted the cottage, but I didn't know it was serious," Quincy said.

"Why didn't you tell me? I asked you if you knew anything about her, and you said you didn't," Clay said. It was entirely out of character for Clay to snap at a superior officer, and she regretted it as soon as it happened.

"Follow me," Quincy said firmly.

Shit. Clay was going to get a bollocking, she knew it. Everything that had felt so exciting and new was now morphing to unhappiness and panic.

Quincy marched her into their operations room, where some of her colleagues were working on plans, then into Quincy's office.

Quincy shut the door firmly and said, "Sergeant, do not raise your voice at me in public again. Do you understand me?"

"Yes, Inspector."

Quincy sat at her desk. "To answer your question, I found out this morning who she was. I was told at the beginning that a diplomatically sensitive person was within the household, and I was to keep an eye on her, but that's all."

Clay held her head in her hands. She had been so happy this morning, lying with Kat in her arms, and now, hours later, Kat was a princess, a princess who had a future that didn't or couldn't include her.

Quincy got up and walked back to Clay and put a hand on her shoulder. "Is this serious, Clay?"

"Yeah, I'm in love with her."

Quincy sat on the edge of desk and sighed. "Clay—"

"It's just typical of me. I always get huge crushes on unattainable women. This time I thought I'd finally met someone that I could love and could love me, and then I find out she's a princess. A princess who's going to be heir to her uncle."

"Being a princess doesn't make her unattainable, Clay. Look at Queen Bea—she fell in love and married a Queen."

"That's different. This is my career, my life, and one day she's going to leave for her new life," Clay said.

"Don't give up on love, Clay. I nearly did through not sharing my feelings and nearly lost the only love of my life."

Clay thought about what Kat said this morning about Teddy. It was never too early to teach her languages, as she would be expected to converse with people all round the world as Queen. That was Kat's future.

"Clay, we need to define your role here. Kaz Rickson is being put under your command. She and Jack will be one on one with the princesses, and you will be on Kat," Quincy said.

"Just when she is out with the princesses?"

"No, this is close protection. Anywhere she goes."

As if this couldn't be any harder than it already was. "How am I going to justify that if she isn't to know about the situation in Vospya?"

"She is being told MI6 have requested protection for her, with the growing unrest in her country."

This was going to be so hard.

CHAPTER SIXTEEN

The drone in the sky buzzed around the Buckingham Palace garden. Bea and Roza were sitting in the sun watching Teddy run around with Lex, while Kat walked around the plants and trees with Anna, trying to get her to sleep.

Around the perimeter Ravn, Clay, Jack, and the new addition to the team, Kaz, stood with Azi. This morning Bea had opened a new community farm in London, but this afternoon she wanted to spend some time with Roza.

Teddy squealed as Lex caught her and lifted her high in the air. Roza sighed happily.

"She's going to be a fantastic parent, isn't she?"

"She will, and so will you," Bea said.

"Hmm. I don't know, but I'll try my best. It worries me that I'll not have enough time when I'm out of the country so often, and even when I'm at home in Denbourg, I'm sometimes doing two or three visits a day to charities and other organizations."

"You can only do your best. My advice is take the baby everywhere you can, especially foreign trips. George and I always try to tailor our overseas trips to suit the girls, but it's difficult. I mean, look at today. George is over in Ireland and won't be home till after the girls are sound asleep," Bea said.

"I suppose it makes you appreciate the family times you have together."

Bea nodded. "It really does. How's Lex's family? Excited about the new baby?"

Roza smiled and her eyes widened. "Oh yes. Faith and Jason are over the moon with excitement, not to mention Lex's sister Poppy.

Faith's been like a second mother to me. They spend every school holiday with us in Denbourg, and Faith pops over even more. Poppy is going to study in Denbourg when she leaves school too."

"Lex must be happy about that," Bea said.

"Oh yes, she adores her little sister." Roza rubbed her back and grimaced.

"Are you sure you're okay to go to the Indian family centre tomorrow? I can go on my own." Bea said.

"No, I'll be fine. It's why I'm here."

The tiny drone whizzed by and reminded Bea it was still there. "Did I tell you that Theo was beginning to win over Azi?"

Roza grinned. "No, tell me."

"He took her to one of his homelessness charity organizations the other day. No media, no publicity, just a private visit to show her what's important to him now, not just drinking and partying. They had dinner alone last night. Theo is determined to win her heart."

"She'd be such a good partner for him. Intelligent and someone who is hugely involved in humanitarian campaigns," Roza said.

"Azi would be a good person for him."

"That's something I worry about," Roza said. "I mean my little child growing up and seeing all the media reports about me, drunk, partying, not doing my job."

"Don't worry about that. You can be an example to them of how you can change your life to the good—you both can."

Lex had Teddy on her shoulders now, and they both waved over.

"Yes, that's true," Roza said. "I'm so proud of Lex. She's embraced working with addiction groups and charities. People really respond to her because she's been through her own drug addiction."

Bea watched Kat lean over Anna's pram and adjust her blankets. "That's what you should worry about, getting a good nanny."

"Yes, I know. Someone like Kat would be great. Could we steal her from you?" Roza joked.

"You couldn't even if I wanted to give her to you. She won't be with us for much longer, and I wanted to talk to you about it," Bea said.

"She's leaving? Why?"

Bea turned around and indicated to Azi to stop filming, which she did happily.

"This is top secret, and Kat herself doesn't know the details, but I have to tell you."

"Sounds worrying. What's going on?"

❖

Katya was glad to see Anna sleeping at last. Anna loved to fall asleep outside in her pram, but it wasn't easy when she heard her big sister shouting and playing with Crown Consort Lennox.

She looked over to where Clay was standing and smiled. She must have not seen her because Clay didn't smile back. Clay had been quiet since she came back from her meeting, unlike this morning when they were making love.

It had been wonderful. In fact, every day since they spent the weekend at the cottage had been so happy. She couldn't remember a time when she'd felt such positivity about the future, excitement, and simple enjoyment of life.

Kat decided to walk over and talk to Clay, but Queen Beatrice caught her eye and waved her over. She made her way over and said, "Ma'am?"

"Will you take a seat beside us? I'd like a little chat," Bea said.

"Park Anna beside me and I'll rock her," Roza said. "It'll give me good practice."

Bea patted the seat between them. "Have a seat, Kat."

"Thank you, ma'am," Kat said. This was strange. Kat was starting to fear some bad news. "Is everything all right, ma'am?"

"Yes, I just wanted a word with you. In fact, the Queen wanted me to have a word with you. She would have done it herself, but she's away all day, as you know."

"Yes, ma'am."

"The prime minister has been informed of your identity."

"He wants me to leave, doesn't he?" Kat said. That was always her fear, that she was living on borrowed time.

"No, no. Not that, we wouldn't let that happen anyway, unless it was completely necessary. No, there's two things. First thing is, it was felt that your uncle should be informed that you were alive, safe and sound here in Britain."

"Really?" Kat squeaked in surprise. Her heart began to pound with excitement. "It's what I've always wanted, but I was always advised it was safer if we both remained anonymous."

"Yes, George says it was felt that with everything going on in Vospya, and your uncle's role of being a figurehead for the revolution, it would help him to know he wasn't alone."

"What did he say? Can I talk to him?" Kat said.

"Not for the moment. Your calls could be intercepted, but I'm sure it will happen before long."

Katya started to cry. She couldn't wait to share her news with Clay, but then she remembered she couldn't. Kat felt guilty, like she was building their relationship on a lie. What would Clay think when she found out she was Princess Olga?

Roza took her hand, and Bea got her a hankie from Anna's bag.

"Hey, don't upset yourself," Bea said.

Kat dried her eyes. "I've dreamed of knowing him since I was a girl."

"You'll get your chance soon. I think when the freedom fighters win the day in Vospya, your life won't have to be secret."

"You think they'll actually win?" Kat asked.

"I don't want to give away any state secrets, but George is quite hopeful," Bea said.

Roza squeezed her hand. "Well, I don't care about state secrets, Kat. You're one of us. My officials think it's inevitable."

"That would make me happier than you could imagine." Kat thought of setting foot on Vospyan soil again, and it made her feel elated. Her parents would be so happy.

"There was one other thing," Bea said.

"Is this the bad news?" Kat asked.

"No, not bad, just different. We want you here, Kat. You are the best person we could ever have gotten to look after the girls."

"But?"

"There's no *but*. Just a change, that's all. With the possibility of the Vospyan government collapse and your identity being made known somehow amongst the chaos, the prime minister would like you to have protection."

"What kind of protection?"

"A close protection officer."

Kat looked around at all the protection officers trying to look inconspicuous in the palace gardens. This didn't make sense.

"Why would a nanny need protection? I've lived my whole life so far in secret without needing a guard."

Bea looked to Roza for support, and Roza said, "Think about it from Britain's angle. If you are kidnapped or injured, Britain would be put in a difficult position. It would be obliged to give the kidnappers what they want or send in special forces to get you back. Lives could be lost, so putting up with security will help the prime minister and George."

"Yes, I see what you mean, but I just don't see my identity coming out."

"When regimes collapse," Bea said, "you never know what can happen."

Kat sighed. She couldn't imagine having a guard on her all the time. As a child she probably had. She remembered a man named Del who took her to school every day. Kat never thought of him as a guard, but he must have been.

"Do you think I'm putting the princesses at risk with my presence around them? If you'd prefer I left—"

"No, no," Bea said. "We want you to stay with us as long as you can. It's just some simple adjustments to the way we do things."

"Who'll be my protection officer?"

Roza smiled. "The adorable Sergeant Clayton."

"Ronnie? Really?" Kat said happily.

Bea nodded. "We're moving someone else in to help with the princesses so that Clay can keep watch over you."

"I suppose I can cope with that." Kat was so happy. Working closely together would help them build their new relationship. "Do you think my uncle Louis and I will ever be able to go back to visit Vospya one day, when this is all over?"

Bea smiled. "I'm sure you both will."

Anna started to cry and wake up from her nap. Bea went over and picked her up from the pram. "It's okay, sweetie. I'm here."

Kat turned to Roza and said, "Thank you for helping me, and listening. Both of you."

"Of course I'll help you. We had the same great-great-grandmother. We're family."

Kat looked over to Clay and smiled at her. She couldn't wait to talk to her about this. Clay had seen her but didn't smile back. That was strange.

❖

Kat walked to Clay's room after again getting one-word replies to her texts. It was so out of character for her, especially since they'd made love at the weekend. Something had been different all through today, and Kat didn't like it.

After her talk with Bea and Roza, she assumed that Clay would want to talk about her new role, but she didn't even come to take Teddy out in the afternoon. Maybe she was busy with meetings or something, but she could have texted back more than yeses or nos.

She knocked on the door and a sombre looking Clay answered.

"Hi, do you want to go down to get dinner together or go out somewhere?"

"No, I think I'll stay in tonight. I'm tired," Clay said.

"You're never tired."

"Well, I am now."

What? "What is going on with you? Has something happened?"

"No, nothing."

Kat was starting to get annoyed now. She pushed past Clay to get into her room. "What is going on, Ronnie? You've been weird all day. Avoiding conversation, sending me one-word replies? I mean, we were in bed together this morning."

"Yeah? Well, things change," Clay said.

"Things change? What are you talking about? How can you be so cold?"

"I don't think this is a good idea."

Kat's anger was burning. This wasn't the Clay she knew. "What isn't a good idea?"

"Us, sleeping together, working together. I think we should just leave it."

Kat felt the tears welling up in her eyes. "I don't understand. Is this just because you've been assigned to protect me? You pursued *me*, got me to open up to you. Was that just to get me into bed?"

Clay said nothing and stared down at the floor.

"I can't believe this," Kat said. "I trusted you. The first one I let inside, and now this?"

"You never trusted me with who you were. Trust has to work both ways, Olga," Clay said angrily.

Her old name coming from Clay's mouth felt so strange to her, so alien. "They told you who I was?"

Clay nodded.

"And that has changed you from this morning?"

Clay didn't know what to say. The look of hurt on Kat's face was killing her. But she didn't know any other way of distancing herself from Kat, and she had to distance herself before they both got hurt any more.

"I don't know who you are. I mean, it was just a bit of fun, wasn't it?"

Kat took a step towards her, and Clay saw the tears in her eyes. "I'll tell you exactly who I am. I'm Princess Olga Bolotov of Vospya and Marchioness of Romka. My father was the King's brother and my only living uncle is the now King Louis in exile. My family was murdered right in front of my eyes. I had a gun placed to my forehead by a rebel fighter, but a soldier rescued me while I watched my nanny being shot. Is that what you want to hear? Does that make you know me better? Or is knowing my true identity just an excuse to dump me?"

Clay was shocked, shocked at the horror of what Kat had gone through as such a small child. It became clear why she was so guarded, why she never let anyone close. She didn't know what to say. What could she say after that? In Kat's eyes she was a callow cad who, after bedding her, now wanted nothing to do with her.

Kat wiped her tears away and said, "I had to become a new person when I arrived in Britain. My own survival depended on it. Even my uncle didn't know until the last few days that I'd survived. Now King Louis and I are the last remaining Bolotovs, but only in name. I'm a nanny. I'm a normal woman. I haven't changed since this morning, but you have."

They really hadn't told Kat about the restoration of the Bolotov monarchy. Clay could tell her and have nothing withheld between them, but then she would bring down the whole weight of her destiny upon her, before it was necessary.

Let her have her ordinary, private life as long as she could. Clay would do anything to make Kat's life better while she could, because before long they would be living very different lives.

"I'm sorry, Kat. I don't think I want a relationship." Those words killed Clay.

"I may be forced to have you follow me around all day, but don't speak to me, don't even look at me, because I'm not interested in anything you have to say, understand?"

Clay nodded. Kat walked away and slammed the door shut. Clay took an angry kick at the trash bin on the floor and it flew across the room.

❖

Alexander stared at the photograph on the holographic screen. The news played on the living room TV as he sat and looked at his phone screen. What was it that bothered him about this photo? He enlarged it, as he had done many times, and he just couldn't work it out.

His attention was drawn back to the TV news where he saw pictures of the vice president of Vospya. His phone rang just at that second.

"Yes?"

"It's Victor, sir. Are you watching the news?"

"Yes, I'm looking at the vice president, but I missed the first part of the report."

"President Loka has arrested the vice president, sir."

"Jesus, has he gone mad? He'll split the government."

"The president is convinced a high-ranking politician is working with the freedom fighters. They seem to know exactly where our soldiers are being deployed. Intelligence is that the freedom fighters will enter the capital in the next day or so, while the UN peacekeepers are gathering to be deployed to our borders as soon as they get the okay from the member states."

Alexander smacked his forehead in frustration. Loka was destroying everything they had worked for.

"Anything more of the royal nanny?"

"No, not yet, sir. I've never seen such security around anyone before."

All for a nanny? Alexander just didn't get it. "Keep me informed."

He put the phone down, lifted his glass of whiskey, and walked over to his balcony. Alexander loved this expensive apartment overlooking the Thames. It represented how far he had come.

As a child and young adult, he'd lived in a small one-bedroom apartment in an overcrowded area of the capital. As a young man, Loka had been the charismatic right wing leader of a terrorist group. Alexander found his home when he went to see Loka speak. He talked about jobs and housing for true-born Vospyan citizens.

The ruling classes had allowed the country to become too welcoming, too liberal, and Loka promised those young men who attended the meeting riches and power. When Alexander looked out over London from his plush apartment, Loka had been proved right.

He had been one of the president's chosen men. One of those brave enough to execute the ruling royal family. Many rebel fighters didn't have courage, but he and his friends did, and Loka was forever grateful.

Loka was in danger of destroying that now. If he was in charge, none of this would have happened. The freedom fighters would have been found right at the start and he would have executed them on Monument Square in the capital.

He'd planned to support the vice president in the grab for Loka's power, but now that idea was gone, unless he could be rescued.

Alexander couldn't let this happen. He couldn't lose what he had worked for, for so long. He had to make enquiries and find out who the right man was to dedicate his loyalty to.

The past week had been one of the worst for Clay since her mum died. Guarding the woman she now knew she had fallen in love with. The emotional separation from Kat had made that crystal clear.

Since that night one week ago, Kat had completely shut down to her, and Clay couldn't blame her. She'd played the cad in order to push her away, and it worked. If only Kat knew that was only to protect them both from inevitable heartbreak when Kat returned to Vospya.

Holly had been well pissed off at her too. Obviously, she had talked to Kat and didn't know the full story.

Clay stood by the car at the door of Windsor Castle, waiting for Kat to come out. It was Kat's day off, and Clay was escorting her to Miss Dora's house. Kat came walking out the door but didn't look her way.

Clay hurriedly opened the front passenger door, but Kat had already chosen the back door, obviously to sit as far away from her as possible. It was the most horrendous feeling to have Kat think badly of her, but what choice did she have?

After losing her mum, it was all too much. She wasn't brave enough to lose someone else she loved. It was just her luck—the first attainable woman she fell for became the most unattainable.

She tried to take the snub on the chin and walked around to the driver's side. She hesitated a few seconds before getting in. One of the worst things about her new role was the silences that she had to endure.

Clay was never good with awkward silences, but intentional ones from the woman she loved were a whole different ball game.

She sat in the driver's seat and shut the door. "Ready for take-off?"

"Yes," Kat said flatly.

Fuck, this was hard. She instructed the car computer of their destination and they set off. The silence was making her stomach twist with tension. A few times she looked up in the rear-view mirror and caught Kat looking back at her but then quickly looked away, but while the self-drive car was doing its thing, Clay couldn't help but look at Kat. It wasn't hard to see that this woman was a princess. She had soft regal features. Too good for her. Clay should have known it from the start.

They arrived at Dora's house. Clay again tried to get around to get the door in time but failed miserably again.

Kat looked at Clay and said, "I'll be about an hour and a half."

"That's fine. I'll be here," Clay said.

Kat just nodded and walked away and into Dora's building. It was so hard to stay angry at Clay. She had to keep reminding herself of what Clay had said to her and what she had done, but it was so divorced from the Clay she knew and the apparent sadness she was showing that it made the task almost impossible.

She arrived at Dora's front door and rang the bell. Before long her former headmistress was welcoming her in.

"Little Kitty Kat. Come in, come in."

Dora ushered her in, took her hand as usual, and kissed it reverently. "Come, we'll get some tea and have a good talk."

Kat sat by the fire while Dora pottered in the kitchen. "Where's your young lady today?"

"What young lady?" Kat played dumb but knew exactly whom she meant.

"You know. That handsome young policewoman."

Dora appeared in the doorway with a heavy tray full of tea and cakes. Kat got up immediately and took it off her.

"Sit down. I'll get this." She carried the tray over to the coffee table and hoped Dora would forget the question.

Dora lifted the teapot and said, "Shall I be mother?"

Kat smiled and nodded. Dora was adoringly old-fashioned.

She poured out the tea and said, "So, your handsome police-woman?" She put down the teapot and added, "Would she mind me calling her handsome? That's the energy she gave out to me, but I'm not up with all the latest terms. I would hate to offend."

"No, I'm sure she would approve of handsome." Kat wanted to rest Dora's mind but also change the subject. She rubbed her hands together vigorously. "Ooh, you made lemon drizzle cake. My favourite."

"I know—that's why I made it."

Kat took a big slice of cake and placed it on a plate. "Yum!" She took a big bite and again hoped the subject would be forgotten.

"So?"

"So what?" Kat asked.

"Sergeant Clay."

"Oh, well. Things have changed."

"What things?"

How could she explain? "Clay is my close protection officer now. She's down at the car."

"I had heard that. The prime minister thought it necessary, and I hear your uncle, the King, knows about you now. That's wonderful."

Kat put her teacup down. "How did you know that?"

Dora took a sip of tea. "I'm kept informed."

Kat felt like there was so much more going on here. "What does that mean?"

Dora sighed. "I suppose it doesn't matter any more, but I'm your MI6 agent."

After church in the morning, Queen Adrianna, Queen Sophia, and their pack of dogs joined George, Bea, and the children for afternoon tea in the drawing room.

Queen Sophia was currently bouncing her granddaughter Princess Anna on her lap, while Teddy was showing her great-grandma her toy horses.

Since it was Katya's day off, Bea was glad of the grandmas' help in entertaining them. Her own mum and dad usually joined them, but they were visiting her cousins in Scotland this weekend.

"Are Roza and Lex joining us?" Adrianna said.

"George? What did Lex say earlier?" Bea asked George.

George, who was reading some papers beside Bea, said, "Sorry? What?"

Bea sighed. "What did Lex say about joining us?"

"Oh, she said Roza had a bad backache, so she'd see how Roza felt later."

"George, do you have to read papers on a Sunday afternoon?" Bea said.

George looked at her guiltily. "Sorry, but a late-night bulletin came through. The prime minister will be calling me later, so I have to understand what's going on."

"You can't stop them," Sophia said. "You want to stop them, but they won't. Eddie was the same."

Adrianna sat back after Teddy ran off around the room with one of her horses. "My Freddie was the same."

George looked up and said, "If you all are quite finished talking about me as if I wasn't here, I'll tell you what it was about."

"Hurry up then, dear," Adrianna said, then held her hands out to Princess Anna. "Give me my little Anna, Sophia."

"What is it, George?" Bea asked.

"The Vospyan Liberty Freedom Fighters have entered the capital. Their numbers have grown and grown. The army has turned against Loka since he arrested and executed their colonel yesterday. It's inevitable that they will take control soon."

"Really, Georgie?" Bea said happily.

"Yes, the UN peacekeepers will enter Vospya when the freedom fighters take the palace, and as it's been agreed, they will lay down their arms."

"How wonderful," Adrianna said. "King Louis will be so happy."

"How soon, George?"

"It could still be some weeks before they fight their way to the palace, but it's in sight."

The drawing room door opened, and Lex walked in with Roza on her arm.

George immediately got up and went over to offer another arm.

"Are you feeling okay?" Bea asked.

"Her back is aching, but she insisted on getting up," Lex said.

"I can speak for myself, Lex. Pregnancy hasn't hampered my power of speech."

Lex said nothing but simply raised her eyebrows. She and George helped Roza ease down onto the couch.

"Could I get a cold drink?" Roza said.

"George, could you buzz for a footman?" Bea said.

"Of course."

"Where is Theo?" Roza asked.

"Off galivanting with his film producer friend," Adrianna said.

Lex smiled. "Has Theo won her over at last?"

Sophia laughed. "I wouldn't say that. He's taken her to see one of his children's arts projects, the exhibition at the National Gallery. Trying to persuade her he really cares about the world and its people."

Adrianna kissed little Anna's soft hair. "About time the boy settled down and got married. I think this strong woman, Ms. Bouzid, could make something of him."

"He's certainly besotted," Bea said.

Roza shifted around in her seat trying to get comfortable. The footman entered and George asked for some ice water for Roza.

"Did you get the late-night bulletin, George?" Roza asked.

"About Vospya? Yes. The prime minister is calling me tonight about it."

"Mine too," Roza said. "Kat will be so happy. Is she here today?"

"No, Clay took her over to visit her old headmistress," Bea said.

George saw the grimacing on Roza's face and remembered how uncomfortable Bea had been this late in her pregnancy. She hoped this wasn't putting Bea off having another child. George would love a third and a fourth, but that was down to Bea, and she would never try to pressure her.

Suddenly Roza cried out, "Oh no, oh no."

"What is it?" Lex said in panic.

"My waters have just broken. It's too early, Lex!"

Lex jumped up in panic. "It's okay, okay. We'll get—"

George saw terror on Lex's face. She grasped her by the shoulders. "Calm down. We'll get her to the hospital. Does she have a packed bag?"

"Um…yes, yes. I can't—yes, an emergency bag."

"Go and get it. I'll call Ravn."

Lex ran off, and Bea and Sophia sat beside Roza, trying to calm her.

"It's too soon, Bea. There's something wrong, just like my mama."

Bea gripped her hand tightly. "Nothing is going to happen."

Sophia added. "The baby is just impatient to see you, Roza."

George finished talking to Ravn and felt Teddy gripping her leg. She picked a worried-looking Teddy up.

"It's okay, Auntie Roza's baby is ready to be born. That's all."

Lex came running back into the room. "I've called Perri. Is she all right?"

"Lex, I need you. I'm not in Denbourg. Our baby won't be born in Denbourg," Roza said in panic.

Lex looked at George. She had to be the one to keep calm in this situation. She used her phone to call Bastian. "Bastian? Operation home soil."

❖

"What do you mean, my agent?" Kat asked.

"I was a young classics professor at Cambridge when I was recruited to MI6. I did a few jobs over the years, here and there. Then you arrived on our shores as a scared, young ten-year-old."

Kat rubbed her forehead. She couldn't quite believe what she was hearing. "But I thought you'd been headmistress for years?"

Dora smiled. "No, my history was fabricated. I left my post at Cambridge, and my whole role was to keep you safe, happy, and with a parental influence. I was there for you, always have been."

"But why?"

"You and your uncle were the only two Bolotovs left. That made you second-in-line to the throne. There might have been a revolution, but Vospya was unstable, and nobody knew if the new regime would last. That made you a very important person."

"But it did last," Kat said.

"Until now." Dora popped another sugar in her tea and stirred it. "Besides, the King wanted you to be looked after. For security's sake he couldn't have you in his household. People would put two and two together. If he couldn't give you a family, he wanted to have one person you could rely on."

Kat put her hand on Dora's knee. "I always have relied upon you."

Dora covered her hand with hers. "I was never blessed with my own children, but taking care of you has been my true blessing."

"Thank you, Dora." Kat wiped tears from her eyes. "Why are you telling me now?"

Dora cleared her throat. She was obviously feeling emotional too. "It seems like the time for honesty. With the civil war as it is, things are in flux, things may change, and I don't want you to think I was lying to you. You mean too much to me."

Kat thought of the way she had to keep her identity from Clay and what a blow it would have been to her. One day a nanny, known to no one, the next a princess from a crumbling royal dynasty. It must have been a shock.

She had felt guilty at withholding who she was, but she didn't consider herself to be lying.

"Thank you for being there for me, Dora. Life would have been very lonely without you," Kat said.

"A parental figure can make you feel less lonely, but that will never substitute for someone who holds your heart."

Kat's thoughts immediately went to Clay downstairs. Had she truly done a complete turnaround in her character and feelings? There was a large part of her that couldn't reconcile the Clay she was falling in love with and the one who'd coldly dumped her.

"So?" Dora said. "Why is Sergeant Clayton not up here having a cup of tea with us?"

"We had a disagreement," Kat said.

"Really? She seemed such a relaxed, easy-going person."

"So I thought too," Kat said.

"Can it not be fixed?"

Kat thought of lying in Clay's arms, of looking into her eyes like they were her soul and seeing nothing but love.

"I didn't end it. Clay did."

"You became close, then, my dear?" Dora asked.

Kat nodded. "Yes. I've never let anyone into my heart, Dora. You know that, and the first time I do—well, it doesn't matter anyway."

"Did this happen when she found out who you were?"

"Yes," Kat said, "after she was assigned to protect me."

Dora topped up both their teacups. "Maybe she's scared, Kitty Kat."

"Scared of what?" Kat asked.

"Of who you are, of who you'll become."

"Who am I?" Katya shrugged. "I'm Katya Kovach, nanny, who'll become a nanny again in the future."

"You were born a princess and will always be a princess, whatever life calls you to do. You're used to titles and a grand family history—Sergeant Clayton isn't. She works for the Queen, a role that she thinks is the greatest honour she could have ever had. That's the respect she has for royalty. Then all of a sudden you are one of them. Think about that, Kitty Kat."

Was it blind panic that had fuelled Clay's coldness?

Her mobile phone interrupted her thoughts. It was Clay.

"Kat, we have to go now."

❖

Roza was sitting in her private hospital bed with George, Bea, and the children around her. Lex was holding their newborn baby boy.

Bea couldn't stop smiling at the look of adoration on Lex's face. She handed Anna to George and went to sit beside Roza. It had all been a panic, but the baby had come so fast that it was only now starting to become real.

"How do you feel, Roza?"

"Still a bit shocked—our little prince has come so quickly. I thought I would be hours and hours in labour."

"Seems like you're good at giving birth," Bea joked.

"Let me see the baby," Teddy said to Lex.

"Okay," Lex sat down in one of the seats so Teddy would be closer.

"Have you decided on a name?" George asked.

"Not yet," Roza said. "We have two lists we were whittling down. We thought we'd have more time."

Bea couldn't help but smile at Roza's evident happiness. She squeezed her hand. "All that worry, and everything went perfectly."

"I know." Roza looked over at Lex and said, "I don't think I'll ever get my little prince back."

Both women laughed. Bea picked up a tub of soil and another of water on the bedside cabinet.

"And whose was this genius idea?"

Lex and Georgina grinned at each other.

"That would Queen Georgina," Lex said. "She knew I was worried about Roza being over here and giving birth, and the Denbourg officials were extremely worried about the heir to the throne not being born on Denbourg soil."

"Don't remind me." Roza rolled her eyes. "I heard about nothing else before I came over for my visit."

George continued, "I knew precedent was set during the Second World War, when some royals seeking refuge in Britain had hotel suites temporarily designated their native soil for a birth, therefore making the child fully native to their country. So I spoke to the prime minister and made this hospital suite a part of Denbourg, and Lex organized the

Denbourg earth and water, so the prince was born on native soil. All organized, no problem."

Bea laughed and shook her head. "You never fail to amaze me, Georgie."

"Diplomatic problems are my specialty." George walked over to the window and peeked out the blinds. "I think every journalist and camera is outside the hospital. We'll need to leave by the back entrance, Bea. We want to keep a low profile."

"How are you leaving?" Bea asked. "Has it been agreed?"

"Perri is bringing me clothes and Lyndsey, my hair and make-up person, to get me ready for the press, but I let Lex negotiate our exit with the media."

Lex stood and brought the prince over to Roza. "I think he wants his mummy. We've agreed with our press team to stand on the front steps for a photo call with our boy, and then we will leave for St. James's Palace."

"Good plan," George said. "If you give them a little, you get more privacy in the coming days."

Bea thought Roza had never looked happier than with her little prince in her arms. She looked over at George. *Hmm, another little prince or princess sounds like the perfect idea.*

Clay was struggling with the silence. All she wanted to do was talk to Kat and tell her everything and explain why she had behaved so badly, but of course she couldn't.

They had been waiting in a private waiting room for half an hour. When she got the call from Clay, they hurried back to pick up the princesses and bring them to the hospital to be with their mothers.

Once George and Bea took the children in to see Roza, there had been nothing to distract them from the issue that hung between them.

Clay looked over to the coffee machine in the corner and said, "Do you want a cuppa while we wait?"

Kat sighed. "Yes, please. I'm tired. I need something to perk me up."

At least Kat was talking to her now. She went over to the machine and said, "How do you want it?"

"Black with two sugars, please."

Clay got two coffees and walked back over and sat down. "Here you go."

"Thanks."

There was silence again, and Clay was desperate to fill it. "Teddy was excited, wasn't she? Another cousin for her to play with."

"I remember being taken to see one of my little cousins at the hospital. The King already had two older children, and I think the third was a surprise. Little Daniel. I always had a special bond with him as he grew up."

It struck Clay that the cousin Kat was talking about so fondly must have been killed too, along with everyone else in the family picture next to Kat's bed. It suddenly felt very real. How did she cope with being so alone, one of only two left?

Clay didn't have a big family. There was only her aunt and her two sons. She was never close to her cousins, but going by the picture she had seen, Kat was.

"I'm sorry about your family, Kat. I can't imagine how awful it must have been."

Unusually candid, Kat said, "It's been lonely."

Clay felt even guiltier about how she'd reacted after finding out who Kat was. It should be her job to comfort Kat, to take care of her, and instead she hurt her.

"Kat? I'm sorry I hurt you that day."

Kat turned to look at her. "Is it only because you found out who I am?"

"Yes, we're in two different worlds."

"How are we? You're a protection officer, and I'm a nanny. That isn't going to change," Kat said.

Clay knew the opposite was true, but Kat wasn't to know that. She replied as honestly as she could. "What nannies have their own protection officers?"

Kat searched her eyes, then got up and walked over to the window of the waiting room.

"All my life I've wanted to melt into the crowd, because there is safety in anonymity. Being born Bolotovs got my family killed, and yet after shunning the limelight, here I am, a nanny with a guard. I know you care about me, Ronnie. I don't believe that cold, uncaring persona you put on that day. You're a kind, loving person, but who I am seems to scare you or make you feel uncomfortable."

Kat was so right. It did frighten her, it terrified her, and she didn't know how to get over it. A future between them was impossible, and when Kat left it would break her heart.

That evening, the Queen took a call from the prime minister. They discussed Queen Rozala's new baby boy and the arrangements made for them to go home, then the prime minister informed her of a new development in their plans for Vospya.

As soon as she ended the call, she asked a page to bring Kat to her. Not too long after, there was a knock at the door.

Kat came in and curtsied. "You wanted to see me, Your Majesty?"

"Yes, sit down, Kat. I wanted to keep you up to date with what's going on in Vospya."

"Has something happened?" Kat asked. She was immediately worried that something bad had happened. Had government forces pushed back the freedom fighters?

"I received a bulletin last night from Number Ten. The freedom fighters have entered the capital and are expected to gain control in a week or two."

Kat gasped and put her hand to her mouth. "You're kidding. Really? Could this really be the end of Loka's regime?"

George half smiled. "We think so. Loka has split his party, arresting rivals, executing the colonel-in-chief of the army—thanks to their defection to the freedom fighters, they have the numbers to finish this. The only ones defending the capital are his personal guard."

Kat couldn't stop the tears running down her cheeks. George got her a tissue and came around the desk to give it to her.

"Here."

"I'm sorry, ma'am. I've—I've dreamed of this since I was a little girl."

George put a comforting hand on her shoulder. "Don't apologize. You've been through so much in your young life. Your parents would be so proud of you."

"I hope that one day I'll go back and visit Vospya, and they'll be looking over me."

George cleared her throat. "There has been a plan in place for some time about the handing over of power, and I've been cleared by the prime minister to explain it to you."

Kat wiped away her tears and tried to gain control quickly. She knew this was important to understand clearly. "Thank you, ma'am."

"As you probably know, the UN has been keeping a close eye on this situation. They wanted to help but at the same time didn't want to be accused of regime change, so the plan is that as soon as the freedom fighters take the palace, or Loka gives himself up, the UN peacekeepers will go in and ensure that the citizens are secure and things are done properly. The freedom fighters will immediately put down their arms, and the peacekeepers will help set up the start of democratic processes."

"Democracy in Vospya," Kat said. "I never dared hope."

"Never give up hope for democracy, Katya. Now, as you know, your uncle, the King, has been a focal point of the cry for freedom, and he has been asked to go to Vospya and…" George hesitated. "Give a speech to reassure and bring people together."

"That's wonderful. At least the relic of the Vospyan monarchy can serve a good purpose. My father would be proud of Uncle Louis."

George cleared her throat. "Yes, quite so. Um—before he does that, he wants to talk to you."

"I can talk to him on a video call? When?" Kat was thrilled.

"No, a video call won't be necessary. He wants to meet you in person."

Kat's jaw dropped. "Meet me? How?" Kat squeaked.

"Last night an RAF transport brought King Louis into Britain. He's staying in an undisclosed location, and if you are agreeable, you will be taken to meet him tomorrow."

Kat felt her hands start to shake. It was all too much to process.

"I know it's all very overwhelming," George said.

Kat couldn't think straight. Her emotions were so mixed up, confused.

"What about the princesses? Queen Beatrice is taking Princess Teddy and Princess Anna to visit one of Prince Theo's local arts projects—Queen Rozala was meant to be there, but Queen Beatrice will be alone if I'm not there to help."

"It's all been taken care of. Holly is going with Queen Beatrice, Lali will be there, and Theo has promised to pull his weight with his nieces. Everything will be fine, I promise."

❖

Clay walked slowly along the corridor. She'd come from a late meeting of the security team. King Louis was in the country, and a carefully engineered meeting between him and Kat, or Princess Olga, was scheduled for tomorrow.

She slung her suit jacket over her shoulder and wondered if Kat had been told yet. Everything would be over soon. Kat would know her destiny and leave her post, and Clay. Clay thought she had been protecting her heart by cooling things off with Kat, but the truth was it had already been too late. Her heart was going to break just the same as if she had carried on with their relationship.

She turned the corner of the corridor that led to her apartment. She was surprised and worried when she saw Kat sitting on the floor, back against the wall, by her room door.

Clay immediately panicked and ran the rest of the way to the door. "What's wrong? What happened?"

Kat looked up at her with watery eyes and said, "I don't know what to feel."

There was a desperation in Kat's voice, and all Clay wanted to do was make her feel better.

"Let's go inside." Clay offered her hand and pulled Kat up.

Once they got in, Kat said, "Do you know?"

Clay nodded. "We've just had a briefing from Quincy."

"My uncle—" Kat stuttered, and Clay pulled her into an embrace.

"I'm here. Tell me what you're thinking."

Kat clung to Clay and drank in the safety and security she felt in her arms. Never letting go she said, "I feel happy, scared, nervous, overwhelmed—just, everything."

"I understand. I'd feel all those things too."

"You'll be there by my side, won't you?" Kat asked.

She felt Clay's muscles stiffen slightly.

"I'll be there with you," Clay said.

Was that quite the same thing, Kat wondered, but before she could think any further, Clay guided her over to sit on the bed.

"I think we need a drink. You're going to meet your family."

Clay got a couple of bottles of beer from the fridge and handed one to Kat. "I'm sorry I don't have wine. This is the best I can do."

"It's fine." Kat took a swig, and the cold liquid tasted a nice change from wine. "Vospya is going to be free in weeks, the Queen said."

Clay sat next to her on the bed. "That is the best news ever. Think of the people like us, living in fear, or the ones that Loka killed, that would have been praying for this day."

"I never thought I'd see Vospya free in my lifetime. They had such a tight hold on the people."

"My history teacher at school said that the flame of democracy is very hard to blow out. I thought those were just words, but I can see what he meant now."

Kat held out her hand, and Clay took it. "It might dim, but not die. At least we always have to believe that." Kat's emotions were calming in Clay's presence. Enough to separate her thoughts from the jumble they had been in. One thought was dominating her mind. "Everyone's going to know who I am, eventually, aren't they?"

Clay was silent.

"I can't work here and be a security threat to the princesses. There will be lots of rogue Loka supporters out there."

"You can't say what tomorrow will bring, but whatever life brings, I know you'll find a way to thrive. You have so much to give, Kat."

Why did she get the feeling Ronnie was certain she wouldn't be with her?

"I love you, Ronnie."

Clay didn't think about herself or her feelings, only Kat's. She kissed her softly, then slowly undressed Kat before undressing herself. They slipped into bed, and Clay kissed every part of her lover, as if it was her last time.

"Touch me, Clay. I want to feel."

Clay was frightened that if she looked in Kat's eyes, she would betray her heart's wants and tell her she loved her. So she kissed all the way down her body, kissing, licking, and making, as best she could, Kat's body feel.

When she tasted Kat, she hummed in pleasure and felt her lover's hand cling to her hair. Kat's hips bucked and waved as Clay licked and sucked at her clit, and before long, Kat squeezed her thighs tightly around her head as her orgasm overtook her.

As Kat's breathing calmed, Clay felt her body shake with sobs. She climbed back up to Kat and stroked her hair. "Hey, what's wrong? Don't cry."

Kat looked at her through tear-filled eyes. "I'm frightened that things are going to change. Are they?"

Clay had no answer to that. So she held her tightly until her sobs quietened, and she slowly drifted off to sleep.

❖

When Kat awoke, Clay was already dressed, sitting in the chair by the bed. She was staring at the floor in front of her, her elbows leaning on her knees in a dejected manner. Gloom hung over the room, and Kat knew this was over as far as Clay was concerned.

"Why does this have to be over?"

Clay looked up with anger and frustration in her eyes. "I love Katya Kovach, but I can't love Princess Olga."

Kat sat up quickly, holding the quilt to cover her naked body. Clay did love her. She knew it. "You can't love one without the other, Ronnie. Why does my former life make such a difference to you? It's only a title—it doesn't mean anything any more."

"You don't understand," Clay said sadly.

"This is ridiculous." Kat got up and started to pull on her clothes, frantically. "I don't mean very much to you, if an old, stupid dead title makes a difference to you."

Kat slipped her shoes on and hurried to the door. When she touched the door handle, Clay said, "I'm sorry. Maybe one day you'll understand."

Kat didn't turn back to look at her, but simply said, "You were the only one I ever let in. I love you, but you're not the person I thought you were, Sergeant Clayton."

Kat left and slammed the door behind her.

CHAPTER SEVENTEEN

The early morning dawn streamed through the bedroom curtains. Bea sat up in bed and smiled when she saw George lying with her hand on Teddy's back. Teddy must have woken and been upset during the night.

Bea loved to see the deep love and affection George had for Teddy. She knew they would have the closest relationship their whole lives. George stirred and her eyes flickered open.

"Good morning, sleepyhead. I woke up before you for a change," Bea said.

George had never lost her military discipline and was usually up and starting her day as if she was still in the navy.

George sat up against the headboard. "Teddy had a nightmare. It took me a while to get her to settle."

"You should have woken me," Bea said.

"You've got enough to do. You deserve the sleep. Yesterday was a busy day."

Bea stroked Teddy's hair. "I wonder how Roza and the baby are this morning."

"Happy but tired, I'm sure," George said.

"Lex looked so happy, didn't she? She couldn't put him down. Thank goodness you got the Denbourg soil and water prepared."

"Yes, it saved the day, although the Denbourg officials want her back home as soon as possible."

There was a knock at the door, and a maid walked in with a tray of tea and coffee. George always started the day with strong, black tea, and Beatrice didn't feel alive until she had her coffee.

"Thank you, Gabby," Bea said to the maid.

Bea turned to her bedside table and said, "Computer, show Anna's room."

On the screen, footage popped up of Anna, wide awake and babbling to herself in her cot.

"I better go and get Anna."

George stood and said, "I'll go. You cuddle with Teddy for a bit."

"Mummy," said a sleepy Teddy. She crawled over to her, and Bea lifted her arm so she could snuggle into her.

"Any messages, computer?" Bea asked.

"*There is one message from Roza.*"

George came back into the room carrying Anna.

"Good morning, sweetheart," Bea said.

George and Anna lay down on the bed. Anna reached out for Bea, and she kissed her chubby little hand.

"There's a message from Roza, Bully. Computer, play message from Roza."

"Hi, you two. We wanted you to be the first to know the name of our little boy. Crown Prince Lennox Augustus George. We wanted to thank you and Bea for always being there for us and supporting us through everything, so our little boy should have your name, George."

"That was so nice of them," George said, smiling.

"It really was. I wonder if he'll go by Lennox or Augustus, after Roza's big brother?"

"I'm sure they'll see what his little personality is first," George said.

"Hmm. Did you remember that we'll have to look after the children this morning? I told Kat to concentrate on getting ready to meet her uncle today. Holly is going to help her get ready."

George sighed. "It's a big day for Kat. King Louis is going to tell her everything. Today she'll become Princess Olga again, if she accepts that role."

"Do you think she will?" Bea asked.

George held Anna close and stroked her hair. "Yes, I think so. She understands duty as well as I do."

"I hope she'll be all right, Georgie."

"We will help, by being there for her," George said.

❖

Holly carried her large toolbox of make-up items along the corridor towards Kat's room. Kat didn't know she was coming to help her get ready for her big day, but both she and Bea thought she would need the support.

George had given Quincy the go ahead to tell Holly who Kat really was. Holly was both surprised and not at the same time. Nobody would expect the nanny sitting by them in the dining room to be a princess, but the more Holly thought about it, the more it made sense.

Kat was quiet, reserved, as if she was always holding back a piece of herself. Plus her manners, accent, mannerisms, spoke of someone who was brought up in an extremely upper-class way.

She arrived at the door to find Clay standing outside, looking glum.

"Morning, Clay. How's Kat?" Holly asked.

"She's worried, nervous," Clay said sadly.

"Is everything okay, Clay?"

Clay gave her an obviously false smile. "Yeah, I'm fine. Should you not be helping Queen Bea get ready?"

"Not this morning. Bea and I both agree that I should help Kat this morning. Sorry, Princess Olga."

"I'm sure that'll help."

Holly patted Clay on the arm. "Don't worry, Clay. She'll be okay."

Clay nodded and Holly knocked at the door. "Kat, it's Holly."

"Come in."

Clay was definitely under stress, and Holly felt a bit guilty for giving Clay a hard time over upsetting Kat. There was obviously more to it. She walked into Kat's apartment and heard her shout, "I'm in the bedroom, Holly."

She went in and found Kat in her dressing gown, looking at three dresses.

"Kat?"

Kat turned to her and Holly bobbed a curtsey.

Kat sighed. "Someone told you?"

"Yes, George cleared Quincy to tell me. Bea thought it would be good if I could help you this morning. I agreed." Holly smacked her make-up box a few times, then set it down.

"Thanks, it would be good to have a second opinion." Kat waved her over. "What dress? I can't decide."

"You're nervous?"

Kat hugged herself. "Yes, I'm meeting the only family I have left, and he's the King."

"When was the last time you met your uncle?" Holly asked.

Kat pursed her lips and thought for a second. "A month before the uprising against the government. We had Sunday dinner at the palace, the whole family."

"Were you a close family?" Holly asked.

A big smile came to Kat's face. "Yes, my family was huge, on all sides. When we all got together, it was crazy. Laughter, arguments, jokes, everything."

"And they're all gone?" Holly said softly.

Kat nodded sadly and wiped away a tear. "I promised myself I wouldn't cry today."

"How are things with you and Clay?"

"Apparently a princess, albeit one with a dead title, is not someone she wants to be with."

Holly shook her head. "I think she's probably confused. I'll sort her out, Kat."

"No, please don't say anything to her. If she doesn't feel strongly enough about me, then it wasn't meant to be." Kat turned her attention back to her choice of dress. "Which one do you think?"

"The blue one. It'll be beautiful on you."

Kat picked up the dress. "Yes, this one. You're right."

"Let's get you ready, then."

Holly went to set up her make-up box, then heard Kat say in a low voice, "I'm dreading that my life is about to change."

Alexander woke to realize he'd fallen asleep at his desk at home, a half-empty bottle of vodka beside him. When he sat up in his chair, his neck was in intense pain from how he had fallen asleep.

He'd spent his time, into the small hours, trying to contact friends in government back home, but he had found it difficult. The situation was descending into chaos, and those he did manage to contact feared the writing was on the wall.

Alexander had to protect himself, and since then he had been making plans in case the worst happened and the Vospyan government fell. There might be reprisals, and he had seen talk of arrests for war crimes if the freedom fighters won the day.

How had it come to this? Alexander had built himself up from rebel soldier to ambassador, and he was possibly going to lose it all. He had done too much, killed too many to get where he was today, to end up in jail or whatever the UN would do with him.

He poured out a large shot of vodka and downed it in one. If there were to be reprisals, Alexander knew he would be at the head of the line. All those years ago, when it was certain that their campaign to overthrow the government was going to be successful, Loka made it clear that the royal family, the Bolotovs, must be eliminated.

Not one of Loka's most trusted lieutenants had risen to the task, frightened that killing the King and his family was a step too far. But Alexander was ambitious and knew if he delivered on Loka's demand, he would be a hero.

Alexander closed his eyes and remembered the day his life and his fortune changed. He led a team of his comrades to Gorndam Palace, where the extended royal family were under royal guard, and killed them one by one.

At first even among his team of young, hungry rebels, the men had found it difficult to shoot the women, the elderly, and the young, but it had to be done. There could be no survivors, and Alexander took pride that he'd led the way, and Loka rewarded him for that.

Sometimes at night, when he closed his eyes, he could still see the eyes of those he had killed that day. The terror in their eyes as he put his gun to their heads and pulled the trigger. All except one that got away.

Alexander jumped up quickly. He frantically opened the file that the Vospyan agents had sent him.

"A young girl, fucking Princess Olga."

The princess had gotten away from him that day, and he had lied to Loka that he'd shot them all, except Prince Louis, who wasn't in the country.

He opened the picture, and said, "A refugee aged ten, were you?"

Alexander enlarged the picture until he saw a distinctive pair of eyes looking back at him. One green, one half green, half blue.

"It's her."

CHAPTER EIGHTEEN

Katya paced around the hotel meeting room. Security was everywhere—undercover security, of course. The word had been put out that a foreign ambassador was staying at the hotel, so Clay told her.

The King's protection officers were on the door outside the meeting room, and Clay was inside. Clay had become quiet, and she could feel her pulling away from her by the second. At the moment she was staring passively ahead.

She sighed. "Clay—"

The hotel room doors suddenly opened and a tall grey-haired man walked in at pace, then slowed as he saw her. She curtsied immediately, and Clay bowed her head.

Kat's heart thudded so hard, and she stopped breathing. Her uncle approached so slowly, and then when he got near, he reached out a shaky hand. "Is that really you?"

Kat nodded. "Yes, it's me."

He cupped her cheek and said, "My little Olga, my little Ollie?"

As soon as she heard her real name from his lips, the tears started to flow. Her uncle opened his arms, and she flew into them and sobbed on his shoulder.

"Olga, you have no idea how much I mourned you and the rest of our family. I felt guilty that I survived and all the rest of the family didn't."

"Me too," Kat said.

Kat pulled back and Louis offered her his handkerchief. "The night I was told about you, I fell to my knees. It was the greatest gift anyone could give me. At first I was angry that I was not told about you before, but I came to realize it was probably the right thing to do. I can't imagine how scared you must have been to be alone at ten years old."

"I was, but Queen George's father made sure I was taken care of, and my former headmistress was a mother figure to me. She still is."

Louis grasped both her hands. "I'll be forever grateful to the Queen's family for taking care of you for me."

"They have been very kind," Kat said.

He put his hand on his heart. "You have me now, Ollie. We have a lot to talk about. Let's have a seat and talk."

Once Kat and the King were seated, Kat looked up at Clay, and she smiled back. Clay wished she could be beside her, an arm around Kat, giving her reassurance.

Tea was brought in for Kat and the King while they chatted. Clay kept staring ahead impassively but listened to every word. She knew what the King would tell her about the monarchy, and she was worried how Kat would react.

"So," King Louis said, "tell me about yourself. I hear that you have always worked hard?"

"Yes, after school I went to Cambridge. Then I went to nannying school. I wanted to love and protect children as my nanny had done."

"Your nanny was a saint. Thank God you got out. You must miss your brother. What a fine man he would have turned out to be," King Louis said.

"I keep the family picture by my bedside. You remember the last big picnic we had? It was for Johnny's birthday."

"I remember. A happy day." He crossed his legs and continued, "I was so happy to see Queen Rozala and Consort Lennox blessed with their new little prince."

"Yes, it was all a bit of a panic yesterday, but it ended well. He is a beautiful baby boy."

"Rozala's family were always great friends to us Bolotovs. Do you remember the family coming to stay with us when you were a girl?"

Kat nodded. "Roza remembers too. We've spoken about it."

King Louis took a drink of tea and asked, "Do you have a boyfriend—"

Kat cut him off, "I'm gay, Uncle Louis, I might as well tell you now."

The King put his teacup down. "You don't have to be worried, Ollie. If you'd let me finish I would have said, do you have a boyfriend *or girlfriend*?"

"Oh, sorry," Kat said.

"I'm gay myself, Ollie. Another reason why I supported the freedom fighters' cause. Loka has harassed, tortured, and killed people like us."

"Did Mama, Papa, and the King know?" Kat asked.

"Of course, dear. You were just a little girl, so you probably don't remember what a free, liberal country Vospya was, before the far right started to garner support. They were great days, and we hope we can bring them back again."

"I wish I could remember more. Sometimes my memories feel like a dream or watching someone else's life," Kat said.

"We will make the country like that again, and you will make memories that are certainly real. Tell me, is there anyone special in your life?"

Clay's chest went tight, and she saw Kat look to her. Maybe she wanted a nod or a smile to give her a clue that Clay still wanted to be together, but Clay remained impassive. It was the hardest thing, when all she wanted was to go over and say to the King, *Yes, we are together and in love, and I will spend every moment making Kat happy*, but she didn't.

She heard Kat sigh and say, "I thought there was someone, but they weren't as interested as I thought they were."

That cut deep. Of course she was interested, but Kat had a big future—away from Britain, away from her.

"Then they are a fool, my dear Ollie. You are beautiful and more special than you know."

Yeah, I am a fool.

❖

Kat was hurting. She'd given Clay the chance. All she'd needed was a smile, any kind of indication, and she would have told her uncle. But no, she just stared into nothing, looking emotionless.

Why did she even bother opening her heart in the first place? Kat wished she'd hadn't.

King Louis sat forward. "Now, on to business. When the rebels took control, I was in Switzerland managing the family business interests."

Kat was surprised. "Family business? What other business did we have other than being royal?"

"The family, now you and me, own BEI Group."

"What's that?" Kat asked.

"Bolotov Equity and Investment Group. We own a portfolio of equity in global companies, real estate, technology companies, extensive art collections that are loaned throughout the world, charity trusts, and much more. The company has grown so much since I was exiled, and it's now worth seven billion dollars."

Kat had to grasp the arm of the chair. "You're kidding."

"No, not at all. The Bolotov Trust funnelled a large portion of our equity income into public funds. Loka and his henchmen thought they would get their hands on the money, but they didn't realize it was run from Switzerland. It was my role in the family to handle business. Your father and your aunt supported the King at home. We all had our roles. The money was safe—it is safe and can help rebuild Vospya."

"Astonishing. How are you going to do that?" Kat asked.

"Did you watch my statement when I accepted the crown?"

"Of course. I was so proud of you. I watched it with my friend—well, she was my friend, but now she's my protection officer, Sergeant Clayton."

Kat indicated to Clay, and the King looked at her, narrowed his eyes, then turned back to Kat. He was probably wondering why she wasn't a friend any more.

"Well, I vowed, as you've seen over the years, I'm sure, that I would never ascend to my brother's title. He died as King, and out of respect I wanted him to remain King. But I was contacted by the Liberty Freedom Fighters, led by Nikola Stam, via several European security agencies, to ask me to publicly aecept my title and put my weight behind their aims."

"It really helped," Kat said. "I've followed the news closely. Queen Georgina says you are going to Vospya to make a speech once the UN peacekeepers go in."

King Louis cleared his throat. "Yes, once they gain power, the freedom fighters will lay down their weapons, and I will appoint an emergency government, with the UN monitoring, until an election can be set up."

"You will appoint?" Kat couldn't understand why the freedom fighters would give that sort of power to the former royal representative.

"That's the other part of what the freedom fighters asked of me. I was asked to take the title, and once they wrest power back—"

"What?"

"They want to reinstate the monarchy, a constitutional monarchy to safeguard democracy. That's you and me, Ollie."

Kat fell back the few inches to the back of the chair. She felt like she'd been punched in the chest. People talked about their lives flashing before their eyes. Kat saw her future flashing before her eyes.

"I know it's a shock," Louis said, "but I'm an older man, Ollie. I'm not going to marry or have any children at this stage in my life. You are my heir."

Kat looked up at Clay. She was actually looking at her. This was why Clay had pulled back from her. Why she had been uncharacteristically cold that evening when they argued.

Clay not only knew who she was, she was aware of what her future was going to be, and she didn't tell her. Clay only held her gaze for seconds before shifting her focus to the floor.

Yes. You knew everything. That made Kat angry.

"Ollie, Nikola and his supporters believe that the people want the security of constitutional monarchy. I know it will change your life, but we have to bring the country together and build it back up to what it was. Will you help, me, Ollie?"

There was no question that her own desire for a normal, boring life had to be forgotten. Her parents would expect no less.

"Of course I will, Uncle Louis."

King Louis clapped his hands together. "Excellent. We have so much to do. We'll set up a trust to fund a grand rebuilding program, to make Vospya the country it once was. Then when the oil and gas operations are fully utilized, the country will have income and jobs. Vospya will have a bright future."

Kat's heart ached. And she would have a life without Clay.

❖

Kat didn't say one word on the way home to the palace, but Clay could feel the anger pouring from her. As Clay parked the car, Kat said, "You never told me. You knew and you never told me."

Before Clay could reply, Kat got out of the car and slammed the door shut. Clay followed her as quickly as she could, and members of staff looked at them quizzically as they went passed.

"Kat, let me explain."

They arrived at Kat's room upstairs and unlocked it and went in, fury clearly showing on Kat's face. Kat threw her bag down on the couch and said, "What's to explain? You kept it from me."

Clay shut the door. "I had no choice."

"Of course you had a choice. I walked into that meeting with my uncle with no idea that my life, the one *I* chose, was over. All you had to do was tell the woman that you supposedly love."

Clay started to feel frustrated and angry. "That's the whole point and why we can't be together. You're not just the woman I love, you are the heir to the throne of Vospya. I was asked to keep it from you, so that you had as long as possible before the enormity of what was to come was explained to you. I'm a police protection officer, and I follow orders. You will never have to do that."

"You think I won't have to follow orders? You work every day with Queen Georgina and Queen Bea, and you think I won't have to follow orders? They are told who to meet, what to do, what is best for them every day of their lives, and the same will be happening to me. In fact, it started today."

"That's different. This is my job," Clay said.

"You think what I will be doing, what George and Roza do, isn't a job?"

"Okay, yes, it's a job, but the expectations are completely different. The Queen has power—it may be soft power, but it's power nonetheless. I refuse to follow orders—I'm out of a job. You are not, Your Royal Highness."

A look of hurt flashed across Kat's face. It was a mistake to emphasize the difference between them.

She turned her back and said, "Just go, Ronnie."

"I'm sorry. I'm sorry I didn't tell you. When I found out, the bottom fell out of my world, okay?"

Kat remained silent and kept her back turned on her. Clay walked to the door dejectedly and left.

CHAPTER NINETEEN

The next week was hard for Kat. Clay guarded her dutifully, and all she wanted to do was turn and throw herself into Clay's arms, but she didn't. What was the point? It would only hurt more when she had to leave.

Every day she was reminded of when she would have to leave. King Louis's team in Switzerland sent her protocols nearly each day, to prepare her for what was ahead. Basically, the King wanted to use her as Vospya's foreign ambassador while he concentrated on domestic matters.

She would be travelling the world, trying to repair the country's reputation, and it needed a lot of repair. Katya didn't consider herself charismatic, and after a lifetime of trying to hide in the shadows, now she had to live in the limelight. The thought scared her. In the meantime, waiting on the fall of the Vospyan dictatorship was nerve-racking.

At least for now, Kat was allowed to carry on taking care of the princesses, but she could not take them out in public, where they could all be targets.

"Look, Kat," Teddy said. "I drew you a cat."

The household was at Windsor as usual on Saturday, and Teddy was busily drawing while Anna was playing with her toys on her playmat. "What a lovely cat, Teddy."

The nursery room door opened and Lali stepped in. "Kat, Queen Roza is here."

"Auntie Roza," Teddy squealed and bolted for the door.

Since Queen Rozala had to cut short her trip and take the new prince home, she wanted to drop in to say goodbye. Also since Roza wouldn't be taking part in the documentary any more, they'd all agreed to give Azi a few shots of them altogether as a family. One big extended family.

"Wait, Teddy," Kat said. "Thanks, Lali."

Lali took Teddy's hand while Kat picked Anna up and walked out of the nursery. They passed Clay standing outside the door, and Kat felt a magnetic pull inside her body. How was she ever going to leave her? The pain, she knew, was going to gnaw at her heart forever.

As she and Lali walked along the corridor, Lali said, "I contacted your friend Artie."

When Bea had asked Kat if she could recommend a replacement nanny, the only name worthy, and the only one she'd trust with the princesses, was Artie.

"You did? What did he say?"

"He was very interested. I'm setting up a meeting between Queen Bea and Artie as Bea's timetable permits."

"Great. I know she'll like him. He's really nice and trustworthy."

Kat was hyperaware of Clay following behind her, and Clay would be aware that Artie being interviewed meant she was ever closer to leaving.

They arrived at the drawing room door, and Lali opened it. Teddy ran in and shouted, "Auntie Roza, Aunt Lex!"

George put her finger to her lips and said, "Shush, Teddy. You'll scare the baby."

Roza was on the couch with Lex, while George was standing beside Bea, who was sitting in an armchair. Azi was preparing her camera on the other side of the room.

Bea stood and said, "I'll take Anna, Kat."

Lex stood and indicated to Kat. "Come and meet our boy, Kat."

"Thank you."

Kat took a seat beside Roza, and George said, "Would you mind Azi taking some footage while you are here, Kat? She has been security cleared."

That meant she knew who Kat really was. "If you like."

Roza smiled and said, "Would you like to hold him?"

"I'd love to," Kat said.

Kat took him, and the new prince wriggled around until he settled. "You're a handsome little boy, aren't you?"

She heard Azi's camera buzz around them as it took some footage.

"We wanted to drop in before we go home to Denbourg," Roza said, "and before you leave for Vospya."

Kat nodded but felt her heart thud with fear.

Queen Georgina said, "Roza, Kat—sorry, Olga—I'm glad we have this time together before we go our separate ways."

Both she and Roza looked up at George and listened, while a page came around with a tray of drinks.

"One day there will be three Queens on the thrones of our respective countries. Not only are we comrades, with an acute understanding of the responsibility that we share, but we share ancestry. We are family, a truly royal family, spread across Europe. I have to tell you that gives me comfort, that two other countries will be led by women who share the same ideals as I do, and who will give everything to maintain democracy and peace, for all our children."

George lifted her drink and continued, "I propose a toast, to royal family."

"Royal family."

"Royal family."

The support and encouragement she got from George and Roza would make things easier, when the time came. She was lucky to have such good friends and family. If only Clay could be part of that family.

The next day, Clay was sitting on her living room floor putting her new furniture together. It had been delivered on Sunday morning, so she would be off work and able to spend the day getting everything put together.

At the moment she was putting together a bookcase, with some difficulty. In the background, cheers and noise came from the TV. Late the night before, the Liberty Freedom Fighters had taken Gorndam Palace, and the last remaining guards had surrendered.

Crowds of Vospyans gathered in the square in front of the palace, celebrating the end of Loka's tyranny. When she'd woken up late last night and saw what had happened, she sent a message to Kat, one of congratulations that she had her country back and to check that she was okay. Kat replied only to say, yes, she was okay.

That one little reply hurt. It felt like she was totally cut out of Kat's life. She wondered how long it would be before Kat truly left the country, and her, behind. Would things have been different if she had embraced Kat's desire to continue the relationship, or would it have naturally come to an end? She would never know.

It was a blessing she had gotten her furniture delivery this morning, as it gave her something manual, something to take her mind off her feelings. She looked up at the TV when renewed shouts and cheers caught her attention.

The news reporter on the ground directed the audience's attention to a statue of President Loka on the square. Citizens had climbed up on the plinth and attached ropes around it and were currently pulling it down. It toppled and crashed to the ground.

"Wow." Clay knew she was watching history. She was torn away from the history making when she heard her doorbell ring.

She was amazed to find a very tired looking Kat at the door. "Kat? Are you okay?"

"I miss having you as my friend," Kat said sadly.

Clay didn't hesitate to take her hand and pull her into the house. "Come and sit down."

Kat looked around the house filled with boxes and packaging. "You got your furniture delivered?"

"Yeah, I'm wrestling with a bookcase right now. Sit down."

Kat plopped down onto the new sofa and ran her hand over the soft, grey covering. "This is nice. I knew we made the right choice."

The *we* in that sentence made Clay sad it wasn't a choice for them. It was just for her.

"You've been watching?" Kat asked.

"Yeah, of course. It's history in the making, and I know how much the freedom of your people means to you."

"Have they just pulled down Loka's statue?"

"Just before you came in. You can't ever stop people's spirits longing to be free, can you?" Clay said.

"No, I'm so proud of their courage. I've been up watching it all night. I can't imagine how happy my family would be, looking down on this."

Clay was brave and took Kat's hand. "They would be, and of you for stepping up."

Kat gave a wry laugh and rubbed her eyes. "I thought I would have more time to prepare, but the international community is rallying around Vospya, and things are moving fast. I've been talking all night to George, to my uncle, to his officials. I didn't mean to answer your message so abruptly last night, but every time I started to compose a new message, someone else wanted to talk to me. The UN peacekeepers are over the border and on their way to the capital. As soon as they arrive, Nikola will hand over arms and responsibility for law and order to them, until the dust settles."

Clay let out a long breath. "There's a lot of work to do, I'd guess."

"I don't know how it will all get done, but it needs to. Uncle Louis is going in tomorrow and will make a speech. Then, all being well, next Friday, I'll leave for Vospya."

Clay could feel her heart ripping. She wanted to say she'd come with her, but she'd pushed Kat away so far that she wouldn't likely be asked again, and she doubted King Louis would approve of a police protection officer being her girlfriend. Those were lines you weren't supposed to cross, professionally.

Clay remained silent, not knowing what to say.

Kat filled the gap in conversation by saying, "My friend Artie is going to probably be the princesses' new nanny. He was my only friend at Landsford School. You can trust him, and please don't be difficult with him."

"Would I?" Clay smiled.

"Yes, you would. Just be your fun-loving, kind self, and you'll get on like a house on fire."

"Do you want some tea or juice?" Clay asked.

"Could I get some coffee? I'm struggling to stay awake."

"No problem."

Clay went to the kitchen and made the coffee, but when she came back, she found Kat had fallen asleep. She got a blanket and placed it over her and stroked the hair from her eyes.

"I love you," Clay whispered.

She walked back to the kitchen and poured away the coffee. Her computer alerted her to an incoming call.

"Hello?" The familiar voice made her spin around, and she realized it was a video call.

There on the screen was Dora. "Dora? Hello."

She smiled warmly at Clay and said, "I hope I'm not interrupting?"

"No, uh, how can I help?"

"I don't know if Kat explained to you, but the last time I saw her, I told Kat that I was her MI6 officer. Always have been."

Clay was not expecting that. Dora in her woolly cardigans and strings of pearls was not who she thought of as an MI6 agent, but that was why she was an excellent choice, no doubt. "Wow, no, she didn't, but we haven't spoken much since then."

"No, I thought that. I take it you have seen the news?" Dora said.

"Yeah, it's amazing. It's what Kat has always prayed for."

"Yes, but not what lies ahead of her. Kat's always been a quiet girl, a loner, but I've never seen her happier than since she met you."

Clay didn't reply. She wasn't making her happier now.

Dora continued, "Now to the business of my call. I was asked to set up this call by a third party, to make you feel more at ease. Sir? Are you there?"

It was lucky Clay wasn't still holding a coffee cup because she would have dropped it on the floor when King Louis joined the conversation on a split screen.

Dora said, "Sergeant Clayton, let me introduce King Louis of Vospya."

"Sergeant, I've seen you before, but we've never met formally. It's nice to talk to you."

Clay finally pulled herself together and bowed. "Your Majesty."

"I don't have long, things are moving at pace here, as you can imagine, but I needed to speak to you, and Dora was asked to introduce us," King Louis said.

"How can I help, sir?"

"My niece has a big life change ahead of her, and I'm trying to put the best people around her to make her comfortable and safe. I would like to ask you to become her head of security."

Clay felt a burst of excitement inside, but then it deflated like a balloon when she realized this wasn't an option.

"It would be a great honour, sir, but I have to decline. Princess Olga and I have—" Clay struggled with her words.

"Ollie is in love with you, I know. I could tell that when we met in London, but I understand from my discussions with her last night, and with Ms. Dorcas here, that you have distanced yourself because of who she is."

Clay nodded. "I'm a police protection officer who fell in love with a nanny, but now she is a princess and heir to the throne of Vospya. I know that's a line that I can't cross."

"Sergeant, I have read reports from your commanding officers and spoken to the Queen about you, and all that I have heard is that you are an exceptional person, personally and professionally. The fact that you love her makes you even more perfect to head up her security team."

"You approve of me?" Clay said with surprise.

"Not only that, but I think she needs you, and Vospya needs you. I'm sixty-five, not an old man, but things are unstable. There will be rogue rebels around for some time, no doubt, and if anything happens to me, Ollie will be vital to the recovery of Vospya. She, we are symbols of our glory days of democracy, and my people will need her. But you will hopefully have a long time together before she has to step into my shoes, time enough for you both to enjoy life first."

Clay was dumbfounded, but slowly the ripples of excitement started to spread throughout her body. "I really appreciate your support, sir, but could I speak to her about it first?"

"Of course. Make your decision, and then let my officials know. Ollie knows how to get in touch with them. I'll say one last thing. Loving and protecting her would be everything to me, and I'd be in your debt. Goodbye, Sergeant Clayton."

"Goodbye, sir."

When his picture left the screen, Dora returned. "She loves you, Clay. Be honest with her and make your decision. But be prepared—this will be a very different kind of life."

Alexander had left his ambassadorial residence when he realized which way the wind was blowing. Luckily, he'd already made plans to escape the country, if he could get past security without being stopped.

He looked around the dowdy, cheap hotel room he was staying in and cursed President Loka. He had ruined what they had with mismanagement and incompetence. So much work had gone into what they had, and it was now in tatters.

But if he played this right, he could survive. His biggest worry was being identified as one of those who executed the royal family. His life wouldn't be worth living then. Someone would talk when the freedom fighters tried to find out where the family was buried.

He looked back up at the TV and watched the replay of Loka's statue being downed and smashed. It was more than a statue—it represented the ruling party's ideals, and now they too were smashed.

Alexander tried to stay calm. He had money, his papers, and travel tickets. First thing in the morning, he would get out of this disgusting liberal country, and who knew, maybe he could band together with other likeminded Vospyans and build a new base of support, behind *him* this time.

That positivity was dashed when a band flashed across the bottom of the TV screen. *President Loka has been apprehended alive.*

That was it. It was officially over. If Loka was alive, he would sing like a bird and bring them all down. A few seconds later, a message beeped on his phone. It was from Victor.

The police came to the embassy and to your residence. There is a warrant out for your arrest. You are to be held and extradited to Vospya. Get out now.

Fuck! How was he going to get through security now?

He was filled with anger and panic. But he was never going to let himself be captured. He opened his bag with shaking hands and brought out his gun. Just beside his gun was the file on Princess Olga.

Alexander took out the picture and traced her face with the end of his gun.

"Princess Olga, the little girl who got away."

Kat's eyes flickered open and she realized she was lying on Clay's chest, and Clay had her arm around her. Her hand was resting on Clay's stomach, just under her T-shirt. She felt so comfortable, loved, and protected, but then Kat remembered sadly that she was leaving Clay in a week.

The TV was off, the coffee was still lying unfinished on the floor, and Clay appeared to be dozing along with her. Kat started to trace her fingertips around Clay's stomach. Her skin felt so soft, so warm. Safe in the knowledge that Clay was asleep, Kat said, "I love you."

"I love you too," Clay said sleepily.

Kat jumped and pushed herself up to see Clay smiling at her. "I thought you were sleeping."

"I was, and then you touched me, and my body started waking up."

"Did you mean that?" Kat asked.

"Mean what?"

"That you love me?"

Clay cupped her cheek. "Yes, I love you, always will. You're a beautiful person, both inside and out, and you're the bravest person I've ever met."

"You believe that, and yet you're willing to let me leave next week? Why are you telling me this now? To make things even harder?" Kat said with frustration.

"Tell me what you want. What you want me to do?"

Clay was confusing her. "I don't understand."

"Tell me what would be your wish, when you leave for Vospya," Clay said.

"My wish would be that you come with me and be with me forever."

Clay grinned. "Forever? Is that all? Okay."

Kat couldn't believe what she was hearing. She jumped up and straddled Clay's waist. "What?"

"I said okay." Clay grinned.

"Okay, you'll come with me?"

"Yes, I'll come and love you forever."

"But why? What's changed?" Kat asked.

"Your uncle called me while you were asleep and asked me to be your head of security. He also reassured me that our relationship would have his blessing."

"You accepted? Really?"

"Really. Wherever you go in the world, I go."

Kat was so excited that she kissed Clay on the lips and lost her balance on top of Clay. Clay tried to hold on to her, and they both rolled onto the floor.

"Ah," Clay said in pain, as she'd made sure she landed first.

Kat laughed. She was so full of excitement.

"I'm glad my pain makes you laugh."

Kat grasped her hair and started to pepper kisses all over her face. "Aww, but I'm happy. You love me, and you're coming with me?"

"Someone has to make sure the heir to the throne doesn't fall off pieces of furniture," Clay joked.

Kat's excitement started to calm, and she felt intense joy sweep over her. She clasped Clay's hand and placed it on her heart.

"I know you're giving up your life to come with me, giving up your career with the police—I understand how big that is."

Clay cupped her cheek. "I'm not giving up my life. You are my life."

Kat felt tears come to her eyes, and Clay said, "Don't cry. I always make you cry."

Kat chuckled and wiped her eyes. "They are happy tears. Stay there."

She jumped up and closed the living room blinds. Clay started to get up, but Kat pushed her back down.

"I want to pin you down this time." Kat pulled off her jumper and threw it aside along with her bra.

Clay immediately cupped her breasts, and Kat leaned over, bringing them to her lover's mouth. She felt Clay try to flip her over.

"No, I'm pinning you, remember?"

Clay rolled her eyes and Kat pushed up her T-shirt, giving her kisses around her stomach. Between kisses she started to undo Clay's belt. "It's not that bad, is it, Ronnie?"

"No, just frustrating," Clay growled.

"You can have your fun later. I need to show you how much I appreciate what you're doing, how much I love you."

Kat pulled at Clay's jeans and underwear. Clay helped by wriggling out of them. She kissed around Clay's lower stomach, and Clay groaned.

"You're bad," Clay said.

"Hey, I'm only starting to explore my sexuality, and you are my only test subject, ever. So get used to it."

Clay laughed, "Okay, I suppose if I must, I must, Your Royal Highness."

Kat stopped Clay's joking by licking all around her clit. Clay only tolerated that for a minute before she said, "Put it in your mouth and suck, baby."

It really turned Kat on making Clay feel hot, making her moan, making her needy. She sucked and swirled until she felt Clay's hand pushing her down onto her sex and keeping her there.

"Yeah, baby. Suck it. That's it."

She loved this. There was so much she wanted to try with Clay, and there was a lifetime to try it.

"Fuck, I'm coming," Clay called out as she gripped Kat's hair with her fingers.

Kat climbed up Clay's body and put her hand on her lover's heart. "I think I won that round."

Clay laughed and then out of nowhere flipped Kat onto her back. She grinned down at her like a Cheshire cat while pulling off her T-shirt.

"You are a bad girl, but I'm going to make you scream."

Kat laughed and said, "I love you, Ronnie. Forever."

"I will love you always."

CHAPTER TWENTY

Clay had to wait till Monday evening for the Queen to have time in her busy schedule. Clay fingered her collar. She felt nervous to go in front of the Queen, even though she was certain she was doing the right thing. Cammy came out of the Queen's office and Clay stood to attention.

"At ease, Sergeant. The Queen's ready for you. She has twenty minutes before she has to get ready for her evening appointment at the film premiere."

"Yes, ma'am. I won't take long."

"In you go, then."

Clay cleared her throat and walked into the office. The Queen looked up from her papers. "Clay, come in."

"Thank you for seeing me, Your Majesty," Clay said.

Queen Georgina put the lid on her fountain pen and put it down. "How can I help you?"

"Ma'am. Just after Christmas, I asked if I would have your blessing to move on, to an overseas appointment."

"I remember. You were in a difficult space at that time, and you said you'd give it a few months to consider it more fully and see if you felt better about your place here with us."

"Yes, ma'am, and I have felt differently, living here in my new quarters at the palace, and the cottage. After my mum died, it meant so much to feel part of this big royal court you lead here—"

The Queen raised an eyebrow. "I feel a *but* coming."

"But in spite of that, I still want to take the opportunity of a placement abroad. Specifically, Vospya."

A smile started to grow on Queen Georgina's face. "With Princess Olga?"

"Yes, ma'am. We are very close—in fact, I love her. King Louis asked me to head up her security team."

The Queen got up and walked around her desk to shake her hand. "If we had to lose you, Clay, then this was the only way I would approve of. You are taking on an important job. Princess Olga's safety is vital."

"Thank you, ma'am. I'm only sorry that I'm leaving the princesses. I love them very much."

"They love you, Clay, and I'm sure you'll still see them a lot. Olga will always be a part of my family's life. We are all a royal family, and I'll be there to support her at every stage."

"Thank you, ma'am. Thank you for everything, Your Majesty."

All the royal family lined up at the Windsor Castle entrance to say goodbye to Kat and Clay. Queen Rozala and Lennox had already left for Denbourg, but Holly, Quincy, Cammy, and Lali were all there. It was a sad day for them all to be saying goodbye to friends who had become like family, but also an exciting day.

Kat had been dreading this new life since she found out about her future, but now that she had Clay, she felt she could do anything.

Kat and Clay kneeled down by Teddy, and Clay said, "You take care of your little sister for me."

"I will miss you and Kat," Teddy said.

Kat looked at Clay and gave her a sad smile before turning back to Teddy. "We'll miss you too, but we'll be back to visit—won't we, Clay."

"We will. I promise."

When they stood up, Clay ruffled Teddy's hair, and Kat kissed Anna, who was up in Bea's arms.

"You be good too, Anna," Kat said.

Bea then pulled her into a hug. "You take care, both of you."

George shook Clay's hand and said, "If you need anything, just let us know."

Kat stood back and looked to all her friends, who she'd already said her goodbyes to, and said, "Thank you all."

"We better get going," Clay said.

Clay escorted her up to the line of cars with blacked-out windows, staffed by her new security team. There would be one in front and one behind. They had already discussed this but Kat said again, "I don't know why you can't travel in the car with me, Ronnie."

"We've discussed this. I only just met your team a few days ago. I need to be seen in command of that team before the world knows about us. Now in you get, Your Royal Highness."

Kat smiled and waved to her friends before slipping into the car. What a difference a week made. Now no longer a nanny but leaving to fulfil her family destiny, but with the woman she loved by her side.

The car started to pull off and she waved her last goodbyes. They were on their way to the airport and would be leaving by private plane. Next stop would be the Vospyan capital of Viermart.

Her Uncle Louis had been received with great joy by the citizens. It had been decided that not long after arriving, Kat, or Olga as she had to get used to being called, would make a speech on the palace balcony with the King and Nikola Stam, the leader of the freedom fighters.

That was something she was not looking forward to. Going from being trained to understand there was danger in being in the spotlight to standing in the biggest spotlight of all was daunting, but at least she'd have Ronnie with her.

The car travelled along the winding country roads leading out of Windsor and she thought of the beauty of Vospya. She had tried to describe to Clay what Vospya was like, and it was similar to England in many ways, although she remembered it had more green spaces and countryside.

Kat expected it to be different in some ways from her memories. A country didn't go through a civil war without damaging the land. She could only hope King Louis and the new democratic government could bring the country back to life.

The news of her survival had been released to the media yesterday, and it had become a sensation. Everyone wanted a picture of her, but they didn't know she was still here. King Louis's fledgling press office let it be known that she had already left the UK, giving her time to leave quietly.

Suddenly Kat's vision was engulfed in a white flash of an explosion, and then she felt hands pulling her out of the car. Before she knew it, she was on her knees in front of a crazed looking man with the muzzle of a gun against her forehead.

He said in their native Vospyan tongue, "Remember me, little girl? I remember you with your strange eyes. You got away from me."

In that instant she was back to that day in the forest when her family were shot dead. She recognized his dead, sadistic eyes.

"I got your bitch of a nanny, but you ran like the royal pig you are. Well, I got you in the end, didn't I?"

In all the panic she was feeling, it was as if her life had come full circle. She only hoped Clay was safe.

Clay scrambled free from the seat belt and shook the protection officer beside her. Her hearing was still whining from the loud explosion ahead.

"Thomas? Are you okay?"

He shook his head to clear his vision. "Yes, ma'am. Stay down a second. We have to be careful." The driver of their car was out cold, and when she looked out of the window, she saw the horrifying sight of Kat with a gun against her head.

"Fuck. Thomas, I need you to go out your side and take his attention. I just need one good shot, but don't take any stupid chances, okay?"

"Yes, ma'am."

Thomas got out, and she heard the man shouting at him. Clay scrambled out of her broken window as quietly as she could. Using the front of the car as cover, she took her handgun out and looked over the bonnet.

The man was shouting at Thomas, "Put your gun down or I'll shoot her."

Thomas must have done that because he then said, "Kick it away."

Clay lined up her shot. She knew she'd only get one chance to end this and get Kat to safety. She took a breath and her heart calmed. One of her greatest attributes was staying calm when the situation required one shot.

This was it. She squeezed the trigger and the bullet ripped right through the assailant's brain. He dropped like a stone, and Kat started to scream as his blood spurted over her.

Clay ran to her side and took her in her arms. "You're okay, I'm here, I'm here."

"It's him, Ronnie. It's him."

"Who?" Clay asked.

"The man who helped kill my family, who killed my nanny, and who nearly killed me."

Clay pulled Kat closer and kissed her head. "He's dead now. He can't harm you ever again."

She watched Thomas search through the man's jacket, with the loudening sounds of sirens in the distance.

He looked up from reading the passport in the man's pocket and said, "It's the Vospyan ambassador who's been on the run."

The man who had been at the palace, who had been amongst them all this time, was the one who killed Kat's family.

"He will never harm you again," Clay repeated.

Kat clung to her with a death grip. "You saved me."

"I told you, I can shoot the wings off a fly."

CHAPTER TWENTY-ONE

There was chaos in the Buckingham Palace cinema room. All the family were gathered to watch Princess Olga's balcony appearance with the King. The children were running around like mad, shouting excitedly, and the adults were about as excited as the children.

George loved the noise and wouldn't have it any other way. When she thought about how Olga's family had been torn from her, it made George appreciate them all the more.

Her own grandmother was there, her mama, Bea's mum and dad, her aunt, her cousins, and then there was Theo and the newcomer to the brood, Azi. Theo had won her over, it seemed, and she slowly started to be included in family gatherings, while still working on the documentary.

At the moment she was fixing his collar and straightening his tie, while he looked at her adoringly. George laughed inside, but she knew that she had the very same look with Bea. She and Bea were sure Azi would make an excellent addition to the family when the time came.

They had also asked Cammy, Lali, Holly, and Quincy to watch this momentous historical moment that their friends were part of.

Bea turned away from her mother and said, "George, when is this supposed to start, because Anna is wriggling like a fish."

The cameras were trained on the square full of people, waiting outside Gorndam Palace.

"Anytime now. Give me my little angel." George took Anna and bounced her on her knee.

"Are you still sure about making another little prince or princess?" Bea asked.

"I'm always sure about that. Teddy and Anna need another little playmate in their lives. Besides, now you have Artie, and you can trust that you can leave them with him in safety."

Bea smiled and rested her head against George's shoulder. She had met Kat's friend Artie, and he was the perfect choice, just as Kat said he would be. "I thought you'd say that." She was silent for a few seconds and then said, "I'm nervous for Kat. She's been through so much."

"I'm sure she'll do fine. She has Clay beside her every step of the way," George said.

"Thank God she does, or that disgusting man could have killed her."

George shuddered. "To think we actually had that man in our home. It horrifies me."

"I know," Bea said. Bea gazed at the crowd on the screen and saw so many rainbow flags. "Look at all the Pride flags, Georgie. They would have gotten you tortured and shot only a month ago."

Teddy ran over and clambered up onto Bea's lap.

"Kat coming on TV yet?"

"Soon, sweetheart." Bea kissed Teddy's cheek.

The focus shifted to the balcony.

George raised her voice and said, "Pipe down, everyone. Princess Olga is about to come out."

A hush descended on the cinema room.

Kat had to hold her hands together, or everyone would see they were shaking. She was standing in the gallery room that opened out onto the balcony, where King Louis and Nikola Stam were addressing the crowd.

The gallery room, much like the rest of the palace, was damaged and decaying. Some damage, like bullet holes in the wall and crumbling plaster, was due to the civil war, and other things like the drab decor were due to poor upkeep of the building by Loka's government.

It was a sad reflection of the palace she had known as a girl. One of the most notable things was the blank spaces on the walls left by the missing fine art collection. Some items had been sold, but most were stored in the palace basement.

It would all be put back together again—it would just take time. A loud cheer from outside brought her back to the present, and she looked around the room for Ronnie. She was standing talking to one of her new team.

Clay had really grown in the short time since they'd left the UK. She hadn't led a protection squad before, but with teachers like Inspector Quincy and Major Cameron, Clay couldn't fail.

Thank God, Clay had decided to come with her to Vospya, or she might be dead now. The fear she had felt looking into that man's dead eyes was overwhelming, but Clay had protected her, as Kat knew she always would.

United Nations peacekeepers were spaced throughout the room, ensuring fair play and security, as were the soldiers down in the public square. It gave Kat heart that their ranks were made up of soldiers from Denbourg and Britain, amongst other of their European neighbours.

Loka had been taken out of the country and would be standing trial in a war crimes tribunal. No sentence could ever pay for his crimes, the thousands of deaths he ordered, but it would give some of the victims closure, at least.

Kat was one of them. Loka had given the location of the mass grave where her family was buried, and once things were settled, they would get a proper state funeral.

Nikola had given his speech, and the King was now onto introducing Kat. The country had taken her to their hearts since the news broke that she was still alive. King Louis explained that she was a symbol that the hope the people had would never die, a part of their freedom that Loka's regime just couldn't kill.

Clay walked over to her and said, "All ready?"

"No, I'm terrified."

Clay took her hands and said, "You will be great. I've got faith in you."

She had helped Kat rehearse for this moment continuously since they'd travelled by plane over to Vospya.

"I hope I live up to their high expectations," Kat said.

"Have faith in yourself. I know you have faith in me. When you're out there, Dora, the Buckinghams, and Queen Rozala and Lennox will be watching you, supporting you, plus I'll be standing right there."

Clay pointed to the wall just beside the doors that opened onto the balcony. "No one will see me, no one will know I'm there except you, and I'll always be there."

King Louis was getting near her cue to come on. "It's time."

Clay kissed her on the lips. "I love you with all of my heart. Go and become the princess you were born to be, Olga."

She quickly flicked through her phone to find the picture of her family all together, which had sat on her bedside all the years since she had been gone. A look of determination came over Kat, and she walked up to the doors. Clay took her place at the side of the doors, out of sight.

King Louis said her name, and a cheer went up. Kat looked to her and mouthed the words, *I love you, Ronnie.*

"I love you," Clay whispered.

Kat walked out onto the balcony, and the cheers and screams grew louder.

Clay stood and listened with pride. The plan was to have Kat dedicate herself to freedom and to swear an oath to defend democracy, giving the people hope that they would have a long and stable future.

She thought about her mother looking down from above and how proud she would be of her. It had been some journey from the streets of London, running with the bad crowd at school, to working in Buckingham Palace, and now loving a princess, but somehow it was all meant to be.

One day soon, they would make their relationship official, but for now the spotlight was on Princess Olga, as destiny always meant it to be.

Katya Kovach the nanny might have walked out there to the people, but Clay knew that Princess Olga would come walking back to her, and Clay made her own private pledge to love and protect her as long as she lived. Another royal family was about to enter the world stage.

The crowd quietened to let Olga speak.

"My mother and father named me Olga after the legendry Queen Olga who took up arms and helped protect our capital during the Second World War. I can only hope that I will have the same courage as my ancestor. But I pledge to you that for as long as I live, I will live to serve the tenets of freedom and democracy."

Olga raised her voice for the final part of her pledge. "For God, for Vospya, and for the people!"

The crowd went wild, and Clay knew Princess Olga had finally found herself.

About the Author

Jenny Frame is from the small town of Motherwell in Scotland, where she lives with her partner, Lou, and their well-loved and very spoiled dog.

She has a diverse range of qualifications, including a BA in public management and a diploma in acting and performance. Nowadays, she likes to put her creative energies into writing rather than treading the boards.

When not writing or reading, Jenny loves cheering on her local football team, cooking, and spending time with her family.

Jenny can be contacted at www.jennyframe.com.

Books Available From Bold Strokes Books

A Far Better Thing by JD Wilburn. When needs of her family and wants of her heart clash, Cass Halliburton is faced with the ultimate sacrifice. (978-1-63555-834-0)

Body Language by Renee Roman. When Mika offers to provide Jen erotic tutoring, will sex drive them into a deeper relationship or tear them apart? (978-1-63555-800-5)

Carrie and Hope by Joy Argento. For Carrie and Hope, loss brings them together but secrets and fear may tear them apart. (978-1-63555-827-2)

Detour to Love by Amanda Radley. Celia Scott and Lily Andersen are seatmates on a flight to Tokyo and by turns annoy and fascinate each other. But they're about to realize there's more than one path to love. (978-1-63555-958-3)

Ice Queen by Gun Brooke. School counselor Aislin Kennedy wants to help standoffish CEO Susanna Durr and her troubled teenage daughter become closer—even if it means risking her own heart in the process. (978-1-63555-721-3)

Masquerade by Anne Shade. In 1925 Harlem, New York, a notorious gangster sets her sights on seducing Celine, and new lovers Dinah and Celine are forced to risk their hearts, and lives, for love. (978-1-63555-831-9)

Royal Family by Jenny Frame. Loss has defined both Clay's and Katya's lives, but guarding their hearts may prove to be the biggest heartbreak of all. (978-1-63555-745-9)

Share the Moon by Toni Logan. Three best friends, an inherited vineyard, and a resident ghost come together for fun, romance, and a touch of magic. (978-1-63555-844-9)

Spirit of the Law by Carsen Taite. Attorney Owen Lassiter will do almost anything to put a murderer behind bars, but can she get past her reluctance to rely on unconventional help from the alluring Summer Byrne and keep from falling in love in the process? (978-1-63555-766-4)

The Devil Incarnate by Ali Vali. Cain Casey has so much to live for, but enemies who lurk in the shadows threaten to unravel it all. (978-1-63555-534-9)

Secret Agent by Michelle Larkin. CIA Agent Peyton North embarks on a global chase to apprehend rogue agent Zoey Blackwood, but her commitment to the mission is tested as the sparks between them ignite and their sizzling attraction approaches a point of no return. (978-1-63555-753-4)

Journey to Cash by Ashley Bartlett. Cash Braddock thought everything was great, but it looks like her history is about to become her right now. Which is a real bummer. (978-1-63555-464-9)

Liberty Bay by Karis Walsh. Wren Lindley's life is mired in tradition and untouched by trends until social media star Gina Strickland introduces an irresistible electricity into her off-the-grid world. (978-1-63555-816-6)

Scent by Kris Bryant. Nico Marshall has been burned by women in the past wanting her for her money. This time, she's determined to win Sophia Sweet over with her charm. (978-1-63555-780-0)

Shadows of Steel by Suzie Clarke. As their worlds collide and their choices come back to haunt them, Rachel and Claire must figure out how to stay together and, most of all, stay alive. (978-1-63555-810-4)

The Clinch by Nicole Disney. Eden Bauer overcame a difficult past to become a world champion mixed martial artist, but now rising star and dreamy bad girl Brooklyn Shaw is a threat both to Eden's title and her heart. (978-1-63555-820-3)

The Last First Kiss by Julie Cannon. Kelly Newsome is so ready for a tropical island vacation, but she never expects to meet the woman who could give her her last first kiss. (978-1-63555-768-8)

The Mandolin Lunch by Missouri Vaun. Despite their immediate attraction, everything about Garet Allen says short-term, and Tess Hill refuses to consider anything less than forever. (978-1-63555-566-0)

Thor: Daughter of Asgard by Genevieve McCluer. When Hannah Olsen finds out she's the reincarnation of Thor, she's thrown into a world of magic and intrigue, unexpected attraction, and a mystery she's got to unravel. (978-1-63555-814-2)

Veterinary Technician by Nancy Wheelton. When a stable of horses is threatened, Val and Ronnie must work together against the odds to save them and maybe even themselves along the way. (978-1-63555-839-5)

16 Steps to Forever by Georgia Beers. Can Brooke Sullivan and Macy Carr find themselves by finding each other? (978-1-63555-762-6)

All I Want for Christmas by Georgia Beers, Maggie Cummings & Fiona Riley. The Christmas season sparks passion and love in these stories by award-winning authors Georgia Beers, Maggie Cummings, and Fiona Riley. (978-1-63555-764-0)

From the Woods by Charlotte Greene. When Fiona goes backpacking in a protected wilderness, the last thing she expects is to be fighting for her life. (978-1-63555-793-0)

Heart of the Storm by Nicole Stiling. For Juliet Mitchell and Sienna Bennett a forbidden attraction definitely isn't worth upending the life they've worked so hard for. Is it? (978-1-63555-789-3)

If You Dare by Sandy Lowe. For Lauren West and Emma Prescott, following their passions is easy. Following their hearts, though? That's almost impossible. (978-1-63555-654-4)

Love Changes Everything by Jaime Maddox. For Samantha Brooks and Kirby Fielding, no matter how careful their plans, love will change everything. (978-1-63555-835-7)

Not This Time by MA Binfield. Flung back into each other's lives, can former bandmates Sophia and Madison have a second chance at romance? (978-1-63555-798-5)

The Found Jar by Jaycie Morrison. Fear keeps Emily Harris trapped in her emotionally vacant life; can she find the courage to let Beck Reynolds guide her toward love? (978-1-63555-825-8)

Aurora by Emma L McGeown. After a traumatic accident, Elena Ricci is stricken with amnesia, leaving her with no recollection of the last eight years, including her wife and son. (978-1-63555-824-1)